365 One-Minute Bedtime Stories

YoYo BOOKS

January

Nibbles

In a big forest, far from here, stands a tall, old oak tree. Tucked among its roots there's a tiny door.

A tiny mouse comes out. It's Nibbles.

'Mummy,' asks Nibbles, 'may I go out to play?'

'Yes, after breakfast,' says Mummy.

She sets a bowl of crushed nuts and a glass of milk in front of him. Nibbles eats and drinks everything up quickly.

'I'll go and brush my teeth,' he says after he finishes.

He puts toothpaste on his toothbrush.

'Yummy. It tastes like strawberries,' smiles Nibbles.

Now Nibbles is ready. He gives Mummy a big kiss and runs outside.

Flopsy

Nibbles runs to the neighbours' house. He grabs the newspaper from the postbox and rings the doorbell.

Ding-dong, it sounds. A large rabbit opens the door.

'Good morning, Mister Sack,' says Nibbles politely. 'I've brought you your paper.'

'Thanks, Nibbles,' smiles Mister Sack.

'Can Flopsy come out to play?' asks Nibbles.

'Of course,' answers Mister Sack. 'But she has to clean her room before she can play. Could you help her?'

Nibbles is happy to do that so he runs upstairs to

Flopsy's room.

'Hello, Flopsy,' says Nibbles as he enters the room.

Oh, my, what a mess! Dolls and dolls' clothes are scattered all over.

'What a messy bunny you are, Flopsy,' says Nibbles.

'I can't help it,' says Flopsy. 'When I play, I always make a mess.'

'But why didn't you tidy up last night?'

Flopsy sighs. 'I didn't feel like it. A little mess isn't so bad, is it?'

Nibbles looks around and smiles. 'Flopsy, this is a total mess. But I will help you.'

They get started. Luckily it doesn't take too long.

'Thanks, Nibbles!' says Flopsy.

'Glad to help. That's what friends are for,' smiles Nibbles. 'Now let's go out and play!'

Hopper

Nibbles and Flopsy are going to visit Hopper, their friend. But he's not at home by the brook where he lives. Where could he be?

'Maybe he's still asleep,' guesses Flopsy.

'No, Hopper is always first to wake up,' replies Nibbles. 'But maybe he has gone out.'

Flopsy shakes her head.

'We have to find him,' says Nibbles.

They start searching. They look under the little bridge. They hunt in the reeds and grass. But Hopper is nowhere to be found.

'Gosh,' says Flopsy, 'I hope nothing bad has happened to him.'

They both go to the edge of the water and peer around for their friend.

Suddenly something green springs out of the grass over their heads. Splash! Water flies all over. Nibbles and Flopsy are startled and completely soaked.

After they calm down, they spot Hopper's head sticking out of the water.

'Ribbet!' he croaks. 'I really got you!'

'Hopper! You rascal!' yells Flopsy, shaking her fur dry and wiping her face.

Then all three of them laugh and laugh at Hopper's joke. That Hopper really is a rascal.

Blinders

Ding-dong!

'I'm coming,' someone calls from the playroom in the mole house.

Blinders, the mole, runs down the hall. Bang! He runs smack into the coat rack and falls head over heels.

'Ow, my head!' he cries, as a jacket falls off the coat rack onto him.

'Who turned out the lights?' yells Blinders confused.

He struggles to get free. But he bumps into the coat rack again. An even heavier winter coat falls down. He sinks under the weight.

It's dark as night now. He tries to crawl out from under the coats. Ha! Finally he sees some light and creeps toward it. Slowly he manages to get out from under the pile.

He stands up and wipes his nose.

Ding-dong, sounds the bell again. Blinders wants to run to the door, but he's tangled up in the jacket.

Smack! He falls against a cupboard. 'Ow!' he cries, 'another bump!'

But then Blinders looks up in fright. On the cupboard, a vase wobbles and tips over.

Blinders jumps forward to catch the vase, but it

slips through his paws. Crash!

Blinders can't believe his bad luck today.

He sits still for a moment, afraid to move.

Then his mummy comes into the hall. She helps Blinders get free.

'Blinders, you've forgotten to put on your glasses again,' she says, while she puts them on his nose.

'Now you won't run into anything any more.'

'Thank you, Mummy,' says Blinders.

Then finally Blinders answers the door.

The Friendship Tree

'Hi, Blinders,' cry Nibbles, Flopsy and Hopper as the door opens slowly.

'Hi everybody,' says Blinders in his soft voice.

'Can you come out and play with us? We are going to our Friendship Tree,' says Flopsy.

'Great!' smiles Blinders.

Whooping and laughing, they run along the path in the woods. They cross the bridge over the brook and dive into the high grass. There, next to the brook, stands an old hollow tree. It's their secret hideout. They call it their Friendship Tree. By climbing up the branches, they get to a hole in the trunk where they can crawl inside. Nibbles and Hopper have made a slide out of an old board, setting it into the hole. One by one the friends slide down into the tree, laughing all the way.

It's nice and light inside the trunk. On one side there's a big hole through which they can see the sparkling brook.

'What shall we do today?' asks Nibbles.

'Hide and seek,' suggests Hopper.

'Leapfrog,' says Flopsy.

'Let's swing,' says Blinders.

Everybody thinks that it's a great idea. They climb up a ladder and out of the trunk.

On an old branch of the tree the friends have hung two swings. Blinders and Flopsy go first. Nibbles and Hopper push them.

Then it's Nibbles' and Hopper's turn to swing. Blinders and Flopsy push them as hard as they can.

Hopper and Nibbles shout with joy.

It's another great day at the Friendship Tree.

The Parcel

Mister Sack, Flopsy's daddy, is delivering the post. His sack is full of parcels and letters. He stops by each house and drops the post into the postboxes.

'Who is this for?' Mister Sack asks himself.

It's for Mister Owl, the mayor. Mister Sack runs to the thick beech tree where Mister Owl lives. He always gets lots of post because he's the mayor of the village. Mister Sack tugs on a long rope that hangs from the tree. Up above, a bell tinkles.

'Who is there?' booms a deep voice.

'It is me,' calls Mister Sack. 'I have a big parcel for you.'

'I am coming,' answers Mister Owl. 'Mmm! That must be my new book,' he says happily.

'A book? It must be a big one,' sighs Mister Sack. 'Poor you,' says Mister Owl. 'But I have something to thank you with.' He hands Mister Sack a juicy carrot. 'That's very kind of you,' says Mister Sack surprised. 'Bye for now, Mister Owl.'

'Bye, Mister Sack.'

Nice Nibbles

Nibbles is helping his mummy in the kitchen. She has chopped hazelnuts, walnuts and acorns into little pieces. Nibbles puts the nuts in a bowl. He mixes them with raisins. Then Mummy adds a spoonful of sweet blossom honey. Now it's ready.

'That will be a feast later, Nibbles,' says Mummy.

'Nut salad is one of my favourites!' cries Nibbles, excited.

Mummy laughs, 'But you will have to wait until dinner time.'

'Mummy,' begs Nibbles, 'may I taste a little now?'

'OK, because you were so nice to help me,' says Mummy. 'You can have a spoonful. But the rest is for later.'

'Thanks, Mummy,' smiles Nibbles. It tastes wonderful.

'As soon as Daddy is done with his work,' says Mummy, 'we can eat.'

'That long?' thinks Nibbles. He gets an idea. If he helps Daddy, they can eat sooner.

He runs to Daddy's workshop. Nibbles' dad is a carpenter. He is building a chair for Miss Mole.

'Daddy, are you almost done?' asks Nibbles.

'Almost, but then I have to sweep the workshop,' he says.

'Shall I do that for you?' asks Nibbles.

'Great!' answers Daddy happily. 'That will save work and time.'

Soon they are done.

'That went fast,' says Daddy. 'You were a great help. Let's eat now.' At the table, Nibbles gets an extra scoop of the delicious nut salad because he helped Mummy and Daddy so much.

Yum-yum!

Three Carrots

Three carrots lie on the table.

Flopsy spots the carrots and climbs up on a chair.

She looks at them one by one. Each carrot looks different. The first is thick and short. The next is long and thin. The last one is the nicest, neither too thick nor too long. But a piece is missing at the tip.

'That's a pity,' says Flopsy. 'Otherwise I'd surely eat this one. Maybe I should take the thick one,' she thinks. She almost takes a big bite. But she stops.

'Who knows? Maybe the thin one tastes much better. Maybe I should eat that one.'

Flopsy puts the thick carrot back on the table. She picks up the thin one.

'This will taste good.'

She almost bites into the carrot. But… again she stops. 'Actually, the carrot with the missing tip looks the tastiest,' says Flopsy, her mind made up.

She grabs it and jumps off the chair. Just as she opens her mouth, the doorbell sounds.

'Now what?' thinks Flopsy. She puts the carrot back and goes to the door.

'Hi, Miss Mouse,' says Flopsy. 'What can I do for you?' Mummy also comes to the door, bringing the carrots with her. 'Hello, Miss Mouse. Here are the three carrots you asked for.'

'Thank you so much,' answers Miss Mouse. 'I ran out. Very kind of you to let me borrow some.'

'Oh, you are very welcome,' smiles Mummy. 'Right, Flopsy?' Flopsy has a different opinion about that!

Digging

9 JANUARY

Nibbles, Flopsy, Blinders and Hopper meet in the woods. Each one has a shovel.

'We are going to dig a very deep hole,' says Nibbles.

'Deeper than anyone has ever dug!' shouts Hopper.

'And we'll put a sign by it that says, NIBBLES, FLOPSY, HOPPER AND BLINDERS DUG THIS,' says Blinders.

'We will be famous!' shouts Flopsy.

'Let's go,' says Nibbles. All four start digging.

After a while Blinders stops. 'Digging is hard,' he says. 'I need a rest.'

Soon Flopsy stops. 'My gosh, I can't feel my paws any more.' Puffing, she sits down.

Nibbles and Hopper continue bravely digging. Only their top halves show above the hole.

Now Nibbles gives up. 'I'm dead tired…' he gasps. He sits down by Flopsy and Blinders.

Only Hopper carries on. He tosses shovelful after shovelful of dirt out of the hole. It's getting more painful. Hopper sinks to his knees. His friends pull him out.

'May-maybe this is deep enough…' he puffs.

Nibbles nods, wiping the sweat off his face. 'It is so deep. Look how beautiful and round it is.'

'Oh yes,' pants Flopsy. 'Very round.'

Blinders takes a look. 'Maybe it's not the deepest, but surely it's the most beautiful hole.'

'Let's put that on the sign,' Nibbles proposes. They all like that idea.

So when you go walking in the forest, watch out for a small round hole with a sign beside it. You'll know who dug it.

Doing Some Shopping

10 JANUARY

Nibbles walks to Miss Squirrel's shop. Carefully he opens the door. A bell tinkles.

'Hi Nibbles, what can I do for you?'

Nibbles gives a shopping list to Miss Squirrel.

'Hazelnuts, acorns, some herbs and a piece of cheese,' she says. 'Let's see.'

She takes the lid off a barrel and scoops out some hazelnuts. Then she takes some acorns and puts them next to the hazelnuts.

'Now the herbs,' says Miss Squirrel, picking out jars from the spice rack. She measures spoonfuls of herbs and pours them into a bag.

'And finally the cheese,' she says, taking a smelly piece of cheese out from under a glass bell. She cuts off a big piece and wraps it in paper.

'Well, that's it. That'll be fifty pence,' she says, putting the things in a big bag.

Nibbles puts the money on the counter. Miss Squirrel gives the big bag to Nibbles. But the bag is almost as big as Nibbles. That's a problem.

'How can you bring that home?' she asks Nibbles. 'The bag is too big and heavy. You can never carry that alone.'

Nibbles smiles. 'I brought my cart with me,' he says. 'It's outside. Could you please put the bag in my cart so I can take it home?'

'How smart of you!' laughs Miss Squirrel, and she takes the bag and brings it to the cart.

Now Nibbles can take the shopping home. 'Bye-bye, sweet Miss Squirrel,' he says and then off he goes with his cart.

Rain, Rain

Hopper and Nibbles are playing outside. Suddenly dark clouds blow in. Soon it starts to rain.

'Shouldn't you put on your coat?' Hopper asks Nibbles.

'Oh, I like rain,' answers Nibbles.

'But you'll get soaked,' worries Hopper.

'I don't mind. You don't have a jacket,' observes Nibbles.

'Because I'm a frog. I live in the water.'

Nibbles gives him a long look. 'If you can stand it, so can I. Come on, let's play.'

They run and jump until they're both drenched. Then it's time for Nibbles to go home. He says goodbye to his friend and runs to his house.

Arriving home, Nibbles feels a cold shiver run up his spine. He doesn't feel well. His head feels hot and his nose starts to itch.

'A... atchoo!' he says. His mummy comes to him.

'Oh Nibbles, you're soaked through. Did you run through the rain without a coat?' she asks.

'Atchoo!' sneezes Nibbles in reply. He's feeling worse every minute.

'Put on dry clothes, quickly!'

She dries the shivering mouse and pulls off his wet clothes.

'Nibbles, why didn't you put on your jacket?'

'I...liked the rain...,' shudders Nibbles. His head feels like an oven.

'Silly you, now you're sick,' says Mummy, angrily. She puts Nibbles to bed and makes hot chocolate for him. Now Nibbles knows why he should have put on his raincoat.

January

The Key

Blinders finds a key on the path. It is gold-coloured and looks very old. He brings it to the Friendship Tree. Nibbles, Flopsy and Hopper are waiting there for him.

'Look what I found on the path. A real an-keet key.'

'Antique, you mean,' Flopsy corrects him. 'That means that something is old and valuable.'

'It looks chic,' says Nibbles.

'Ribbet! Who knows? Maybe it's the key to a treasure chest,' says Hopper.

'Quick, show us where you found it,' says Nibbles. 'Maybe we can find the treasure, too.'

Blinders takes his friends to the place where he found the key.

'It was here on the path,' he says.

Hopper frowns. 'If we look hard, maybe we'll find the treasure chest.' The friends search under every branch and stone. But they can't find the treasure chest.

Then Mister Owl, the mayor, passes by.

'Hello!' he says. 'Did you find a key, by chance?'

The amazed friends look at each other.

'You mean this one?' says Blinders, holding out the key.

'Yes, indeed. That's the one! Thanks!' Mister Owl shouts happily.

Blinders gives the key to Mister Owl.

'We thought maybe it belonged to a treasure chest,' says Flopsy.

Mister Owl laughs.

'A treasure chest?' he chuckles. 'Not exactly.'

'No,' continues Mister Owl, 'it's the key to my shed. That's where I keep my rubbish bin.'

A rubbish shed? They all burst out laughing.

Waiting for Daddy

Nibbles and his little sister, Misty, sit in front of the window. They are waiting.

'What's taking Daddy so long?' asks Misty.

'He should be here just about now. The hands of the clock have moved a whole quarter of an hour,' says Nibbles, pointing at the clock. Misty doesn't understand the clock and its hands, but she believes her brother.

'Why does waiting take so long?' sighs Misty.

The children peer out of the window. No sign of Daddy.

'Be patient,' says Mummy. 'He will show up.'

But the children are excited. They press their noses against the windows, looking for Daddy. Where is he?

'He is probably talking to somebody,' says Nibbles. Misty sighs deeply.

'I hope they stop talking soon,' she says.

But then they both jump up. There's Daddy! They run to the door and open it. They shout, 'Daddy! Daddy!' as he walks up the garden path.

In his hand he has a brown bag from the bakery. There are two honey biscuits in it.

One for Misty and one for Nibbles.

'You look starved,' smiles Daddy when he sees the two eager faces. Then he pulls the biscuits out of the bag and gives one to each of them. They immediately attack the biscuits.

Those honey biscuits are just sooo delicious.

Curious Nibbles

Nibbles stands in front of the gate at Daddy's workshop. A big sign above the gate says 'Carpenter Mouse.' Inside, Nibbles' daddy makes things out of wood. Tables, chairs, cupboards and beds. Sometimes toys, too. Nibbles has heard his father say something about a new toy he's making.

'That'll be fun,' Daddy told Mummy.

Of course, that makes Nibbles very curious.

Slowly, Nibbles opens the gate. He peers through the opening. The warm smell of wood fills his nose. Then he opens the gate a bit more and peeks in.

He can't see a lot. Big boards are standing in the way. Inside, he hears his father hammering.

As quietly as he can, Nibbles sneaks into the workshop. He hides behind a board, then carefully looks at Daddy. Daddy is throwing a cloth over something. Then he turns around and looks straight at Nibbles. Nibbles is scared out of his wits.

'You thought I didn't hear you, right?' laughs Daddy. 'But I hear very well. You can't fool me.'

Disappointed, Nibbles comes out of hiding.

'It's not finished yet,' says Daddy, pointing at the mysterious thing under the cloth.

Full of awe, Nibbles looks at the thing under the cloth.

'When will it be ready?' Nibbles wants to know.

'Tomorrow,' answers Daddy. 'You have to be patient for one more day.'

Poor Nibbles. He has to wait.

Daddy's Surprise

Next morning Nibbles gets up early. He runs to his sister's room.

'Misty, are you awake?'

Misty jumps up and gets out of bed.

'Are we going to look?' she asks.

Nibbles nods. Together they go downstairs. They come to the door of the living room. Their legs are shaking.

'Open the door,' says Misty to her brother.

Slowly, Nibbles takes the doorknob and turns it. The door opens.

In the living room stands a huge thing. A cloth covers it.

'Look, Daddy's surprise!' exclaims Nibbles.

They run to it.

'Can we take the cloth off?' asks Misty to Nibbles.

Nibbles nods. 'Daddy said we could.' So Nibbles takes a corner of the sheet and pulls it down carefully.

'Wow!'

Mummy and Daddy hear cheering from the living room. Curious, they peek around the door.

They see Nibbles and Misty sitting on a big rocking horse. They rock and rock, laughing and whooping with delight.

When the kids see Daddy, they jump off the horse and give Daddy the biggest hug ever. They think that he is the coolest daddy in the whole world.

The Fairy Tale Book

Misty, Nibbles' little sister, has received a fairy tale book for her birthday. It has lovely pictures. Nibbles wants to read the book. But Misty refuses. She says that the book is hers.

Nibbles looks glum. He really wants to read it!

'Please, Misty,' says Nibbles using the sweetest voice he has.

'No,' says Misty angrily. 'It's my book.'

'But you can't even read,' says Nibbles.

'Neither can you!' answers Misty, angry.

For a moment Nibbles doesn't know what to say.

'Yes I can,' he blurts out. 'I can too read. Didn't you know?'

Misty gives Nibbles a disbelieving look.

'Shall I show you?' proposes Nibbles. 'I'll read you a story.'

Misty doubts it. Can her brother really read? Hesitantly she gives him the book.

Nibbles sits down on the sofa with the book.

'Come, sit down next to me,' he says. 'Then you can look at the pictures.'

Misty crawls up next to Nibbles on the sofa.

'A long time ago in a forest far away from here…' starts Nibbles. Misty listens attentively. Her brother can really read! She didn't know that.

But Nibbles can't read at all. He just pretends. He looks at the pictures and then makes up an interesting story to go with them. But Misty doesn't know. With his little trick, Nibbles gets a look at her book.

Cold

It's so cold this morning! Nibbles hurries to the Friendship Tree.

When he arrives, he sees his friends waiting for him. They are also warmly dressed.

'My daddy says it froze last night,' says Blinders, while he blows clouds of breath into the cold air.

'And it froze really hard too,' says Hopper, pointing. 'The branches are covered with frost. The brook is completely frozen. The water has turned to ice.'

'It looks beautiful,' smiles Flopsy from under her thick woollen hat.

Hopper clambers out through the hole and bounces to the edge of the brook. He bends over and touches the ice carefully.

'What are you doing?' asks Nibbles.

'Watch,' says Hopper. He knocks on the ice.

'It's rock hard!' shouts Hopper delighted.

Hopper carefully tries a couple of skating steps on the ice. He can slide! He goes faster and faster.

Then Hopper falls on the ice. Luckily he isn't hurt.

'And it's also very slippery,' he laughs.

Flopsy, Nibbles and Blinders clamber onto the ice. They hold each other to stand up. They see who can slide the furthest. It's glorious fun.

If it were up to them, it could freeze every day.

January

The Biscuit Tin

It's raining. Blinders is inside, building a castle with his toy blocks.
But he doesn't have enough blocks to build a tower. What now?

Blinders has an idea.

There's a big biscuit tin in the kitchen. Blinders always thought that the tin looked like a tower. He starts to ask Mummy if he can borrow the tin for his castle, but the telephone rings. It's Mummy's best friend. She chats and chats. Blinders doesn't want to wait until Mummy finishes her phone call. He decides to borrow the tin now. He will tell Mummy about it later.

Finally Mummy hangs up the phone. Blinders is busy playing. So busy he forgets to tell her that he borrowed the biscuit tin.

Mummy sees that it's time for a snack for Blinders. She goes to the kitchen and looks for the biscuit tin. Surprise! The tin is not there.

'Who took the biscuit tin?' she asks. 'Maybe it was Blinders? Maybe he ate all the biscuits and hid the tin? That would be very naughty of him.'

She goes to Blinders.

'What are you doing with the biscuit tin?' she asks. Even before Blinders can tell the whole story, Mummy grabs the biscuit tin. She pops off the lid. The tin is full! Not one biscuit is missing.

Then Blinders tells the whole story to Mummy. Mummy understands. Blinders couldn't ask her, because Mummy couldn't listen.

'Blinders is such a sweet boy,' thinks Mummy. 'I think I'll give him two biscuits.'

The Snow Bunny

A thick blanket of snow has fallen out of the sky. The whole forest is white and silent.

An alarm clock rings in Mister Sack's bedroom. He yawns and gets out of his bed.

Mister Sack is the postman. He is always the first one up in the whole village. Post should be delivered early in the morning, in Mister Sack's opinion.

He puts on his winter coat and his warmest hat. But when he opens his door, he sees a wall of snow.

He can't get out of his house.

'What now?' thinks Mister Sack. 'I really must deliver the post.'

But then Mister Sack has an idea. He pushes up his sleeves.

'I'll dig a tunnel through the snow. After all, I am a rabbit! We rabbits are the best diggers in the forest.'

Mister Sack starts to dig a tunnel to the road. He pops up out of the snow and looks at the forest. It is beautiful today. Then he runs to the first house on his route. But he can't find the letterbox there. It must be under the snow!

'How am I going to solve this?' thinks Mister Sack. 'I'll just have to dig again.'

Super fast, Mister Sack digs his way to the letterbox. Then he pushes the post through the slit.

'So! On to the next letterbox,' says Mister Sack, and he hurries on his way.

That one is under snow, too. And so Mister Sack digs another tunnel.

This way, he delivers all the letters right on time. Isn't that good of Mister Sack?

The Fish

20 JANUARY

Hopper sits on the edge of his water lily pad, dangling his feet in the pad, looking out over the chilly water. He's bored. All his friends are off with their mummies and daddies.

'I wish I had somebody to play with,' he sighs. Suddenly he sees a movement in the water. Then he hears a tiny splash.

Hopper looks down but doesn't see anything. Then he sees something moving.

A fish comes up for air.

'So you're bored?' he asks.

'Er... yes,' says Hopper a bit scared.

'Let's play together,' proposes the fish.

That sounds like a good idea to Hopper. But... what game can you play with a fish?

Hopper thinks.

Then he takes a ball and throws it in the water. Like a shot, the fish swims after the ball. With his tail he swishes the ball back to Hopper. Then Hopper leaps into the water with a splash. He throws the ball back to the fish and they play a game of water football. It's really fun! Hopper isn't lonely any more. He's made a new friend.

January

A Letter for...

Flopsy is writing a letter. She draws a crown with lots of candles on top and writes her name.

'Done!' she says.

She folds the letter and puts it in a beautiful pink envelope.

Now she has to write the name of the person the letter is for. Luckily it's not very long. Mummy wrote it for Flopsy so she can copy it. First part of a circle, open on one side, with a little line. Then a funny letter with straight lines and a curve. Next a mountain, with another little line. Then the last letter – just a mountain.

'That wasn't too hard,' thinks Flopsy.

She sticks the stamp that Mummy gave her on the envelope.

'Daddy, could you please deliver this letter?' she asks.

'You're lucky that I'm the postman,' he smiles. 'You don't have to go to the postbox.'

The next day, a pink envelope falls into an old lady's letterbox. She picks it up and opens it. Then she sees the beautiful drawing that Flopsy has made for her birthday. It's Flopsy's grandmother. Happy birthday, Gran!

Hopper Wants to Play Football

It's snowy outside, but Hopper wants to play football. He takes his ball and goes outside. Flopsy, Nibbles and Blinders are making a snowman.

'Does anybody want to play football?' he asks.

'No,' answers Nibbles, 'we will have plenty of time for football when the snow melts.'

He puts the ball on the snow and kicks it. The ball rolls slowly over the snow and soon stops.

'You see?' smiles Nibbles. 'The ball can't roll in the soft snow.'

Hopper looks mad. He really wants to play football!

He tosses the ball high in the air. The ball bounces off a branch that's covered with snow. The branch wiggles and the snow falls off it. Right on top of Hopper.

Hopper is buried in snow. Brrr, that's cold! Snow goes inside his collar and melts on his face. Hopper shakes the snow off, laughing.

It looks like playing football in the snow isn't a good idea after all. Anyway, he will help his friends with the snowman now.

January

 ## The Shape

It's dark in the forest. The village lies under a thick blanket of snow. All the lights in the houses are out. Only in the tree house of the mayor, Mister Owl, is a light still on. Mister Owl is up late. All evening long, he has written letters and signed papers.

'Finally,' he yawns, 'it's time to go to bed.' He signs his last letter.

He blows out the candle on his desk and stands up. He takes a quick glance outside.

'So beautiful, all the snow outside,' he mumbles satisfied.

But what is that? Mister Owl presses his beak against the window. Did he see something?

Yes, someone's standing there. It's hard to see, but there's a shape out there.

'Who is outside at this hour?' he mumbles. But then a thought goes through his mind like lightning.

'Maybe it's a burglar?'

'Oh, gosh,' says Mister Owl, worried. 'I have to chase off that burglar.'

He runs to the kitchen and grabs a large pan. Quickly he puts on his thick coat because it's so cold outside. Then silently he goes to the front door. Mister Owl sneaks up to the shape. He gets his pan ready to give a hard whack. The shape stands deathly still. Mister Owl is really close to the shape now.

'But...' whispers Mister Owl. 'That's not a shape. It's the snowman the children made yesterday. I

fooled myself.'

Relieved, Mister Owl goes back to his house. Now he can go to sleep.

 ## Tug-of-War

Hopper has found a long, strong rope. 'Let's play tug-of-war,' proposes Blinders.

'How do you do that?' asks Flopsy.

'Easy,' says Blinders. He takes a piece of chalk and draws a line on the floor.

'We make two teams. Flopsy and Nibbles will be one team. Hopper and I are the other team. Each team grabs an end of the rope. Then we pull as hard as we can. The strongest team will pull the other team over the chalk line and win.'

Quickly each team grabs an end of the rope.

When Blinders gives the starting signal, the two teams start to pull as hard they can. It's exciting! At first it looks like Flopsy and Nibbles are going to win. But a second later it seems like Hopper and Blinders will. But suddenly, *SNAP!* The rope breaks.

Flopsy and Nibbles crash into the wall of the Friendship Tree. Fortunately they aren't hurt.

Hopper and Blinders, however, fall through the hole in the wall…

As soon as they can get to their feet, Flopsy and Nibbles run to the hole.

Then they burst out laughing.

Hopper and Blinders are lying on the ice of the frozen brook. Blinder's glasses are tipped at a funny angle on his nose. Hopper's hat is over his face, but he still has the rope.

'Lucky the brook is frozen,' laughs Flopsy. 'Otherwise you would be soaking wet!' Indeed. All's well that ends well.

The Penguin

Nibbles is a penguin today. He makes a bill from paper, puts it on his snout and waddles stiff as a board to the living room.

Quack, quack, he says.

'What's that funny animal, a duck?' asks Daddy.

Quack, quack. 'I am a penguin,' answers Nibbles.

'A penguin?' says Daddy to Mummy. 'Don't they live at the South Pole in the snow and ice?'

Quack, quack, says Nibbles jumping.

'I think they eat fish,' says Daddy.

Quaaack, says Nibbles. Nibbles doesn't like fish. With his flipper, Nibbles points at some honey biscuits.

'Oh, look,' laughs Mummy, 'This penguin prefers honey biscuits.'

'That is a crazy penguin,' smiles Daddy as he stands up. 'I'm going outside. Would the crazy penguin like to join me?'

Nibbles nods.

'Then put on your coat, because it's cold.'

Nibbles shakes his head no.

'Oh, I see,' says Daddy, 'penguins love the cold.'

The penguin nods approvingly. They go outside.

'Brrr… so cold,' thinks Nibbles. He starts to shiver. He'd better go back inside.

When Daddy comes in later, Nibbles is lying on the sofa close to the hearth. His bill is gone.

'What now?' asks Daddy. 'Aren't you a penguin?'

Nibbles shakes his head. 'I'm a sloth now. They live in the jungle where it's always warm. And the best part of all – they laze the day away.'

The Sledge

Nibbles and Flopsy are playing with a sledge. They pull it up the hill and then slide down, crowing with joy.

'That was great! Let's do it again!' shouts Flopsy.

'OK!' says Nibbles. 'We'll pull the sledge back up.'

'No,' says Flopsy. 'I don't want to go up that hill again.'

'How come?' asks Nibbles surprised.

'I want to go up that hill,' says Flopsy firmly, pointing at a very high hill.

'Isn't that dangerous?' asks Nibbles.

'Don't you dare?' replies Flopsy.

'Of course I dare,' says Nibbles, acting tough.

Together they pull the sledge up the hill.

'Ready?' shouts Nibbles to Flopsy when they reach the top.

'Okey-doke!' shouts Flopsy back. Nibbles pushes off and together they slide down the hill.

They go really fast. They scream and laugh. But suddenly the sledge bumps into something. The children fly through the air. Two pairs of boots are sticking out of the snow. Fortunately the snow is soft.

A moment later Nibbles and Flopsy crawl slowly out of the drift. They're completely covered with snow. They have cold, wet snow in their collars and up their sleeves and trouser legs. They don't like it.

After they shake off the snow, they pick up the sledge. It's still in one piece.

'Shall we do something else?' asks Flopsy quietly.

'That sounds good to me,' answers Nibbles. 'I've seen enough snow for today.'

The Tea Party

Flopsy's mummy gave her an old teapot and some tea cups to play with. She takes them to the Friendship Tree.

When Nibbles, Hopper and Blinders arrive at the tree they see Flopsy working busily.

'What are you doing, Flopsy?' asks Nibbles.

'I'm making tea,' she says. 'We're going to have a tea party. A cup of hot tea is great in this cold weather.'

The boys think that's fine.

'I also have chocolate cake,' says Flopsy, while she puts the yummy-smelling cake on a plate.

The tea is ready. Flopsy pours a cup for each of

them. The other three take a sip of the tea.

'Yuck!' snorts Nibbles. 'That tea is nasty!'

'Ugh!' yells Hopper, spitting it out. 'Blech.'

Blinder makes a face too. 'What kind of tea is it?'

Flopsy thinks about it for a moment.

'There are pebbles, branches, some mud from the brook, and an old sock in it.'

The three look at her with wide eyes.

'Don't you like it?' she asks surprised.

'No! Not at all,' they answer.

'Here, have a piece of cake,' she says apologising.

Suspicious, Nibbles asks, 'You didn't make it yourself, did you?'

Flopsy laughs. 'No, Mummy made it.'

That's all the boys need to know. They gobble it up.

A strange tea party-cake, but no tea!

A Little Accident

Nibbles is running through the house, in and out of rooms, up and down the stairs. Suddenly he stumbles and falls down hard on his knee.

'Ouch,' he yells. His knee really hurts.

Nibbles sits up and looks at it. He's got a cut.

Mummy comes in. She heard Nibbles fall.

'Are you hurt?' she asks, concerned.

Nibbles nods and points at his knee.

Mummy takes a long look at his knee. It's bleeding.

'Come, let's fix that,' says Mummy. She gets some antiseptic and a plaster from the cupboard.

She puts some bad-smelling antiseptic on the cut. That stings a bit. Nibbles doesn't like it, but he knows he has to have it. Otherwise the cut can get worse and hurt a lot more.

Nibbles does his best not to cry.

'There,' says Mummy, 'That's over. Now we just have to put the plaster on it.'

Nibbles likes that part a lot better because Mummy has a lot of nice plasters with pictures on them.

He chooses the plaster with superheroes.

'That looks tough,' says Mummy after she puts on the plaster. It hardly hurts at all now.

Nibbles can laugh again.

'Mind where you run in the future, Nibbles,' says Mummy.

Nibbles will do that. He doesn't need any more plasters!

Thaw

29 JANUARY

Hopper is playing on the frozen brook. He slides from left to right on the ice. He likes that.

The sky is a beautiful blue today. The sun is shining brightly too.

'What lovely weather,' sighs Hopper happily.

Here comes Flopsy. She stands still at the edge of the brook.

'Hi, Hopper,' she says. 'Are you still playing on the ice?'

'Yes,' answers Hopper. 'Lovely skating. Do you want to join me?'

'No,' says Flopsy, 'Mummy says I can't.'

'And why not?' asks Hopper, teasing her.

'Mummy says it's getting warmer. The ice is beginning to thaw, so it's dangerous to be on the ice.'

'Thaw?' asks Hopper as he continues to slide happily. 'What's that mean?'

'That's...' Flopsy starts to say. But then the ice cracks under Hopper's feet. He is scared. Then it cracks again. Hopper looks at Flopsy with wide eyes.

SNAP! goes the ice. Hopper falls through the crack into the freezing-cold water. 'Hopper!' screams Flopsy. 'Look out!'

Luckily Hopper can swim very well. Flopsy helps him out of the hole. She brings the soaked Hopper to the edge of the brook.

'That's what I meant,' says Flopsy. 'The ice melts because the sun is getting stronger every day now. That's what they call thawing. It's dangerous when the ice starts to thaw because it gets thin and you can fall through.'

'I've noticed,' shivers scared Hopper. Fortunately he got away with it this time.

The Newcomer

30 JANUARY

Mister Sack, the postman, comes down the path.

What's that, at the edge of the village?

Somebody is working really hard.

Mister Sack decides to take a look.

'Good day,' he says to the stranger.

It's a badger. He looks friendly. 'Good day to you too,' smiles the badger. Politely he shakes Mister Sack's paw.

'I'm Mister Tie.'

'Nice to meet you. I'm Mister Sack,' smiles the postman. 'What are you doing?'

'I would like to come and live here,' answers the badger. 'That's why I'm building a house.'

'Well, that's a tough job,' sighs Mister Sack.

The badger shrugs. 'Oh, I don't need much. If I work a couple of days really hard, my home should be ready.'

Mister Sack thinks for a while. 'Just a moment,' he says. 'I'll be right back.' And he tears off.

When he comes back a bit later, he has brought the entire village.

'This is Mister Tie,' explains Mister Sack. 'He would like to live in our village. Let's help him build his house.'

Everybody likes the idea. And they all start to work. After one day of building and digging, the house is ready.

'This is great,' exclaims Mister Tie satisfied. 'I could never do that alone.'

'But that's not all. We're also giving a party for our new neighbour,' smiles Mister Sack. He points to the path.

Here come Nibbles and his friends. They are bringing cake and fruit juice with them. It'll be a great party.

Mister Tie

Nibbles and his friends run to Mister Tie's house.

When they arrive there, they see Mister Tie dragging a ladder.

'Hello there!' he shouts happily.

'Hello Mister Tie,' they answer.

'What are you doing?' Flopsy wants to know.

'I'm going to hang a sign on the front of my house,' says Mister Tie.

A sign? The children are curious.

'You see,' continues Mister Tie, 'I'm a tailor. And that's why I'm going to put up this sign so everybody can see what I do for work.'

'You're a tailor?' asks Nibbles. 'So you can sew really well?'

'Yes, I can,' answers Mister Tie. 'Why? Is there a hole in your trousers?'

'No,' smiles Nibbles shyly.

'What kind of things can you make?' asks Flopsy curiously.

'Everything,' says Mister Tie while he screws the sign solidly in. 'Dresses, jackets, vests, trousers…'

'And swimming trunks?' Hopper wants to know.

'If somebody asks me? Yes,' laughs Mister Tie. 'You should come and have a look when my shop opens.'

'We'll do that,' answer the children.

'Fine. See you soon.'

'Bye, Mister Tie.'

February

Shadow

Nibbles is sitting on a settee in the lounge this evening. Behind him is a big lamp. He's turned it on.

On the wall behind him he sees a huge shadow. It's his own.

'Hello, shadow,' says Nibbles. He waves at the shadow. It looks as if his shadow is waving back.

Nibbles wiggles his body. The shadow wiggles immediately, just like he does.

Then he sticks out his arm. So does the shadow. It doesn't matter what Nibbles does – the shadow does exactly the same thing.

'Strange thing, a shadow,' thinks Nibbles to himself. Couldn't you ever move too fast for it?

He comes up with a plan. Silently, because maybe the shadow could hear something.

Suddenly he jumps behind the settee.

'Now I'm curious,' he thinks. He peeks – there's nothing to be seen on the wall except the shadow of the settee.

He sticks his head out a little.

Oh no! He sees the shadow of his ear sticking out from the settee's shadow. When he ducks behind the bench again, his ear's shadow disappears. You can't win. Nothing is faster than a shadow!

The Tailor

Today Mister Tie's tailor shop opens. The whole village has come to see it. Everyone is very curious to see what Mister Tie can do.

Nibbles and Flopsy are there. First they look in through the windows. The shop is full of clothing.

'Mister Tie has made all of those himself,' Nibbles says to Flopsy.

'Let's go in and have a look.'

Mister Tie sits in a corner, working behind his sewing machine.

'Hello, children,' he says with a smile. 'Have you come by to have a look at things?'

'Yes,' says Flopsy, 'but I also wanted to ask you something.'

Mister Tie raises his eyebrows. 'Oh, really? What can I do for you?'

Flopsy pulls out a cloth doll. One of her legs has torn loose.

'Aha, I see,' smiles Mister Tie. 'Shall I mend her for you?'

Flopsy gives the doll to Mister Tie. He gets to work with a needle and thread. Before long the doll's leg is back in place.

'This eye is also a bit loose,' he says, looking carefully at the doll. 'I'll fix that too for you.'

In a while Flopsy's doll is as good as new. My, is Flopsy happy!

'Thanks so much, Mister Tie.'
'Happy to help you, Flopsy.'

Nibbles' Nose

Nibbles has played outside all day with his friends today. But now it's time for him to go home.

Nibbles goes skipping home on the path in the woods.

Suddenly he stops and stands still. What is that?

Nibbles sticks his nose up in the air and sniffs.

'What can that be?'

He sniffs again, as hard as he can. Now he can't smell anything. Nibbles stands motionless on the path.

There! There it is again! This time he's definitely smelt something.

'I've got to get home!' he cries.

Nibbles starts to run. He goes as fast as he can. He comes upon Mister Owl.

'Hello, Nibbles!' he says. But Nibbles has no time to answer. His little legs carry him toward home at top speed.

Mister Owl can't understand. 'The youth of today,' he snorts.

Nibbles arrives at the front door, panting. The smell is strong now. There's no doubt. With shaky paws, he opens the door.

A wonderful, sweet scent greets him. He hangs up his jacket on the coat rack and runs to the kitchen.

Mummy just opened the oven door. She pulls out a tray of freshly-baked biscuits.

They're Nibbles' favourites!

'Did you see how well I could smell them?' he asks.

With a nose like Nibbles', you always know where to find something delicious.

Blocks

'Blinders, would you like to watch telly with me?' asks Hopper.

Blinders doesn't feel like it. He wants to play with blocks.

'Oh, come on,' insists Hopper. 'Watch telly with me.'

'But I want to play with blocks,' says Blinders.

'Blinders, don't be so mean,' whinges Hopper.

'Hopper, I have already told you. I want to play with blocks.'

Hopper gets angry. 'Blocks are for babies.'

'That's not true,' says Blinders, getting angry too.

'It is too. Blocks are for babies,' barks Hopper.

Mummy Mole comes between them. 'What's going on here?' she asks.

'Hopper wants me to watch telly with him. But I want to play with blocks,' says Blinders.

'Bah, don't be a baby,' teases Hopper.

'But Hopper,' says Mummy Mole angrily, 'you call Blinders a baby because he wants to play with blocks. You and he both are still young. There's nothing wrong with that, is there? What you are doing certainly is babyish. To keep on asking him to watch telly when he doesn't want to is babyish too.'

Now Hopper gets it.

'I've been a bit selfish, right?' he asks embarrassed.

Blinders and Mummy Mole nod.

'Hey, Blinders,' asks Hopper sweetly, 'would you like to play with blocks with me?'

Blinders looks at his friend happily.

'You bet, Hopper,' he laughs.

Hopper and Blinders build a really high tower of blocks together and have a great time. Just as kids do.

Miss Crow

Here comes Miss Crow. She lives at the very top of an old beech tree.

Her house is the highest in the forest.

Miss Crow is really old. Her wings are a little shabby. Today she's looking at the woods a bit sadly. Flopsy spots her.

'Miss Crow, you look so down. Can I help you?'

'Oh, my dear,' she replies, 'I can't get up to my nest

any more. My wings are too old to get me up that high. What can I do?'

Flopsy looks up. The nest really is high. Suddenly she has an idea.

She runs to the mayor and tells him about her plan. The mayor calls all the villagers together. Then he explains Flopsy's plan to them.

Immediately everybody gets busy. Four big birds fly to the nest.

They tie ropes to the nest. Then they lift the nest up. Carefully, they fly lower with the nest. They put the nest on an old stump.

Meanwhile Nibbles' father has made a ramp. They set the ramp up against the nest. Now everything is ready. Miss Crow can't believe her eyes.

Hesitantly she walks up the ramp and settles into her nest. She's so fond of the old thing! 'Thank you, everyone,' she cries.

And Flopsy? She knows that from now on, she can visit Miss Crow any time and get a lovely biscuit.

the woods. But the thick, dark rain clouds keep coming closer, faster and faster.

Suddenly Nibbles trips over a branch. Then there's a clap of thunder, this time right over their heads.

'Flopsy, go on, keep running!' yells Nibbles, who's lying on the ground.

Flopsy stops. 'No way,' she says firmly. She runs to Nibbles and helps him back up.

Now the first drops of rain are falling noisily.

'Come on, we have to keep going,' yells Flopsy. She drags Nibbles along, but he can hardly keep up with her.

Finally they get to Nibbles' house.

'We made it! Just in time!' Flopsy cries.

Crack! Another clap of thunder shakes the woods. Luckily they are just at the door. The two friends run inside as fast as they can.

'Without you I would have been soaked.'

'No problem. That's what friends are for!'

And so it is. That's why you have friends.

The Storm

A big storm is coming. Dark clouds are filling the sky.

Nibbles and Flopsy are hurrying home.

In the distance thunder rumbles. Each of them glances around. They don't like thunder. Not at all.

'Come on, Flopsy, let's run.'

They run as fast as their feet can carry them through

Rotten Weather

7 FEBRUARY

The storm continues. Mister Sack, the postman, is making his rounds. Good weather or bad, the post must be delivered. Mister Sack races from postbox to postbox in his old rain jacket. The wind blows through it. But Mister Sack stays cheerful.

When he arrives at the mayor's house, he pulls a letter out of his sack. Just as he tries to put it into the postbox, the wind grabs it. Whoops! The letter flies into the air.

'Oh brother,' grumbles Mister Sack.

He races after the letter. The wind blows it up and down.

Then the wind dies down. The letter floats to the ground. Mister Sack hurries over to it. But just as he reaches for it, the wind picks it up again.

'Oh no!' cries Mister Sack, 'I have to keep on chasing it.'

Mister Sack runs all over the forest. Now and then he has to run through deep puddles.

At last, the wind dies down again.

Slowly the letter flutters to the ground.

Mister Sack hurries over to it. Oh no! It's going to land in a puddle!

He makes a long leap and just barely catches the letter. Then he lands in the puddle himself.

Poor Mister Sack is soaking wet. Luckily the letter has stayed dry. Mister Sack stuffs it quickly into the letterbox.

The things a postman has to do…

The Reward

8 FEBRUARY

Flopsy is carrying a heavy shopping bag. It's hard, but she does her best.

She brings the bag to Miss Crow, who is too old to do her shopping herself now. That's why Flopsy does it for her.

Miss Crow is very happy to see Flopsy.

'You are such a sweet girl,' she says. 'Here, have a biscuit.'

'Thank you very much,' says Flopsy, licking her lips.

'Do you know what I think is so nice?' asks Miss Crow while Flopsy takes a quick bite of the biscuit.

'When I was a young crow, I did the shopping for an old fox. I found that so nice to do. And each time I got a little reward for doing it.'

'Ish dat sho?' asks Flopsy, her mouth full of biscuit.

Miss Crow smiles. 'Yes, and now that I've become old myself, I think that it's marvellous that somebody would do my shopping for me. I hope that, when you are an old rabbit, there will be someone who does your shopping for you.'

'I hope sho too, Mish Crow,' says Flopsy as she pops the last piece of biscuit into her mouth.

Miss Crow gives Flopsy a big hug.

'But Miss Crow,' says Flopsy, her mouth finally empty, 'what reward did you get from the old fox?'

'What do you think? A delicious biscuit, of course.'

All Torn Up

Mister Owl is expecting an important guest today.

Miss Falcon from the Ministry of Forest-Dwellers is coming for a visit. That's why Mister Owl has put on his finest suit.

'Now, I'll just put on my mayor's sash, and then I'm ready,' he says.

But the sash falls on the floor. When he bends over to pick it up, there's a ripping sound.

What was that? Oh, no – Mister Owl's trousers have ripped open. What now?

Mister Owl has an idea. He runs down the path through the woods, still wearing his torn trousers. He goes into Mister Tie's shop.

'Mister Tie,' he cries in alarm, 'you've got to help me!'

'What can I do for you, Mister Mayor?'

'My… uh,' mumbles the owl, while he points to his trousers.

'Oh, I get it,' laughs the tailor. 'Give me your trousers.'

Mister Tie gets a needle and thread and gets busy. He neatly mends the torn trousers.

'So that's done,' he says in a moment. 'But you need to think about getting a new suit. This one is all worn out.'

While Mister Owl puts on his trousers, he says, 'Tomorrow I'll come by for a new suit. But I have to run to City Hall now. Until then, goodbye, Mister Tie.'

Mister Owl runs off down the path. 'And thanks!' he yells back.

When Miss Falcon arrives, Mister Owl is in fine shape to welcome her. Without any holes in his trousers.

February

The Suit

Ding-dong, sounds the doorbell in Mister Tie's shop.

'Good morning, Mister Owl.'

'Good morning, Mister Tie. I've come for that new suit. You are right, this one's worn out.'

'It certainly is. What do you have in mind? Something with checks?'

'No, no checks. I, um…' Mister Owl leans a little closer to Mister Tie. 'I've heard that vertical lines make you look… thinner. Is that so?'

'Yes indeed that's true. Let's look at stripes, then.' Mister Owl looks at the beautiful fabrics Mister Tie shows him. He's not sure which one to pick.

'I would take this one,' helps Mister Tie. 'This colour will look good on you.'

'Think so?'

'I'm sure. Now I just need to measure you so I know how big to make your suit.'

As soon as that's done, Mister Tie starts working. Later that week the suit is done. Mister Owl puts it on and stands in front of the mirror.

'It looks great, doesn't it?' says Mister Owl with a broad smile. Mister Tie is a very good tailor!

And those vertical stripes really do make you look thinner.

The Monster

Nibbles, Blinders and Flopsy sit in the Friendship Tree, waiting for Hopper. Suddenly they hear footsteps.

'That's Hopper,' says Flopsy.

But instead, an ugly beast appears in the entrance. It has a black face and red eyes. The friends scream!

'Ha-ha-ha-ha!' laughs the monster, 'you scaredy-cats!'

Then the friends get it. It's Hopper, wearing a mask.

Hopper laughs and takes it off. 'You should have seen your faces! And your screaming – I've never seen such cowards.'

Blinders, Flopsy and Nibbles are still trembling. They didn't like being tricked.

Hopper is laughing and starts to sit on the bench. But Nibbles yells, 'Watch out! A spider!'

Hopper screams and leaps high in the air.

Now it's Nibbles' turn to laugh.

'Fooled you!' he yells. 'There was no spider there!'

'You should have seen your face,' mocks Flopsy. 'And your screaming!'

'Yeah, I have never seen such a coward,' grins Blinders.

Now it's Hopper's turn to feel like he's been tricked. He gets a little of his own medicine.

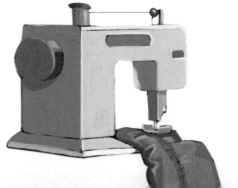

February

Bath Time

Nibbles and his sister Misty are lying in the bath with their ears under water. They love that, because everything sounds different that way.

They hear Mummy's voice. It sounds like she's in a submarine.

'Nibbles and Misty, I'm coming soon to dry you. A visitor is coming,' calls Mummy.

'What did you say?' ask the two underwater mice, laughing. 'We can't hear what you're saying.'

They lie as still as they can in the water. They hear Mummy's footsteps coming toward the bathroom. Then they hear the door bell sound.

Mummy goes downstairs. With Mummy gone, it's totally quiet under the water. The only sound comes from the water gently lapping the sides of the bath.

Now they hear two pairs of footsteps. Mummy is not alone – someone is with her.

'Look, Auntie Hamster. Here they are. But they can't hear you, you know.'

Nibbles and Misty look toward the open door. There stands the aunt who can tell the best stories in the whole wide world.

'Hello, my dears,' they hear Auntie Hamster say in an underwater voice.

Nibbles and Misty jump up excitedly.

'Auntie Hamster!' they cry.

'Oh, look – they can hear us!' laughs Auntie Hamster.

Nibbles and Misty shake the water out of their ears. They don't want to miss a single word of Auntie Hamster's stories.

Auntie Hamster

Nibbles and Misty are sitting on Auntie Hamster's lap. She's a real adventurer. Every time she comes to visit she has a new, exciting tale to tell them.

'Did I ever tell you about the time a tiger followed me? See, I was walking quietly through the jungle when suddenly a huge tiger appeared before me. I immediately started to run. But the tiger came after me, growling and roaring. I had to get away!

Then I had an idea. I began to run round and round a thick tree with lots of roots at its feet. The tiger followed me. I ran until I was exhausted. Then, in a flash, I hid myself under the roots of the tree.

My plan worked! The tiger didn't see me duck in, and he kept running round and round the tree. He ran until he was totally out of breath – and fed up. All of a sudden he collapsed in a heap, just as I had hoped he would.

I crept out from under the roots and escaped. And that's how I escaped the claws of that ferocious tiger. How about that?'

It's perfectly still. Nibbles and Misty are staring at Auntie Hamster with wide-open eyes. They don't believe a word she said. But they don't say so, because

even if not one word is true, she can tell a story so well!

Sheriff Hopper

'Wow, Hopper, you look really cool,' says Nibbles as Hopper arrives at the Friendship Tree. Hopper is dressed like a cowboy. He's got on a big hat, cowboy boots and his daddy's waistcoat.

'Howdy, partner,' he says, folding his arms across his chest. 'I'm Sheriff Hopper, and I keep law and order in the village.'

'Yeah, you look like a sheriff,' says Nibbles. 'But you've made a mistake about your weapon, I think.'

Hopper looks at Nibbles in surprise.

Nibbles points to the sword that's hanging from Hopper's waist.

'Cowboys never have swords.'

Hopper doesn't know what to say.

'Are you sure…?' he asks hesitantly.

'I'm afraid so,' answers Nibbles.

Disappointed, Hopper sits down on a stool. 'So I'm not such a cool sheriff, huh?' He sighs deeply. 'What shall I do? I really wanted to be a sheriff.'

Suddenly Nibbles runs outside. 'I'll be right back!'

Hopper watches in surprise.

A moment later Nibbles is back. 'Here. Put this on your vest. Sheriffs always wear a gold star. Now you can be a real sheriff, after all.'

'Really?' asks Hopper relieved. 'Then you can have my sword.'

'Super,' cries Nibbles. 'I have always wanted a sword. Now I can finally really be a knight. *En garde!*

So everybody is happy!

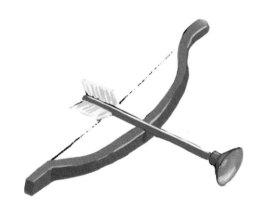

The Go-Cart

Nibbles' and Misty's father is a carpenter. There's nothing he can't build.

Today he's made a little go-cart for them. It's going to be a really nice one. There are places for two passengers and it has four wheels. Daddy has painted it beautifully too.

Now they can start playing with it.

They take turns riding in the car and pushing it. They have so much fun!

But it makes you tired to push so much. After a while they both need a rest.

'Hey, look,' Nibbles says to his sister, 'here comes Mummy.'

Indeed, she's coming toward them, struggling with two heavy shopping bags.

'My, these weigh a lot,' she says, setting them down.

'Why don't you put them in our cart?' suggests Nibbles.

Mummy thinks that's a great idea. She sets the shopping bags in the cart. Nibbles and Misty can just fit in with them. Mummy picks up the shaft on the front and starts to pull them along.

'This is a lot better,' she laughs. 'I'm going to take your cart with me when I go shopping from now on.'

Nibbles and Misty think that's a super idea. That means that every time Mummy goes shopping they will get a free ride. Fantastic!

Disco

Flopsy has brought a radio to the Friendship Tree. Today she's playing disco.

'Disco what?' asks Blinders.

'A disco,' explains Flopsy, 'is where you go if you want to have a good time dancing.'

'But I don't know how to dance,' says Blinders.

'Dancing is easy,' laughs Nibbles. 'You just move as you want to the music. Watch.'

Nibbles, Flopsy and Hopper jump up and down while the music booms.

Blinders keeps still.

'Blinders doesn't know how to dance,' teases Hopper, jumping around himself.

That makes Blinders angry. 'That's what you think,'

he says. He pushes his glasses firmly down on his nose and begins to spring and wiggle like crazy. He jumps left, right, forward, backward. He whirls around and waves his arms.

Blinders dances so fast that he loses his balance. He smacks into Nibbles. Nibbles bangs into Flopsy. Flopsy falls against Hopper. In one second they are all on the floor.

Ow! and *Oooh!* fill the air.

One by one they stand up.

Blinders sets his glasses right on his nose.

'I… uh, I think I did my best but I went too far.'

'You might say that,' says Flopsy, rubbing her sore leg.

Then another great song starts on the radio.

'Shall we dance some more?' asks Nibbles.

'OK,' answers Flopsy, 'but Blinders has to be a little less crazy this time.'

They all burst out laughing. Then they get back to their disco and have a ball.

Heavy Work

Mister Sack, the postman, has bad luck today. He has to deliver a big parcel to Mister Salamander. It's heavy as lead. Mister Sack bends over to pick it up.

'Now I have to take this to that annoying Mister Salamander. That stingy character has a terrible postbox. It's in such bad shape that when I try to put a letter in it, I'm always afraid that the whole thing will fall apart. He really should buy a new one.'

A while later, really tired and sweating like a horse, Mister Sack arrives at Mister Salamander's door with the heavy parcel. He rings the bell. A moment later the door opens.

'Here… here is a parcel for you,' pants Mister Sack.

'A parcel for me? How nice,' cries Mister Salamander in surprise.

Curious, Mister Salamander begins to open the parcel. Mister Sack sinks down exhaustedly to sit on the doorstep.

'Hey, look,' exclaims Mister Salamander in delight, 'it's my new postbox!'

Mister Sack can't believe his ears. But it's true: here's a beautiful, brand new, bright red postbox.

'I ordered it especially for you,' explains Mister Salamander to Mister Sack. 'I thought that you'd be happy if I got a new one. That old one is a wreck.'

Mister Sack is really happy. He just wishes it weighed a little less.

February

Alphabet Soup

Mummy has made soup. Wonderful smelling vegetable soup. Nibbles and Misty can't wait to try it.

Especially because Mummy has put letter-shaped pasta in it.

At the table, Mummy serves the soup. Fragrant steam rises to Nibbles' face.

Suddenly he recognises that there are lots of little letters in his soup.

'Mummy, look. That's the first letter of my name, right?'

Mummy looks at his bowl.

'Yes indeed, Nibbles. That's an N.'

Nibbles fishes out the N with his spoon. Then he sees another letter that he knows.

'That's the second letter of my name!' he cries.

Mummy looks again. He's right! He fishes out the letter I with his spoon. This is fun: now the first and second letters of his name are in his spoon.

There's another. And another.

In a little while he has fished out all the letters of his name with his spoon.

'Look, Mummy, I have spelled my name!' he exclaims proudly.

'That's wonderful, Nibbles. But please eat your soup now,' answers Mummy. 'Otherwise it will get cold.'

Nibbles takes one last look at the letters in his soup spoon. Then he sticks them all in his mouth.

'Oops,' he thinks to himself, 'I just ate my name up.' He doesn't know what to think.

But then he tastes the flavours of the letters and the soup. It's delicious.

'I'm glad I have such a delicious name,' he decides. Hungrily, he eats up the rest of his soup. Yum!

An Exciting Book

Nibbles and Flopsy are going to visit Blinders.

When they come into his bedroom they find Blinders sitting on his bed. Blinders is reading a book. Or pretending to, since just like the others, he can't read yet. But he wants to fool his

friends.

'Hello, Blinders,' say Nibbles and Flopsy. 'What are you up to?'

'I was just reading this book,' answers Blinders.

Nibbles and Flopsy look at Blinders with surprise.

'I didn't know you could read,' says Flopsy.

'It's not that hard, you know,' offers Blinders.

'Really?' asks Nibbles amazed. But then both Nibbles and Flopsy look at the cover of the book. They look at each other and wink.

Nibbles goes to sit next to Blinders on the bed.

'What sort of a book is it?' he wants to know.

'It's… um… a book about an explorer.'

'How do you know that?' asks Nibbles curiously.

'It says so in the book,' stammers Blinders.

'Have you noticed what a beautiful cover this book has?' Flopsy asks Nibbles.

Nibbles nods. 'Yes, and see the nice pictures on it. But something's a little wrong.'

Curious, Blinders takes a look. Then he sees it. Oh boy, he's got the book upside down. Nibbles and Flopsy knew it all along.

'I just wanted to fool you a little,' laughs Blinders. 'But you caught me!'

They have a good laugh together.

On the Bench

A new neighbour has come to live in the village. It's Miss Hedgehog. Miss Hedgehog has quills, like sharp needles, on her back. But she can't do anything about that. That's her nature.

Mister Owl has invited her to the village hall to welcome her.

'Please have a seat,' he says, offering her a place on the settee.

'I think I'll stand,' says Miss Hedgehog, but Mister Owl insists that she take a seat. So Miss Hedgehog gracefully sits on the soft cushions.

'May I offer you a cup of tea?' he asks her.

'Yes, but…' But Mister Owl has already disappeared into the kitchen to make tea.

A moment later he pours Miss Hedgehog a cup of tea.

'Would you like milk or sugar?'

'No, thanks. But what I wanted to say…'

'Please go ahead,' murmurs Mister Owl as he carefully sips from his cup.

'What I wanted to say is that it's not a good idea to have me sit here. With all the quills on my back I am stuck now to your soft settee.'

'Heavens!' cries Mister Owl surprised. 'I'm so sorry!'

Mister Owl needs all his strength to pull Miss Hedgehog loose. Luckily he's able to free her.

'Next time, just let me sit on a wooden stool. That's much better.'

Indeed, you only ask a hedgehog to sit on your settee once.

Miss Hedgehog

Nibbles, Hopper, Flopsy and Blinders are picking early spring flowers at the edge of the forest. They choose the best blossoms and gather them together into a huge bouquet. It looks lovely.

Then they walk along the path.

A little later they come to Miss Hedgehog's home. Nibbles rings the bell. Miss Hedgehog comes immediately to open the door.

'Good morning, Miss Hedgehog,' says Nibbles.

'Good morning to you all,' says Miss Hedgehog.

'Welcome to our village,' sing the friends together, handing the flowers to her.

'What beautiful flowers!' exclaims Miss Hedgehog, touched. 'Thank you so much! You are so nice. What lovely youngsters!'

'We're happy to give them to you,' says Nibbles. The four friends stand around, looking at Miss Hedgehog expectantly.

At first Miss Hedgehog doesn't get it. But then she sees the hungry eyes of the four rascals.

'Oh, and now you expect a little something from me, is that it?' she asks apologetically. 'I'll be right back.'

When she comes back, she's got a biscuit tin in her hands. The faces of the friends light up. They each get a honey biscuit. Delicious.

'You must come by any time you want to, especially if you feel like having a biscuit. Agreed?'

'Agreed!' they answer delighted. 'See you soon, Miss Hedgehog!'

The Elephant

Today Nibbles is an elephant. He's put an old sock on his nose. That's his trunk.

He crawls on all fours into the lounge. Every now and then he stops and swings his trunk from side to side. Real elephants do that. He's seen that on telly.

Nibbles comes up to a house plant. It stands in a big pot on the floor.

'Elephant is hungry,' says Nibbles. He tries to eat some leaves.

But this elephant is too small. He has to stretch to

reach the lowest leaves.

How do elephants do it? Of course – they use their trunks to reach them. Nibbles has seen that on telly too.

Nibbles pretends his arm is his trunk and grabs a branch. He pulls it toward himself.

But what happens next? To his surprise, the branch breaks off. Nibbles stands there with the branch in his hands.

Here comes Mummy into the lounge. She sees Nibbles with the broken branch. Then she sees the plant, missing its branch. She gets angry.

A bit later Nibbles is standing in the corner. He's being punished. He still has his sock around his nose. An elephant being punished in a corner.

Do real elephants also have to stand in the corner when their mummies punish them?

The Photographer

Flopsy's mummy is letting her use her camera.

'I am a photographer,' she says to Nibbles. 'And you will be my model.'

'What should I do?' asks Nibbles.

Flopsy considers. Then she runs to the dress-up chest and pulls a silly hat out of it.

'Here, put this on.'

Nibbles puts the silly hat on his head. 'And now?'

Flopsy considers again. 'Go and stand up on that stool.'

'Why should I?' Nibbles wants to know.

'I want to make a nice portrait of you. You have to do something special so I can do that.'

Poor Nibbles climbs up on the stool.

'Now smile really hard.'

Nibbles smiles his biggest, toothiest smile. Flopsy grabs the camera and starts taking pictures.

After a while Nibbles asks, 'Are you about done? I'm getting fed up with standing on this stool.'

'Almost,' says Flopsy. 'True art takes time and patience.'

Flopsy keeps on shooting pictures. After quite a while she's done. Nibbles is glad it's over.

The next day Nibbles drops by to visit Flopsy to see the photos for which he had to pose so long.

'Could I please see the pictures?' he asks.

Flopsy begins to blush. Cautiously she picks up the folder of photos that is lying on the table. Nibbles opens the folder and takes the pictures out.

Oh no, they are all fuzzy. Some show only an arm or a leg. Nibbles starts to laugh and laugh. Flopsy has lots to learn before she can be a good photographer.

The Vampire from the Woods

Hopper has found a book about vampires. They look awful. But that's cool, he thinks. He would like to be a vampire too.

Hopper runs to his toy chest. His knight's cape can do well as a vampire cape. Then he goes looking for vampire teeth. Found them.

He's ready now. He's the Vampire from the Woods.

'But,' he thinks, 'it's still daylight. Vampires don't go out during the day. No, they only go out at the night. As soon as the sun sets I'll go out. I'll hide in a dark corner and wait until somebody comes by. Then I will jump out of my hiding place and give him a good scare. That will be funny.'

Hopper waits until it gets dark.

My, it takes a long time. A vampire has to have lots of patience.

Finally it's night.

Hopper slips outside. Boy, is it dark. The moon is shining spooky light through the trees.

'Brrr,' shivers Hopper, 'this isn't going to be easy.'

Suddenly Hopper hears something rustling in the branches. He screams.

'What… what was that?' he asks with a shaky voice. He doesn't hear anything else.

Hopper has had enough of this. He runs as fast as he can inside. He throws his vampire teeth, cape and vampire book in the corner. Then he jumps in

bed and hides under his covers.

No, Hopper doesn't want to be a vampire any more. It's too scary.

Blinders is Sick

Who's that, suffering in the corner? It's Blinders.

He doesn't feel good. Chills run up and down his back and he feels hot and cold at the same time. He really just wants to lie down and sleep.

'You have a fever,' Mummy says. 'Stay warm and rest inside today.'

Blinders had agreed with his friends to play outside today. But he doesn't feel like that any more.

Mummy brings him warm blankets and covers him up. The bell sounds.

It's the doctor. He takes Blinders' temperature. 'You have the flu,' he says. 'You need to stay in bed and rest for a few days.'

The doctor gives Mummy some medicine. Blinders needs to take it so he can get better. Bah! It tastes awful, Blinders thinks. But he drinks it down anyway.

'Good little patient,' says Mummy.

After the doctor leaves Mummy takes care of Blinders. She puts his favourite books by his bed. She makes yummy herbal tea and mixes in some honey because Blinders loves that. And she lets Blinders watch telly if he wants.

So there Blinders lies. Nice and warm, wrapped up and being cared for by the best nurse that ever was. In some ways it's nice to be sick.

A Dress for Flopsy

Flopsy and her mummy are going to see Mister Tie, the tailor. Mummy wants him to make a dress for Flopsy. In a few days it will be Flopsy's birthday and Mummy wants her to look her best.

Mister Tie lays some fabrics on the table. Flopsy can pick out the prettiest. She picks some pink fabric with tiny white flowers on it.

Mister Tie picks up his measuring tape. It's a long thing with lots of marks and numbers on it. That's how Mister Tie can know exactly how tall Flopsy is so that the dress fits her perfectly. He also measures around her tummy. He needs to know that the dress will not be too tight or too loose.

'So, that's the first step,' says Mister Tie. 'Tomorrow you can come and get your dress.'

But Flopsy wants to stay longer. She wants to see how he makes her dress. Mister Tie likes this.

He gets busy with paper and the fabric. He draws forms on the paper and puts them on the fabric. Flopsy has no idea what he's doing.

Then Mister Tie takes his scissors and cuts the fabric into the shapes he drew on the paper. He takes the shapes to his sewing machine.

'Now I'll sew all these pieces together,' he explains. The sewing machine makes a soft rattling sound. Before long a dress starts to take shape.

'Whew! It's getting late,' says Mister Tie. 'I'll do the rest tomorrow.'

Flopsy can hardly wait!

February

Trying On the Dress

Mister Tie goes into his workshop. He turns the sign that says *CLOSED* over so now it says *OPEN*. Then he opens his door.

Somebody is waiting there. It's Flopsy.

'Good morning, Mister Tie,' she says. 'Is my dress ready?'

'Yes indeed,' laughs Mister Tie. 'You can try it on now.'

The dress looks lovely. Flopsy can't wait to put it on.

'Careful,' warns Mister Tie, 'there may still be pins here and there.'

Cautiously Flopsy pulls her dress on.

It fits perfectly. She looks in the mirror. She can't believe her eyes.

'I look like a princess,' she says astonished.

'If it's your birthday tomorrow, then you are a bit of a princess, aren't you?'

Flopsy is so happy. She throws her arms around Mister Tie and gives him a big hug.

'Ow!' cries Mister Tie.

Flopsy lets Mister Tie go, scared by his cry. Mister Tie rubs his leg.

'I think there's at least one more pin in your dress.'

He bends over and pulls the pin out of the dress.

'That one I forgot,' he laughs. 'OK. Now that your dress is completely free of pins I declare it finished.'

Now the party can begin.

The Birthday Girl

Today is Flopsy's birthday. It's time to celebrate!

Here come Hopper, Nibbles and Blinders. They each are carrying a present.

'Happy birthday, Flopsy,' they sing.

First Nibbles gives the birthday girl a long, narrow package. When she unwraps it, she sees two long poles.

Flopsy doesn't really know what to think. 'Uh… thank you, Nibbles,' she says finally.

Then she gets a box from Hopper. Curious, she opens it. There's a net in it…

'What's going on here?' thinks Flopsy. 'What could I do with a net?' But since she's very polite, she says thank you very nicely to Hopper.

Then Blinders gives her the last present. Flopsy really hopes that Blinders has a nice present for her. She tears off the wrapping paper. Two tennis racquets and a tennis ball sit inside the box.

Now Flopsy gets it! It's a tennis set!

The poles that Nibbles gave her will hold up the net that Hopper gave her.

Hopper, Nibbles and Blinders burst out laughing. 'You should have seen your face when you unwrapped the two poles,' they chuckle. 'You had no idea what they were for, did you?'

Flopsy sees that her friends have really fooled her. 'You are such rascals,' she says. 'But you are the best friends in the whole world. Let's play tennis!'

A Meeting

Miss Hedgehog, the newest neighbour in the village, is doing her shopping.

She passes by Mister Tie's tailor shop. Since she's never been there before, she looks in through the shop's window. Just by chance Mister Tie looks out at the same time. The two look at each other eye to eye through the glass.

Mister Tie hurries outside.

'Have I frightened you?' he asks concerned.

'Not at all. I just didn't expect to be looking right into another pair of eyes,' she laughs.

'Neither did I. May I introduce myself? I'm Tom Tie. I am a tailor.'

'Nice to meet you. I'm Helen Hedgehog.'

'Please come in. May I offer you a cup of tea?'

'That would be lovely. Thank you.'

A bit later they are sitting together and chatting.

Mister Tie explains that he hasn't lived very long in the village himself.

Then Miss Hedgehog glances at the clock. She jumps up suddenly. 'Oh no, is it so late already? I needed to go to Miss Squirrel's shop. But it's closed now. I don't have anything left to eat at home.'

Mister Tie calms her. 'Don't worry. Please stay and have dinner with me. I would enjoy that very much.'

Mister Tie and Miss Hedgehog have a really nice time together that evening. They talk until late into the night. Miss Hedgehog can't remember when she had had such a nice dinner.

March

 ## Spring Cleaning

Flopsy is helping Mummy clean the house. Every nook and cranny must be cleaned. Together, they push a big chest out from the wall. Behind it they find a doll lying in the dust.

'Look at that,' says Mummy. 'How long has she been here?'

'A long time,' says Flopsy. 'I can't even remember when I played with her last.'

'You know, you have so many toys,' says Mummy. 'Maybe while we are cleaning, you could put aside the toys you don't play with any more.'

'Good idea,' nods Flopsy. They go back to work. Flopsy lays out all her toys. She puts the ones she doesn't want any more into a bag. Then she puts the ones she wants to keep neatly away. The bag is full.

'What are you going to do now with that bag?' asks Mummy.

'I'm going to give them to my friend. She has a little sister. I bet she'll be happy to get so many new toys!'

How nice of Flopsy. It's good she found that doll in the dust!

 ## Paper Flowers

'What a pretty flower,' says Flopsy to Miss Crow. 'Does it smell good?'

'It's not a real flower,' smiles Miss Crow. 'I made it myself, out of paper.'

'How beautiful!' exclaims Flopsy in surprise. 'Can you teach me how to do that?'

'Of course. I need some more,' answers Miss Crow. A little later they are at the table.

First Flopsy has to fold a piece of green paper into a triangle. That will make the stem.

While Miss Crow cuts a wire and wraps it with cotton, Flopsy cuts lots of paper petals. Miss Crow puts them all around one end of the stem. The flower is done.

'Cool!' says Flopsy. 'Can we make another?'

'Why, sure,' answers Miss Crow. Together they make a lot of flowers, until they have a bouquet ready.

'I'm going to give this bouquet to Mummy,' says Flopsy.

'That will really make her happy,' beams Miss Crow. A little later Flopsy comes home.

She gives her bouquet to Mummy.

'Thank you! What beautiful flowers!' says Mummy. 'Do they smell good?'

Flopsy laughs out loud. And you know why.

March

The Bookshelf

Blinders wants to read a big, fat book that's sitting high up on the bookshelf.

It's a book that explains everything. Daddy calls it an encyclopaedia. But Daddy has told Blinders not to touch it. He's afraid that Blinders will damage this expensive book.

But Blinders wants to look at it. He's going to be really careful, so Daddy won't notice anything.

Silently, Blinders takes a stool and sets it in front of the shelf. He climbs onto the stool. He reaches for the book. Bother! He still can't reach it.

Maybe if he stands on tiptoes he can.

Yes, he can just touch the bottom of the book.

Carefully, Blinders wiggles his fingers and slowly he moves the book forward. Now he reaches up with his other arm to hold it better.

Suddenly the book slides out and falls. Unfortunately, it hits Blinder's head! Blinders and the book fall to the floor.

Daddy comes running into the room. When he sees the book and Blinders on the floor, he knows what's happened. He feels Blinder's head. He's got a bump where the book hit him. Daddy looks at the book and starts laughing.

'Blinders, you aren't going to believe what page is open in this book.'

'It's about B, for Bumps!'

But Blinders isn't laughing. He rubs his head and is glad Daddy isn't mad at him.

Everything that Grows...

Nibbles is watching a gardening show on telly. A man in a straw hat is explaining how to take good care of your flowers.

It sounds interesting. Nibbles decides to try a little gardening himself.

In the garden shed he finds a flowerpot. Next to it is a bag of compost. He scoops up some compost and puts it into the flowerpot.

With a trowel, Nibbles digs up some flowers from the garden, roots and all. He plants the flowers in the flowerpot. Now a little plant food, some water, and the job's done.

Nibbles is proud of himself. It looks very pretty.

With a lot of work he carries the heavy pot into the living room.

'These beautiful flowers belong here,' thinks Nibbles.

Suddenly he hears a shout from the garden. Mummy is waving her arms in the air. Daddy comes running. They dash into the house.

'Nibbles!' exclaims Mummy angrily. 'What have you done with my flowers…?'

Mummy puts her hand to her mouth.

Together, Mummy and Daddy look at the flowerpot on the coffee table. Droopy flowers hang over the edge. Dirty water drips out of the bottom. And the plant food stinks!

It was a long day for Nibbles after that. First, he had to put the flowers back in the garden then he had to clean up the puddle on the coffee table. Gardening is a lot harder than he thought.

Flying Hopper

Hopper wants to fly. He wants to be the first frog who ever flew. He pictures his name in the newspaper: 'Hopper the Flying Frog.'

He's drawn a lightning bolt on an old t-shirt and put his red trainers on.

He looks like a real stunt man.

He's also got a plan. He needs four things: a strong plank, a barrel, a rope and a log.

Hopper goes over to a big tree. He puts the log on the ground. He lays the plank on top of it. It looks like a seesaw.

Then he takes the rope and throws it over a branch of the tree. He ties one end to the barrel. Then he pulls on the rope and the barrel goes up in the air.

He ties the rope to the trunk.

Everything's ready now. The show must go on!

Hopper stands on the seesaw. He unties the rope from the tree trunk. Suddenly the barrel falls down. It lands on the seesaw. It flips up and shoots Hopper into the air.

The next day Hopper's picture is indeed in the newspaper. You can see him hanging from a branch of the tree. Below you see a whole lot of people looking up at him. The fire brigade is busy trying to get Hopper unstuck from the tree with their long ladders.

But Hopper was lucky. The newspaper didn't make too much fun of him.

Fish Feeding

Flopsy and Nibbles are standing on the bridge over the brook. They watch the fish coming to the surface now and then.

Nibbles has an idea. 'Let's go home and get some food for the fish,' he says. They run home.

Flopsy is the first one back to the bridge. She has a bag full of breadcrumbs. When she tosses a handful into the water, the fish go wild.

'Easy does it,' says Flopsy. 'There is more than enough for everyone. Look, here comes Nibbles. He has more for you.'

Indeed, here comes Nibbles. He has a bag too… filled with sweets.

'Are you going to feed them to the fish?' asks Flopsy cautiously.

'Uh, yeah…' answers Nibbles.

Flopsy breaks out laughing.

'Nibbles, come on – fish don't eat sweets! They like breadcrumbs and worms, not sweets. We can't use your sweets,' says Flopsy.

Nibbles thinks this over.

'Oh no? Just watch this.'

He takes some breadcrumbs from Flopsy's bag and throws them into the water. 'One for the fish….' Then he takes out two sweets and sticks one in Flopsy's mouth and the other in his own. 'And one for us.'

That way everyone is happy – the fish and the fish-feeders.

The Hole in the Path

There has been a big hole in the path in the woods for a long time.

One day Hopper has had enough of it. He decides to repair it. He takes his shovel and wheelbarrow and goes to the path.

'Hey, Hopper, what are you doing?' asks Nibbles when he spots him.

'I'm going to fill in this silly hole so that the path will be all smooth again,' answers Hopper.

'And what are you going to fill it with?' asks Nibbles curiously.

'With sand from that pile there,' says Hopper. He points to a place where there's a heap of sand in the middle of the path. 'That way this hole gets filled and the sand pile over there disappears. That will give us a nice flat path.'

Nibbles thinks that's a great idea. 'I'd love to help you, but I'm going to the shop for Mummy.'

'No problem,' says Hopper. 'I can fix this myself.'

Before long Nibbles comes back. The hole is completely filled up.

'Hey, Hopper, good work!' he calls to his friend.

'I think so too,' says Hopper really pleased.

But then Nibbles looks at the place where the sand pile was. There's a big hole in the path. 'But what's that, Hopper? I thought you were going to make the path smoother.'

'Well, uh… When I moved the pile of sand from over there, the hole wasn't completely filled. So I dug up a little more…'

Hopper filled one hole and made another!

Cake

Miss Hedgehog has baked a cake for Mister Tie.

She puts the cake in her basket and covers it with a napkin. Then she sets off.

She has barely started when Nibbles, Flopsy, Hopper and Blinders start to follow her. With his sharp nose, Nibbles has smelt what Miss Hedgehog has in her basket. Smacking his lips, he runs after her.

'Hey, you rascal, this isn't for you. It's for Mister Tie,' says Miss Hedgehog.

What bad luck for the friends.

A little later Miss Hedgehog goes into Mister Tie's house. The friends stay outside. They press their noses against the window and peer inside.

They see Mister Tie welcome Miss Hedgehog and watch as she takes the napkin off her cake. Mister Tie waves his arms in the air with happiness.

Later they see the two having tea and happily eating the cake.

Suddenly Mister Tie looks out of the window. He sees four noses glued to the glass.

He says something to Miss Hedgehog. They stand up and go outside. They give a piece of cake to each of the friends.

'When we saw your hungry eyes staring at us, we didn't have the heart to eat the cake up all by ourselves,' smiles Mister Tie.

'So that's it,' thinks Nibbles as he takes a big bite of delicious cake, 'the persistent always win.'

March

The Stool

Mister Owl sits down in his favourite chair at home. All of a sudden it falls apart and he's sitting on the ground.

He picks up the pieces and goes straight to Mister Mouse. Nibbles' father is a carpenter and can repair the chair.

'Well, well, let's see what I can do,' says Mister Mouse, examining the pieces.

'The legs are broken. Have you put something heavy on this chair?'

'No,' answers Mister Owl, blushing. 'I… uh, I just sat down as usual.'

Nervously he tries to close his jacket. But it won't close. His fat tummy gets in the way.

'I'm afraid that you're a little too heavy for this chair. I will make stronger legs for it. Perhaps you're a little overweight? It's not very healthy to be heavy, you know.'

Mister Owl knows that he's become heavy recently. He knows he should go on a diet but he can't get started.

'Please have a seat. I will fix your chair in no time,' says Mister Mouse.

'Thanks a lot,' answers Mister Owl. He goes to sit on a chair in the corner.

There's a noise and then a crash. Mister Owl is sitting on the ground for the second time today. Maybe it's time to start that diet?

The Cupboard

Mister Owl has decided to start his diet today.

So he goes to Miss Squirrel's shop and buys a huge basketful of fruit and vegetables. From now on he's going to eat healthy things.

But there's a problem. He has a whole cupboard full of sweets, biscuits and cake. What can he do with that?

'No,' he says to himself. 'I have to get rid of these sweets. Otherwise I won't lose a bit of weight.'

He takes the sweets and biscuits and dumps them into a bag. 'That leaves the cake,' he says.

'It's incredibly delicious. Do I have to throw that out too?' he asks himself, while licking his lips, and his mouth watering.

Mister Owl takes a piece of the cake. Slowly he brings it to his mouth. At the last second he doesn't eat it, though.

'I can't do this,' he mutters. 'This is no way to start a diet.'

He throws the cake into the bag, just like all the rest.

'OK, it's all cleaned up,' he sighs after he tosses the bag into his dustbin.

Good for you, Mister Owl. You should be much thinner soon.

Sold Out

Nibbles is running an errand for his mother.

When he gets to Miss Squirrel's shop, he sees that she's standing with her hands in her hair.

There are a few customers in the shop, all talking to each other.

'It's a real shame,' he hears one say.

'It's unheard of,' says someone else.

'You wouldn't expect that from anyone,' snorts a third person.

'What's going on, Miss Squirrel?' he asks.

'You know that Mister Owl has started a diet, don't you? Well, this morning he bought all my fruit and vegetables. I don't have any left in my shop. It's a disaster.'

'Can't you order more fruit and vegetables?'

'I've done that, but they can't deliver them until this afternoon. My customers want to buy NOW. Otherwise they won't have time to prepare them for dinner tonight.'

Nibbles thinks it over. Maybe there's a way he can help Miss Squirrel.

'If you can give me all your customers' orders, then I'll go to the big market with my cart. I can load everything you order into it and come back. That way your customers will get their food quickly and they can eat tonight.'

Everybody thinks that's a great idea.

That afternoon Nibbles delivers all the orders to the customers. It wasn't much work. And best of all, everybody he visited gave him a nice biscuit as a thank-you! Yum.

March

Snacks

Miss Crow is old. She can't go shopping any more. The shopping bags are too heavy for her. So Flopsy helps her. The bag is full and pretty heavy.

Flopsy carries the heavy bag along, but suddenly one of the handles breaks. The sack falls on the ground. A carton of eggs falls open. All the eggs smash on the ground. What a slimy, drippy mess! Luckily all the rest of the things are OK.

In a moment Flopsy arrives at Miss Crow's house with the broken sack.

'Oh, you poor child, that's too heavy for you. I see that a handle broke. That made it twice as hard.'

Flopsy begins to cry.

'But why are you crying?'

'When the handle broke there was a carton of eggs that broke open when it hit the ground. All the eggs broke,' sobbs Flopsy.

'Poor you. You don't need to cry. It was an accident. I'm just so glad you can help me with my shopping. A few eggs are nothing to cry about.'

Miss Crow hugs Flopsy until she stops sobbing. Then she opens a packet and takes out two biscuits.

'Here, these are for you because you've been such a dear.'

'And your eggs?' asks Flopsy.

'I can go to the shop myself. I need a little exercise. And I can certainly carry a carton of eggs home by myself.'

Dirty Feet

It has just rained. The path by the Friendship Tree is a pool of mud. When Flopsy, Blinders and Nibbles arrive, they decide that they will leave their muddy shoes by the door before going in. That way the Friendship Tree will stay clean.

A moment later Hopper arrives. With boots on.

'Hopper,' says Nibbles, 'better take your boots off. They're covered with mud. You'll make everything dirty.'

Hopper looks at his boots. 'What are boots for? They are meant to get dirty.'

'Yeah, but they'll make our playroom dirty,' says Nibbles.

'Don't be so picky,' says Hopper, and he walks all over the room with his dirty boots, leaving a trail of mud behind him. The others protest loudly.

'Everything is getting filthy from your dirty boots,' yells Blinders angrily. Hopper doesn't pay attention. Suddenly Hopper slips on a bit of mud. He lands right in the patch of mud he's brought in.

'Bother!' he yells, as he sees that his jeans are covered in mud now.

'That's what you get,' says Flopsy angrily.

Hopper goes to the entrance and takes his boots off. 'I don't want to make it any dirtier here, do I?' he asks, sulking a little.

'Indeed,' says Nibbles angrily. 'Now you have to clean up your mess, you slob.'

That afternoon Blinders, Flopsy and Nibbles play a table game. And Hopper? He cleans up his muddy mess. Poor Hopper.

Mister Sack and the Fallen Tree

Mister Sack, the postman, is on his rounds again. Suddenly he spots a fallen tree.

'What's going on here?' he asks himself.

The tree is uprooted. Its roots stick up in the air like fingers. Mister Sack looks at the place where the roots used to be.

But what does he see there? It looks like… a letterbox.

Mister Sack grabs his reading glasses and bends down to the letterbox. The name is almost impossible to read.

'The… Troll Family?'

'Am I going crazy? Trolls don't exist. Or do they?' Suddenly he hears a bell ringing. Where is that sound coming from? He looks around but sees nothing.

'It seems to be coming out of my postbag,' says Mister Sack a little dazed. Mister Sack digs in it. He pulls a letter out. That's what is making the sound.

'Mister Sack,' says the letter, 'it's time.'

'Time for what?' asks Mister Sack astonished.

'Time to get up. You need to deliver the post.'

Suddenly Mister Sack wakes up.

'Good, you're finally awake,' says his wife.

Poor Mister Sack wipes the sleep from his eyes.

'It was a dream,' decides Mister Sack. 'The crazy letterbox, the letter…'

'Do you feel OK?' asks his wife.

'Oh yes,' Mister Sack replies, sitting on the edge of the bed. 'I just think that I need a holiday.'

March

the rope is almost on the ground she jumps. The rope sweeps under her. When the rope is almost back to the ground, she jumps again.

'Hop, hop, hop,' she laughs.

Mister Owl watches with wide eyes.

'Now it's your turn again,' says Flopsy. She gives the skipping rope to him.

Mister Owl twirls the rope and… springs over it.

When the rope is almost back to the ground, Flopsy calls out, 'Jump!' That way Mister Owl knows when he must jump. It gets better and better. Mister Owl can't believe it.

The fat is going to melt away now!

Skipping Rope

Mister Owl has his tracksuit on. He's really working on his diet. He is eating healthy food and also doing exercises. That is why Mister Owl is going to do some rope skipping today.

He goes outside and begins to twirl the rope. Hop! He jumps in the air. But the rope snags on his beak. He has to start over.

This time the rope snags on his fat tummy.

'This isn't going very well, is it?' he suddenly hears.

Flopsy appears. 'You need to turn the rope faster,' she says. 'Let me show you.'

Flopsy takes the rope from him and twirls it. When

Burnt

Nibbles watches Mummy ironing.

She takes a shirt and lays it on the ironing board. It's full of wrinkles. She smoothes them out with the iron. The iron hisses. A big cloud of steam comes out of it. Soon all the wrinkles are gone. Mummy puts the shirt on a hanger so it will stay nice and smooth.

After Mummy has ironed several shirts, she puts the iron on its rack beside the ironing board. Then she gathers them up to take them upstairs to the wardrobe.

'Ssst!' goes the iron. A cloud of steam comes out of it.

Nibbles creeps up and stands close to it. He can

feel the heat rolling off it.

How does it work?

Carefully, Nibbles sticks out his finger to touch the iron. He wants to know how hot it feels. He touches it…

'Ssst!' hisses the iron. 'Ow!' yells Nibbles, pulling his finger back in shock. It's totally red and hurts awfully. He starts crying and calling for Mummy.

She's beside him in a second. She holds his finger under cold water. After a while Nibbles sees a blister on his finger. Mummy spreads cream on the blister and puts a bandage over it.

Nibbles looks at Mummy and thanks her with a hug. He's learned his lesson and will never touch the iron again.

surprise. She wonders what he means.

She checks her calendar.

'Sunday? But that's just the day after tomorrow,' she says to herself. 'You know what? I'll write him a little note to say that I'd be happy to join him.'

Miss Hedgehog gets busy. She writes her answer to Mister Tie in her very best handwriting.

Then she puts her letter in an envelope. She puts a stamp on it and drops the letter into the postbox.

'Mister Sack will make sure that Mister Tie gets my letter tomorrow.'

How exciting. What will the surprise be? She wishes it were Sunday already…

Miss Hedgehog Receives a Letter

The doorbell rings at Miss Hedgehog's house. She opens the door, full of curiosity.

'Good morning, Miss Hedgehog,' says Mister Sack, the postman. 'Here's some post for you.'

'Oh, thank you!' she exclaims. Then she goes back inside to read her letter.

With very polite words, Mister Tie, the tailor, has invited Miss Hedgehog to visit him on Sunday. He promises a lovely picnic in the woods and a

March

Mister Tie Receives a Letter

'This is weird,' says Mister Sack, the postman. 'Yesterday I delivered a letter to Miss Hedgehog that was written in beautiful handwriting. And today I have one for you. Here you are, Mister Tie.'

'Thanks,' answers Mister Tie. 'Did she read the letter?'

'I think so,' says Mister Sack. 'But I don't know what was inside.'

A light goes on in Mister Sack's head.

'Tell me, have you written such letters before?'

Mister Tie blushes a bit.

'Yes indeed, I'm very fond of Miss Hedgehog.'

'Now I get it,' smiles Mister Sack. 'I can guess now who this letter is from. See you soon, Mister Tie.'

'Bye, Mister Sack. And thanks.'

Mister Tie opens his envelope. Mmm, it smells like roses.

It is indeed from Miss Hedgehog.

Mister Tie beams with happiness as he reads her answer.

'She said yes,' he says dreamily.

Then a shock rolls through him. He has so much to do! He's got to prepare the picnic!

Fortunately the surprise for Miss Hedgehog is ready. He just needs to prepare one little slip of paper.

'That's nothing,' he says to himself relieved.

But then he jumps up and runs to the kitchen. He picks up his baking pans, eggs and honey and gets busy. Mister Tie works all evening. If anyone had passed by on the path through the woods, they would have seen his light still burning.

Whew! He's almost ready. It should be a really fine day tomorrow.

The Picnic

The sun is shining. In the woods, two figures walk side by side. It's Miss Hedgehog and Mister Tie. They are having their picnic today.

At a beautiful spot they stop and Mister Tie lays a rug on the ground. Then he takes things out of his picnic basket.

There are honey biscuits, a strawberry pie and a chocolate tart.

Mister Tie pours a glass of juice for himself and one for Miss Hedgehog. They clink glasses.

'Here's to a fine day,' says Mister Tie.

Then Mister Tie puts his glass down quickly.

'Before I forget, I have a little surprise for you.' He pulls a large package out of the picnic basket.

'This is for you, Miss Hedgehog. I hope you like it.'

'Thanks very much,' says Miss Hedgehog, with a sparkling smile on her face. She opens the gift.

'Oh, how beautiful!' she cries. She takes a beautiful dress out of the wrapping paper.

'I made it especially for you,' says Mister Tie a bit shy. He hopes she likes it!

'Thanks so much, Mister Tie. I've never seen such a beautiful dress.'

Miss Hedgehog leans over and gives Mister Tie a kiss on his cheek.

Mister Tie feels warm inside. He's so happy!

The two of them spend a lovely day in the woods. They walk, eat the delicious food and sip the juice. But we should leave them alone now. You don't want to disturb a couple that is falling in love.

The Temptation

20 MARCH

Nibbles and Flopsy just bought some delicious honey biscuits. Munching away, they go by Mister Owl's house. He's busy with a skipping rope.

'Hello Mister Owl,' says Flopsy. 'How's your diet going?'

Mister Owl stops skipping. Huffing and puffing, he looks at the youngsters.

'Are those... are those honey biscuits that you are eating?' he asks, wiping his sweaty face.

'Uh, yeah...'

'Could I taste a little piece?'

Flopsy and Nibbles look at each other in surprise.

'But Mister Owl,' Nibbles says, 'that's not good for... for...'

'Your figure,' helps out Flopsy.

'Pardon?' he asks weakly.

Then Nibbles has an idea.

'Mister Owl, remember how your chair broke?'

'Uh... yes,' answers Mister Owl.

'My father has finished fixing it. You can come this week to get it. Daddy has put stronger legs on it. That way you won't break it any more.'

Then Mister Owl remembers that embarrassing moment. That was why he decided to start his diet. No, he doesn't want to be that fat ever again. Suddenly the honey biscuit is gone from his mind.

'I have to get back to my skipping rope,' he says. 'See you later.'

March

Boomerang

Nibbles has a boomerang.
'What is that?' Hopper wants to know.

'A boomerang. It's a throwing thing. If you throw a boomerang away, it comes back to you.'

'That's handy,' says Hopper. 'Give it a try.'

Nibbles throws the boomerang as hard as he can. *Wop-wop-wop* goes the boomerang as it spins away through the air.

Hopper and Nibbles see the boomerang making a big curve. But then it disappears behind a tree.

'Hey, I can't see it any more,' says Hopper.

'Don't worry. It'll come back,' says Nibbles.

The two friends look around.

'Do you see anything?' asks Hopper.

'Have a little patience, Hopper.'

But the boomerang has vanished.

'If you ask me, that worthless boomerang is lying somewhere on the ground,' says Hopper.

Then they hear a *wop-wop-wop* sound behind them. The boomerang hits them on their heads.

'Ow!' they yell, rubbing their heads. The boomerang is back.

Singing

In the Friendship Tree the friends are all singing.

'Row, row, row your boat…' sings Nibbles.

'Gently down the stream,' adds Hopper.

'Merrily, merrily, merrily, merrily, life is but a dream,' they sing together.

'Hopper, you're off key,' says Flopsy.

'What can I do about that?' he asks. 'Sometimes I don't sing very well. Let's do something else then, instead of this silly singing.'

'No!' say the others. 'Singing is fun!'

'So what can we do?' asks Hopper.

It's silent for a while.

'I have an idea!' exclaims Blinders. 'We'll form a choir and you can be the director.'

'The direct-what?' asks Hopper.

'Director,' explains Blinders. 'Directors stand in front of a choir and use their arms to beat the time.'

That sounds great for Hopper.

A bit later Nibbles, Flopsy and Blinders are standing side by side. Hopper stands in front of them with his arms in the air.

'Ready?' he asks. Then he counts to three. The others join in.

'Row, row, row your boat…'

Now it sounds a lot better. Why not, with such a fine director?

March

Roger Fox

23 MARCH

Who's sneaking along the path through the woods this evening? It's Roger Fox.

During the day you never see him because he is asleep. He's a scoundrel. What's he up to tonight?

Oh no – he's creeping up to Mister Sack's house. He peeks through the keyhole. The door swings open, creaking. Roger Fox slips inside.

Using his flashlight, he looks over the living room. Suddenly the light falls on a chest. He wants to take a look inside.

Carefully he creeps across the room. As silently as he can, he opens the chest. It's filled with silver cups, plates and silverware. Roger can use these things. He takes a big sack out of his jacket.

Greedily, Roger sticks his paw out toward the shiny things.

Boom! All of a sudden Roger feels a big thump on his head. He sees stars. He turns around and sees Mister Sack, the postman. Mister Sack is standing in his pyjamas, holding his postbag that's full of post.

'Do you know how much this weighs? If you like, I'll let you feel it again,' says Mister Sack threateningly.

But Roger Fox doesn't wait. He wants to get away from strong Mister Sack and his heavy postbag.

'Don't you dare come back, you ugly rascal,' he hears Mister Sack shout as he runs out.

Mister Sack can count on that. Roger Fox will never come back.

Sam Stork

24 MARCH

All the creatures who live in the woods have come to Mister Sack's house. There was a break-in last night. But luckily Mister Sack threw him out.

'What if he comes back?' someone asks.

'We need someone who can protect us,' says another.

'We need police protection,' says Mister Owl, the mayor. 'I put an advert in the newspaper.'

Suddenly a big stork comes flying in. He lands exactly next to Mister Owl.

'Are you looking for a police officer?' he asks.

Mister Owl looks at the stork in surprise.

'How do you know that?'

'I'm a police officer. I know lots of things,' says the stork, nodding seriously.

'Amazing,' says Mister Owl. 'We're looking for a police officer because…'

'Because there was a break-in last night? I know. I'm a police officer. I know lots of things.'

'Then you already know…'

'Who it was? Of course. It was Roger Fox. I'm a police officer. I know lots of things.'

'Fantastic!' cries Mister Owl. 'And you are…?'

'Sam Stork. And you are Mister Owl. I know that because…'

'… you are a police officer,' interrupts Mister Owl. 'You've already mentioned that. Can you go after Roger Fox?'

'You can count on me,' Sam bows, spreads his wings, and stands straight up. Everybody looks at him. Suddenly Sam takes off. He flies straight up, smacks into a branch, then falls back to the ground.

Poor Sam. He knows everything, except where branches over his head are.

The Police Station

Mister Owl has had a police station built for Sam Stork.

There's even a prison cell with strong bars.

'We'd better test them,' says Sam.

Mister Owl and Sam go into the cell. They slam the door shut after themselves. Sam grabs the bars. He pushes and pulls them as hard as he can, but they don't move.

'Good and strong, huh?' asks Mister Owl.

'Indeed, I thought so. I'm not a police officer for nothing.'

'Great, then I declare the police station open,' says Mister Owl.

He goes to open the cell door. But it's locked.

'Sam, would you please open the door?'

Sam feels his pockets. The keys aren't in his left pocket. They aren't in his right pocket. They aren't in his chest pocket. Where has he put them?

Mister Owl watches with alarm.

'You haven't lost the keys, have you?'

Sam points to the wall on the other side of the police station. The keys are hanging there on a hook, out of reach.

'Well, then there's only one thing to do,' decides Mister Owl. 'We've got to call for help.'

They yell as loudly as they can. Luckily, it's not too long before someone hears them and lets them out of the cell.

One thing is sure: nobody will ever escape from it!

March

The Red Bike

Nibbles has found a tin of red paint in the garden shed. Red is his favourite colour.

Then Nibbles spots his bike. There are rust spots here and there. Nibbles thinks that's terrible. His bike needs a new coat of paint.

With a screwdriver he pries the tin open.

Nibbles dips a brush in the paint and starts painting the bike. In an hour he's done.

'Nibbles, where are you?' he hears Mummy call.

'I'm in the garden shed!' he answers.

'What are you up to?' Mummy asks as she comes into the shed. Then she sees Nibbles. His nose, hands and clothes are covered with paint spots.

'I painted my bike,' says Nibbles proudly.

Mummy looks at the bike. Then she begins to laugh.

'Well, you certainly did. You painted the wheels, tyres, handlebars and even the chain. You didn't need to do all that.'

'I thought it was prettier that way.'

'You're a funny fellow. If you think it's prettier that way, then that's OK with me. But to cover yourself in paint is not so OK. We're going to have to give you a good scrubbing tonight.'

That evening Mummy scrubs Nibbles hard in the bath. But he is still happy because he now has the most beautiful bike in the world.

Racing

'Hey, look at my cool bike!' yells Nibbles to Hopper. 'I painted it yesterday.'

'Wow, that looks super. Do you want to race?'

That sounds great to Nibbles.

'Sure,' he says. 'Where do we start?'

'There, by the big oak tree. We will go up to Miss Squirrel's place and back. Whoever gets back first wins.'

'OK.'

'1-2-3 Go!' yells Hopper. The two race off.

They pedal as fast as they can. At first Hopper is ahead. As they get to Miss Squirrel's house, Hopper slows down. Nibbles passes him.

'Yesss! Now I'm ahead!' thinks Nibbles. 'Now just…'

Suddenly Flopsy steps into the way of the racers. She doesn't see them coming.

'Look out!' yells Nibbles. He brakes as hard as he can. His tyres slide over the ground. Hopper is braking as hard as he can too. He just barely avoids hitting Nibbles.

Lucky moves! They avoided an accident. Panting and shaking, the friends look at each other.

'Hi Nibbles! Hi Hopper!' says Flopsy. 'Do you feel like racing? Who can be the first to the old oak tree?'

But they don't want to race any more. They came so close to an accident! Racing on public paths is not a good idea, they now know. Unexpected things can happen if there's someone in the way.

thing. It waves its arms and nods its head.

'Hello, little friends!' says the puppet. 'Do you know who I am?'

'You're Punch!' says Nibbles.

'Exactly! Say, do you know what's under this cloth?'

'No,' answer Nibbles and Misty.

'Shall we take a look?'

'Yesss!'

The puppet takes hold of the cloth. 'Count to three with me. 1-2-3!'

With a tug, the puppet pulls the cloth away.

A marvellous puppet theatre appears.

'Wow!' exclaim Nibbles and Misty. The curtains open slowly. The show begins…

Daddy and Mummy certainly can think up wonderful surprises…

 ## A Big Thing

Once again, Nibbles' and Misty's father has built something for them.

It's nearly done. Mummy is hanging two little curtains on it. When that's done they throw a big cloth over the whole thing. That way it will be a surprise.

Daddy drags the big thing inside.

Nibbles and Flopsy look at it in astonishment.

'What is it, Daddy?' asks Misty.

Daddy just smiles about his secret.

Mummy comes in and goes behind the big thing.

Suddenly a puppet pops up and looks over the big

March

The Detective

Police officer Sam Stork is strolling through the woods. Suddenly he notices a little path.

'Hmm. I haven't been that way before. I think I'll take a look,' he thinks.

He follows the path until he comes to a thick oak tree. The path stops there. Sam walks around the tree. What does he see there? There are footprints. Sam bends his long neck toward the ground so he can see the prints better.

'Strange, these look really new,' he mumbles to himself. 'Someone has been by here just a moment ago.'

Sam looks around him. There's nobody to be seen.

'Who's been here and where has he hidden himself?' Sam asks himself. 'Maybe behind the tree?'

Sam walks around the tree but sees nobody. Yet if there are footprints, somebody has been here.

'Perhaps the bad guy is walking round the other side of this tree just to keep from being seen. I have to surprise him. I'll run really fast around the tree. That way I can catch him.'

Sam runs around the tree several times, but still doesn't see anyone.

'Dagnabbit!' he snorts. 'This fellow is pretty smart!'

But then Sam looks at the many footprints on the ground. They have exactly the same shape as… his own feet.

Poor Sam. There was nobody on the path. The footprints were all his. He was chasing himself the whole time.

The Leak

It's raining really hard today. In Miss Hedgehog's house there's a dripping sound.

'Oh no, a leak in my roof.'

Quickly she gets a bucket. She sets it under the leak.

'Good,' she says relieved. But just as she says that, she feels some drops on her neck. She lets out a shriek. Another leak!

She gets another pan. She barely has it in place when two new leaks begin to drip rain in her house. Her roof is beginning to leak like a sieve!

Suddenly somebody knocks on her door. Quickly Miss Hedgehog opens it. It's Mister Tie.

'I was passing by and I heard you scream,' he says. 'Is everything OK?'

'Oh, Mister Tie,' says Miss Hedgehog overcome, 'it's leaking everywhere.'

Mister Tie takes a look around the little house.

'This whole roof needs to be fixed. I'll get my tools quickly.'

He runs out into the pouring rain. A little later he's back with a ladder and tool kit.

Mister Tie climbs up to the roof. There's a lot of banging and clanging. One by one the leaks stop. After an hour or so he clambers down his ladder. Miss Hedgehog lets him in quickly.

'You're a real hero,' she sighs.

'Hap… hap… happy… to help… Aaat-chooo!'

Oh, brother. Miss Hedgehog is nice and dry now, but Mister Tie has caught a cold. It was so nice of him to help her!

Catching a Cold

Mister Tie is really sick with his cold. He closes his shop and turns his sign toward the wall.

'Aaat-chooo!' Mister Tie grabs a handkerchief and blows his nose.

He hardly has any more handkerchiefs left, he's been sneezing so much. What misery.

Sighing, he gets to work. He has a lot to do. Finish some orders, repair some things, clean the shop… Everything takes a lot of effort. After a while he has chills and a fever.

Just then Miss Hedgehog comes by.

'I wanted to thank you for your help yesterday,' she says.

But then she sees Mister Tie is feeling sick. 'You look like you have a fever!'

She feels his forehead. It's burning hot.

'Poor you! You belong in bed.'

'I don't have time for that. So much still to do…' sighs Mister Tie.

'Don't you worry about that. I'll take care of your shop. You just go and rest.'

Miss Hedgehog puts Mister Tie to bed. 'Go to sleep now,' she says. 'I'll take care of your shop just fine.'

'Thanks,' says Mister Tie. He closes his eyes and falls fast asleep.

Miss Hedgehog tiptoes from the room. Before she shuts the door, she glances back at Mister Tie.

'You took care of me yesterday,' she says softly. 'Today I can take care of you. Sleep well, Mister Tie. You'll get better soon.'

April

Cleaning

'Mummy, may I be excused?' asks Nibbles, pushing back from the table.

'Let's clear the table first,' answers Mummy.

'But I said I'd play with Flopsy and Hopper,' whinges Nibbles.

'You can, but first help me clean up. Will you take the plates?'

Nibbles pouts and crosses his arms. He turns his back and stands really still.

Mummy clears the glasses away.

'Still standing here? You'll be late for your friends.'

Nibbles frowns and tries to look even crosser. It almost hurts.

Mummy has filled the sink. She acts as if Nibbles isn't there. She looks out of the kitchen window.

'I think I see Hopper coming. If you don't clear the plates soon, your friends will have to play without you. The plates won't clear themselves, you know.'

Nibbles knows there's no way out of this.

Sniffling, he picks up the plates and puts them by the sink.

'That didn't take long, did it?' smiles Mummy.

Nibbles doesn't answer. Still pouting, he pulls his shoes on and runs to look out the window. Deep down inside he knows that Mummy is right. It didn't take any time to clear the plates. If he had done it right away, he'd be playing right now with Hopper. Really, he's been kind of silly.

The next time Mummy asks him to help clear the table, he'll just do it. Then he can start playing right away.

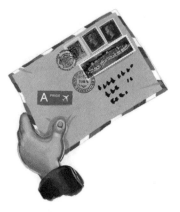

A Letter from Far Away

Mister Sack, the postman, has a letter with lots of stamps on it.

'This came from far away,' he thinks.

The letter is for Mister Owl. Mister Sack rings the doorbell and hands him the letter. He really wants to know who sent it.

'It's from my nephew Wilbur,' says Mister Owl after he opens the letter. 'He lives in the far North.'

'The far North? Isn't it cold there?' asks Mister Sack.

Mister Owl nods. 'My nephew is a snowy owl. They are white as snow and can handle the cold just fine.'

Mister Owl reads the letter.

'How nice! He's coming to visit tomorrow.'

'I'm really curious about your nephew. I wonder what life is like in the far North.'

'Cold. Without a doubt. I'm glad I live here in the forest. The weather is pleasant here.'

'Except when it rains cats and dogs and I have to deliver the post,' mumbles Mister Sack.

'Poor you, that's true,' says Mister Owl kindly. 'See you tomorrow, Mister Sack.'

'See you then, Mister Owl.'

Nephew Wilbur

'Nephew Wilbur!' exclaims Mister Owl as he opens his door.

Before him stands Wilbur, the white snowy owl, all the way from the far North. They hug each other happily.

'It's been such a long time. Come in, come in!'

Mister Owl picks up Wilbur's suitcase and carries it inside. 'Did you have a good trip?'

'Yes, mostly. Some snow here and there and a little icy rain now and then, but that's not unusual for me.'

Mister Owl shivers. 'Brrr, all that cold. Doesn't it bother you to have cold weather all the time?'

'Not at all,' laughs Wilbur, 'I love it.'

'To each his own,' sighs Mister Owl. 'How about a cup of tea?'

'Iced tea?' asks Wilbur.

'As icy as possible,' nods Mister Owl.

'Yes please, then.'

Mister Owl pours the tea over some ice cubes and they float around in the cup.

'Would you like a piece of cake?'

'What kind?'

'Why, ice cream cake, of course.'

Then yes, Wilbur will have a slice.

They chat for hours. Then it's bedtime. Mister Owl leads Wilbur to his room.

'It's the coolest bedroom in the house,' he says.

'Oh really?' asks Wilbur curiously.

'It's in the cellar. It's chilly there all the time. I thought you'd like it best.'

'That's great,' laughs Wilbur.

Strange bird, that Wilbur.

April

Where Has Wilbur Gone?

4 APRIL

'Where's Wilbur?' worries Mister Owl. His nephew Wilbur, from the cold, far North, is visiting for a few days. Because he finds most rooms too warm, Mister Owl has given him the bedroom in the chilly cellar.

But when Mister Owl went to wake Wilbur up this morning, Wilbur was not in his bed.

'Maybe he didn't like his bed and he's on the sofa in my workroom.'

Mister Owl goes to his workroom. There's no sign of Wilbur. He decides to look in the kitchen.

On the kitchen table he sees all the things that should be in the refrigerator: milk, butter, eggs, vegetables…

'What in the world?' Mister Owl asks himself.

Then he hears a strange, rumbling sound coming from the refrigerator.

'What's going on?' he mumbles. He cautiously opens the door.

Inside he sees Wilbur, snoring away.

Wilbur wakes up with a start.

'Oh, sorry! I didn't mean to wake you up.'

Wilbur yawns and stretches. 'No problem. I slept well in your refrigerator. It was much too warm in the cellar. But your refrigerator is a perfect place for a snowy owl to sleep.'

It's not easy having a snowy owl as a house guest.

The Poster

5 APRIL

'Hey, look what I've got!' calls Hopper to his friends, who are waiting for him at the Friendship Tree.

'A poster!' they yell together.

'And look what's on it!' Hopper unrolls the poster and shows it to them.

There's a bunch of flowers on it.

'What a beautiful poster,' says Flopsy. 'Let's hang it up on the wall.'

They look for a good place.

Hopper thinks about it. 'I don't have any tacks with me. Do you?'

Of course not. Who walks around with tacks in his pocket?

That's a problem. They can't hang up the beautiful poster. What next?

Nibbles has an idea. In a corner he spots a few clothes pegs and some string. He ties one end of the string to a hook on one wall and the other end across the room. Now they have a clothesline.

Nibbles picks up the poster.

'Could you please give me a clothespin?' he asks. Blinders hands two clothespins to Nibbles, who clips the poster to the line, just like Mummy does with the washing.

'Look at that!' he says proudly.

'Nibbles, you are super,' exclaim the friends all together.

Nibbles thinks so too, but doesn't say it. It's nice to hear somebody else say that, though.

Quack-Quack!

Hopper lies stretched out, daydreaming beside the stream. It's a beautiful day. He feels the warm sun on his back. Butterflies flit around and the birds sing in the trees.

'Lovely,' he mumbles as he stretches, half asleep.

Suddenly he jumps. What's that sound?

Hopper looks all around. There's nobody to be seen.

'I must have been dreaming,' he thinks, relaxing again.

Just as he's almost asleep, he jumps again.

Quack!

This time he's sure he heard it. He looks around again, but still doesn't see anyone.

Here it comes again: *Quack!*

Is some duck playing a joke on Hopper?

'I'm going to figure this out.'

Silent as a cat, he creeps through the high grass. He's going to teach this joker a lesson.

Quack! he hears again.

Now Hopper can tell where the sound is coming from. Not from the stream, but from the woods. He slinks toward the sound.

Quack!

'Got you!' yells Hopper, jumping out of the grass.

But instead of surprising a duck, he scares Misty, Nibbles' little sister. She jumps and starts to cry, pulling on a string that is tied to a yellow plastic duck on tiny wheels behind her.

Quack! it goes.

Poor Hopper.

67

Mister Owl Catches a Cold

7 APRIL

Mister Sack, the postman, calls to Mister Owl, 'Good morning! I have some post for you!'

'Gub-moaning,' mumbles Mister Owl. He looks very tired.

'You aren't looking well, Mister Owl. Are you sick?'

'Yes,' answers Mister Owl in a hoarse, whispery voice. 'I've got a rotten cold.'

'Poor you! Did you catch it walking in the rain?'

'Not at all. I caught it from my nephew Wilbur – you know him, the snowy owl from the far North? Aaat-choo!'

'You've told me about him. He feels too warm all the time, right?'

'Exactly. He puffs and sweats all the time. So I've kept the doors and windows open so that the cold wind could blow through my house. Aaat-choo!'

'Brrr,' shivers Mister Sack. 'I can see how you caught your cold now.'

'Yesterday he left to go home to the icy far North. He asked me to come and visit him. Very kind of him, but I told him I'd have to think it over. I think Wilbur is great, but it's really cold up there.'

'I see what you mean, Mister Owl. If you do

decide to visit him, you'd better take lots of warm clothes.'

'I certainly will.'

'I have to run now. Hope you get well soon.'

'Thanks. See you, Mister Sack.'

Miss Squirrel's Problem

8 APRIL

Miss Squirrel has a problem. The doors and windows of her shop really need to be re-painted. If her shop looks bad, nobody will buy things from her.

But she doesn't have time to do it herself. Nibbles stands beside Mummy in the shop while Miss Squirrel explains her problem.

'Maybe I can help you,' he says. 'My friends and I like to paint. Maybe we can do it for you.'

Miss Squirrel thinks that's a great idea. She promises them a whole bag of sweets if they can start today.

Nibbles doesn't have to think that over. He runs off to gather his friends.

A bit later Nibbles, Hopper, Flopsy and Blinders arrive at the shop, in their oldest clothes. Miss Squirrel has a tin of paint for each of them. The friends get busy.

Nibbles scrubs off the dirt and old chips of paint first. Then Hopper paints one coat. When that's dry, Blinders puts on a second coat of paint. Now the doors and window have two new coats of paint that will last for years.

Flopsy wants to make this the most beautiful shop in the whole forest. So she paints beautiful flowers on the door and window frames. When it's all done, Miss Squirrel comes to see. She can hardly believe how lovely it looks now. She gives the friends a huge bag of sweets. So everybody is happy!

Dolls and Toy Animals

Nibbles and his sister Misty are playing with dolls.

Nibbles is the father and Misty is the mother. They have loaded Mummy's pushchair with dolls and toy animals and now they are going for a walk.

'That's quite a family,' laughs Mummy when she sees the youngsters go by. 'Do they behave themselves?'

'Most of them do,' says Misty.

'Except Bummel, the bear. He's always up to something.'

'Right,' says Misty. 'You have to watch him.'

'That's the way it is with kids,' laughs Mummy.

They take the whole family to Mummy and Daddy's bedroom. It's bedtime now.

They lay the dolls and animals on the big bed.

Bummel the bear doesn't want to sleep, though. But Nibbles talks him into getting under the covers.

Then Misty picks up a big story book. She opens it to the place where the bookmark is, and begins to read. She can't really read yet, but that doesn't matter. Mummy has read this book so many times to her and Nibbles that she practically knows the story by heart. The dolls and animals listen carefully.

Misty closes the book while Nibbles turns off the light. All the dolls and animals are asleep now.

Even Bummel the bear? Yes, even him.

April

A Pen

Sam, the police officer, comes running into his office. He needs to write something down quickly so he won't forget.

He looks to see if there's a pen anywhere on top of his desk. No, the pen is not in its place.

He opens a drawer. Nope, not there either.

'Bother!' he cries. 'Where did I put that pen?'

Maybe it's been stolen?

'No, that can't be. I would know that if it was. I'm a police officer, after all. I know everything,' he thinks to himself.

'Of course!' he yells, feeling his pocket. It was there all the time. Now he can finally write down what he wants to remember. But...

Oh no, he's forgotten what he wanted to write down.

Aha! Now it comes back to him. He wanted to remember to buy more pens so he'd have some, even if he lost this one.

That's a good idea, don't you think?

Dead Fly Bread

Miss Hedgehog has baked something that smells delicious. Just as she takes it out of the oven, Nibbles knocks on her door.

'Hello, Miss Hedgehog. It smells like you've baked something really good.'

'Nothing's safe from that nose of yours,' she laughs. She puts a loaf of bread with black things in it on the table.

'What kind of bread is that?' Nibbles wants to know.

'It's currant bread.'

'It looks like it's full of dead flies,' says Nibbles doubtfully.

'Those are currants. They are sort of like raisins,' laughs Miss Hedgehog.

Nibbles licks his lips.

'Go ahead, try a piece.' She cuts a little piece and gives it to Nibbles. He barely has time to say thank you before his mouth is full of the currant bread.

'It's delicious!' he cries. 'I have to go now, though. Thanks!'

'I'm happy you liked it,' smiles Miss Hedgehog. 'Have you really never had currant bread before?'

Nibbles shakes his head. But that's not true. Mummy buys currant bread now and then. But if Miss Hedgehog knew that, she wouldn't have given Nibbles a taste, would she?

What a little rascal that Nibbles is!

April

The Bear is Loose

'Raaarrrr!' growls Nibbles. Today he's a grizzly bear. A book with pictures of them lies open next to him.

Nibbles stands up like a bear. His legs are far apart and his arms are high in the air. He really does look terrifying.

Growling and grunting, he lumbers into the living room.

'Whoa! What have we here? A bear in the house?' asks Daddy, who's sitting on the sofa.

'A *grizzly* bear,' corrects Nibbles.

'Oh, they are dangerous,' says Daddy, putting his hands in front of his face and acting scared.

The bear walks toward the sofa with heavy steps. The closer he comes, the louder he growls. Daddy whimpers with fear.

Now the bear is really close to Daddy. He reaches out with his claws.

Suddenly Daddy stretches his arms out. He grabs the bear and pulls him onto his lap. Then he starts tickling. The bear can't stop laughing. Daddy shows no mercy toward the wild bear.

When Daddy finally stops tickling, the bear is totally exhausted from all the laughing.

'Ooo-hooo,' gasps Nibbles as he gets his breath back.

'I didn't know it was so easy to tame a wild bear,' laughs Daddy. 'First I have a grizzly bear in front of me, and then he turns into a teddy bear!' He gives Nibbles a big bear hug.

The Serenade

It's late at night. In a few houses there are still lights on. A dark figure with something on its back moves along the path through the woods.

The figure goes straight to Miss Hedgehog's house. It stands directly beneath her bedroom window. Above, a light is still burning.

'She's awake. That's great,' thinks the figure.

Then he takes something in his two hands...

Miss Hedgehog is reading in bed. It's time to shut her book and go to sleep.

Suddenly she hears something.

Ploing, ploing it goes.

She sits straight up in bed.

Now the instrument begins to play – it sounds like a guitar.

Miss Hedgehog springs out of bed and runs to the window. She looks below. She can't see very well in the darkness.

Curious, she opens the window. At the very moment she sticks her head out of the window, a voice begins to sing.

Hey, she knows that voice!

It's Mister Tie, playing his guitar and singing under her window. A real serenade.

Miss Hedgehog listens to Mister Tie's beautiful song enchanted. When the song is over, she hears Mister Tie say, 'Sleep well, dear Miss Hedgehog.' Then he goes away.

'What a lovely fellow he is,' she thinks to herself as she closes her window.

She certainly will have pleasant dreams tonight, don't you think?

A Nice Time!

There's a lot of cheering and strange sounds outside. Curious, Nibbles and Misty run out to see what's happening.

Just then the circus trucks go by.

Nibbles knows what that means. It's circus time! He grabs his sister's hands and they dance around the room. Misty doesn't know what's happening.

'Tomorrow the circus will start,' Nibbles explains. 'The best time of the year!'

'Circus!' cries Misty. 'Yippee!'

Flopsy runs up to them. 'Did you see it?' she calls out excitedly.

'Yes!' answer Nibbles and Misty together.

'It's going to be great!' crows Flopsy.

They run to the village square in front of Mister Owl's house.

They see Hopper and Blinders coming as fast as they can.

Circus workers are already busy there. The three circus trucks are parked in a circle. The friends recognise them from last year.

'The red one is the fish tent,' says Blinders.

Nibbles points to the green tent. 'That's where the merry-go-round is. I'm sure of that.'

'And that one over there,' says Flopsy, 'is where I want to go. That's the ball toss game.'

The friends watch for a long while. It's too bad they have to sleep a whole night before the circus opens. They can barely wait.

April

Throwing Balls

15 APRIL

The day is here at last! Nibbles gets to go to the circus with his friends.

First they ride the merry-go-round and then they go fishing for prizes.

Finally they go to the ball toss tent. They buy a lot of balls. The idea is to throw them at bottles and knock them down. The friends throw and throw, until one bottle finally falls down just as they run out of balls. It's time to see what they've won.

The man behind the counter, an old weasel, gives them a big plush doll that looks like a dwarf.

'We'll put him in our Friendship Tree,' says Blinders.

'He'll be our mascot,' suggests Nibbles.

'Our what?' asks Hopper.

'Our mascot,' explains Nibbles. 'It's like our emblem or our flag. It stands for us.'

The four of them look at the dwarf doll closely.

'I think he should be called Tobias,' Nibbles says finally.

The others think that's a good idea.

'Come on, let's take him to the Friendship Tree,' says Flopsy. The four take him there and find a nice place for him in their clubhouse. Then they run back to the circus as fast as they can.

Because there's still so much to do there!

The Merry-Go-Round

16 APRIL

It's the second day of the circus.

Everybody from the village is there, including Nibbles, who has come with Daddy, Mummy and Misty.

Daddy has bought tickets for the merry-go-round. It's full of laughing youngsters.

When the merry-go-round stops turning, Nibbles and Misty can get on. Misty chooses a pink bicycle and Nibbles picks a prancing white horse. When the merry-go-round lady comes around they give her their tickets.

Suddenly someone comes running up. It's Mister Owl, panting a bit.

'Miss, could you wait a second? I want to buy a ticket.'

The lady looks at Mister Owl in surprise.

'Aren't you a little old for this ride?' she asks sternly.

Mister Owl looks guiltily at her.

'Yes, I suppose so,' he says, 'but… I love merry-go-rounds so much.'

He looks at the lady with pitiful eyes. 'Please? May I?'

The lady shrugs her shoulders. 'Sure, why not?' she sighs.

Mister Owl quickly buys his ticket and sits on a brown horse. The horn sounds and the merry-go-round begins to turn.

Mister Owl can't contain his happiness. Nibbles and Misty are almost a bit afraid of him, but he doesn't mean any harm. He just loves it so much! And it makes him so happy.

Balloon Contest

The circus is still going strong in the village.

There's a funny clown walking around. He's got a weird hat and a red clown's nose. He keeps on shouting, 'Come try the balloon contest! Come try the balloon contest!'

Flopsy runs after him. She catches up with him.

'Hello, princess,' he says to her, 'would you like to try? It costs just one coin.'

Flopsy has exactly one coin. She can do it!

She gives him her coin. He takes out a card and writes down her name and where she lives.

She can choose a balloon from a box filled with balloons in all sorts of colours. She picks out a bright red one.

'Good choice,' the fellow assures her. He tests the balloon and then fills it with gas. Then he ties a string to it. He ties the card with Flopsy's name onto the string too. Now the balloon is ready.

Flopsy takes the balloon from him. It tugs gently on the string. It seems like the balloon can hardly wait to take off.

Flopsy is excited.

She takes a last look at her balloon. Then she counts to three and lets it go.

The balloon takes off really fast. She watches it until it disappears into the clouds.

Where in the world will it land? Maybe you're as curious as Flopsy is about that.

April

Clothes Wardrobe

This morning Nibbles has just finished washing himself. He's waiting for Mummy to bring his clothes. But Mummy is busy with Misty.

'Mummy,' calls Nibbles, 'where are my clothes? I can't find them.'

'I'm sorry, I didn't have time to get them ready for you. If you want, you can get them yourself.'

That sounds good to Nibbles. He runs to his room and opens his closet.

This is going to be hard. Which trousers and t-shirt should he pick?

Nibbles looks through his clothes, one by one. Finally he picks a t-shirt that he hasn't worn in a long time. It's at the bottom of a pile of shirts. He pulls the shirt out, throwing the others all over the place.

He puts it on and looks for some some trousers. He finds a pair that are also at the bottom of a pile. He tosses the others on the floor and puts the ones he wants on. Now he just has to button and zip up. OK, he's ready.

Just then Mummy comes in. When she sees all the trousers and t-shirts scattered all over the floor, she gets mad.

'Do you know how long it takes me to get your clothes nice and neatly folded? Look what you've done.'

Nibbles looks around at the mess he's made. With a sigh, Mummy begins to fold everything and put it away.

And Nibbles?

He tiptoes out of the room...

A Letter for Flopsy

Flopsy's father, Mister Sack, comes home late from work. He has a letter for Flopsy. There are lots of stamps on it. The letter has come from far, far away.

'I delivered a letter that looked like this to Mister Owl, a while ago,' he says.

Flopsy isn't listening. She grabs the letter from

76

him. She almost never gets mail, so she's really curious. She tears the envelope open. With trembling hands she pulls the letter out. There's also a little card with it.

She recognises that card. It's the card from the balloon contest, and it shows her name and address. She gives the letter to her father, since she can't read yet.

'My goodness!' he cries, 'it's from Wilbur, the snowy owl! Remember him? He's Mister Owl's nephew, the one who lives in the far North. He says he found your balloon. So he sent you this letter to prove it.'

Flopsy can't believe her ears. How could her balloon go all the way to the far North?

'Tomorrow morning, first thing, you can take this to Mister Owl,' says Flopsy's father. 'You will probably win a nice prize.'

'A prize?' asks Flopsy surprised.

Her hands tremble even more as she takes the letter and card back from her dad.

'But now it's bedtime,' he says.

He doesn't have to say that twice. Flopsy can't wait for the next day to come!

The Prize

20 APRIL

Flopsy wakes up very early this morning. She's so curious about what she has won in the balloon contest. She runs as fast as her bunny feet can carry her to Mister Owl's house. He's the mayor of the village.

He greets Flopsy as he opens his door.

'Good morning, Flopsy,' he says in a friendly voice.

'Good morning, Mister Owl,' she answers.

'I have come to get the prize for the balloon contest.' Flopsy hands him the card and the letter that she got yesterday.

'Look at that! It's from my nephew Wilbur. What a surprise!'

As he reads the news that Flopsy's balloon has flown all the way to the far North, he has to sit down.

'I declare that you have won the first prize.'

Flopsy jumps for joy.

'Come with me,' Mister Owl says. 'We will see what your prize is.'

They go to a room where all the prizes are stored. Which one will be hers?

Flopsy sees a big package that has a tag with a large number 1 tied to it.

'There it is!' she cries.

'Right!' replies Mister Owl. He picks up the package and gives it to Flopsy.

It's a table game. It looks like it will be a lot of fun to play. Flopsy can't believe her good luck.

What fun it is to win a balloon contest!

April

The bed creaks a little louder too. But Blinders doesn't hear that now. He's thinking only about one thing: touching the ceiling. That's what he wants most. Blinders is getting out of breath, but he doesn't want to stop. With a last, mighty jump he bounces as high as he can. But he just can't reach the ceiling, even though he goes a little higher than before. The ceiling is just too high.

Blinders comes down hard and lands with a smack in the middle of his bed.

Craaack! goes the bed. The mattress suddenly sinks. Blinders is in the middle of a hole.

'Uh-oh!' he cries. 'I shouldn't have done that!'

Indeed, Superman. Your mission is over.

Superman

Blinders is jumping on his bed. He loves to do that. He's Superman, and he waves his fist as he jumps high in the air. That's what Superman does on a poster that Blinders has on his wall.

Superman wears a red cape. Blinders has a red t-shirt wrapped around his shoulders.

Each time he lands on his bed, Blinders bounces up again as high as he can. He wants to touch his ceiling. His bed creaks with each jump.

If Blinders is going to touch his ceiling, he will have to jump harder and higher. He says to himself, 'Try harder, Blinders! Try harder!' And it works. He bounces a little higher.

Tobias Is Hurt

Flopsy, Nibbles, Blinders and Hopper are sitting in the Friendship Tree. In the middle of the circle stands Tobias, the toy dwarf that they won at the circus.

Suddenly Flopsy exclaims, 'Look! Tobias is hurt!'

The others come closer. 'Where?' they ask her.

Flopsy points to Tobias's thigh. 'Here, see? There's a hole. Some of his stuffing is coming out.'

'Oh no!' say the others. 'We've got to do something.'

Flopsy has an idea. She looks outside for two long sticks. She ties an old rag between them. Now they have a stretcher. They carefully lay Tobias on it.

Blinders and Flopsy run ahead on the forest path, making siren noises. Nibbles and Hopper follow them with the stretcher.

They rush to Mister Tie's shop.

Mister Tie has heard the siren coming and he's waiting for them.

'Mister Tie, our friend Tobias is hurt!' cries Flopsy as they carry him inside.

Mister Tie lays Tobias on his worktable, reaches up and turns the light on.

'Quickly, nurse,' he says to Flopsy, 'needle and thread.'

Nervously Flopsy gives Mister Tie a needle and thread.

Then Mister Tie goes to work. He carefully sews the hole shut.

'So,' he sighs in relief, 'the patient is saved. He just needs lots of rest and good care.'

That's not a problem. Nibbles, Flopsy, Blinders and Hopper will take good care of him.

Cream Cake

Flopsy is curious about whether Mister Owl has lost any weight on his diet. Mister Owl broke his chair when he sat on it and decided to go on a diet and do more exercise. That was long ago. Flopsy decides to find out.

She hides behind a tree. Here comes Mister Owl. He doesn't look any thinner. Flopsy decides to follow Mister Owl.

He goes to Miss Squirrel's shop.

He looks over his shoulder to see if anyone is around before he goes in.

Flopsy waits until Mister Owl comes out again. He has a box. The kind of box a delicious cake would fit into.

Mister Owl goes home, followed by Flopsy. He goes inside.

The kitchen window is open.

Flopsy hears Mister Owl put the box on the table and open it.

'Mmm,' he murmurs, 'this cream cake will taste great.'

Flopsy hears Mister Owl eat the whole cake up.

'Just delicious!' he says. 'That cake was just wonderful.'

Then Mister Owl sits down on a chair.

Crack! Hears Flopsy, and then a louder sound.

'Bother! Another chair broken, because I weigh so much. I've got to get back on my diet.'

'Right, Mister Owl,' thinks Flopsy, 'it might go better without cream cakes.

April

The Scent of Clean Sheets

Mummy comes into the living room with a laundry basket full of clean sheets. While the children play downstairs, she goes upstairs to make the beds.

It's a bit of work, but Mummy knows how nice it is to have clean sheets.

Now she goes to get the youngsters. It's bedtime. Misty and Nibbles have their pyjamas on already. When Mummy reminds them that they have clean sheets, the two disappear up the stairs.

'Don't forget to brush your teeth,' she calls. They are busy doing just that. Then Mummy sits down on a bed with them to read them a story. They listen carefully.

'Time to get to bed,' she says, closing the book.

Flopsy climbs into her bed, Nibbles into his. He smells the clean sheets. Wonderful! They have the smell of fresh flowers. The sheets feel smooth too. He pulls the sheet up to his ears. He just knows he will have good dreams with such nice sheets around him.

After Mummy gives him a good-night kiss and then turns out the light, Nibbles breathes deeply. He lies on his back and smells the freshness in the sheets. Then he shuts his eyes and slowly falls into a lovely night of sleep.

Post for Mister Sack

Mister Sack, the postman, is on his rounds. He has delivered almost all his letters already. There's just one left.

'Look at that!' he laughs happily. 'A letter for me!'

Even though Mister Sack delivers hundreds of letters every day, he almost never gets mail himself. So it's no surprise that he's happy to get this letter.

'I'm going home to read this in peace and quiet.'

Mister Sack goes home, imagining what there could be in that letter. Could he have news that he's won a lot of money? Or could it be a letter

80

from an old friend?

He gets to his house. He hangs up his jacket on the hook and puts his sack in the corner. He walks into the kitchen and makes a cup of tea for himself.

With the tea in one hand and the letter in the other, he goes into the living room. Carefully he puts the tea down. Then he sits on the sofa.

'Let's have a look.'

Mister Sack opens the envelope slowly. He pulls out the letter and reads it.

'What a disappointment,' he grumbles. 'How is that possible? I got another one of these once before. It was a bill for my electricity.'

Poor Mister Sack. That's not fun.

Blinders Has a Birthday

It's Blinder's birthday. He's invited his friends to a birthday party.

He looks out of the window excitedly. He is waiting for his first guest to arrive.

He's really curious about his presents. On his invitation he wrote that he only wanted things to eat, because he does love to eat.

Here come his friends. Blinders rushes to the door.

'Happy Birthday, Blinders!' say his friends together. Blinders invites his friends into the living room. They hand him his presents.

Blinders begins to open one quickly. There's a whole bag of sweets in it.

'Yes!' cries Blinders. He begins to open the second package.

'Careful,' says Flopsy, 'if you aren't careful the whole thing will fall.'

'Oh, wow, it's a strawberry tart,' exclaims Blinders happily. 'Thanks, Flopsy.'

Now the last package. That's from Hopper.

Blinders rips the wrapping paper off.

'This is a toy you can eat,' says Hopper. Blinders can't imagine what that is.

Inside the box there's a bulldozer made out of chocolate. Blinders can do a lot of building with it. If he doesn't eat it first.

That evening, when Blinders has to go to bed, there's not much left of any of his gifts. The whole day long, he's done nothing but eat them. He's got a bit of a stomach ache.

Next year, he's going to ask for normal presents that he can play with.

They last longer. And don't give you a stomach ache.

April

Urgent Needs

Nibbles and Misty are watching an exciting film in the living room.

Mummy gave them a glass of juice before she started the film.

'Take it easy,' she said to Nibbles when he asked for another glass, but he wanted a second one anyway.

Towards the end of the film Nibbles feels like he has to go to the bathroom.

'Just forget it,' he thinks to himself. 'The film will be over soon.'

But the film goes on and on. Nibbles is in trouble and the film doesn't seem to be near the end at all.

He can't stand it. He jumps up and runs to the bathroom.

'Whew, what a relief!' he thinks. He flushes the toilet, washes his hands and runs back to the living room.

The film is over and he missed the best part.

Oh well, he should have listened to Mummy. If he hadn't been so eager for that second glass, he'd have seen the film through to the end.

Wings

Hopper wants to be the first flying frog.

His last try wasn't much of a success, but now he has a solution.

In a book, he has been studying pictures of wings.

He's made some out of sturdy cardboard.

With the wings tightly strapped to his arms, he goes to a long stone that is near the brook. Hopper stands on it. Carefully he waves his wings back and forth. The wind is perfect. The sun sparkles on the water. He gets ready to take off.

'I am a bird,' thinks Hopper, 'and I am going to fly.'

He takes a run and begins to flap his wings like

crazy. At the end of the rock, he jumps forward into the air.

And he feels like he is really flying…

Downward, alas.

With a splash, Hopper lands in the water. His wings float off his arms. He swims to the shore disappointed.

He sees his wings slowly sink to the bottom of the brook.

Poor Hopper. It seems like he's going to have to be a normal frog the rest of his life.

The Raft

The four friends have agreed to meet at the shore of the brook. They are going to build a raft from a few boards they've found.

While Hopper and Nibbles tie the boards together with some rope, Blinders and Flopsy make a mast out of a beautiful flag.

'It looks so nice,' says Nibbles when the raft is done.

'We need to baptise it,' says Blinders, 'just like they do real ships. Somebody famous needs to break a bottle on the front of our raft.'

'Break a bottle?' asks Hopper. 'What sort of bottle?'

'A bottle of lemonade,' says Flopsy. She runs home and comes back a little later with a bottle of lemonade.

Flopsy steps onto the raft. 'Hereby I baptise our raft,' she says proudly, while she cracks the bottle against the mast.

'Look out!' yells Nibbles suddenly. Flopsy jumps quickly from the raft to the shore.

The mast has crashed into the water and the flag is all wet. Now the raft breaks apart and the boards start to float down the brook, one by one.

These four sailors better stay on shore.

Box of Chalks

Nibbles has received a box of coloured chalks from Mummy. She knows how much he loves to draw.

On the pavement by his house he makes one drawing after the other. Soon the whole pavement is filled with drawings. After that he starts drawing on the wall of the house and before long all the walls are covered with drawings too.

Now Mummy comes along. First she sees the drawings on the pavement, and she loves them.

But when she sees the walls, she suddenly finds the drawings not so nice. The whole house is covered! Nibbles, who's still busy drawing, hears Mummy yelling all of a sudden. She sounds angry.

He runs to her as fast as he can. She points to the walls of the house. But what can he say? They look so pretty. He just doesn't know when to stop.

Mummy is not happy. She gives Nibbles a bucket of water and a sponge. Nibbles has to clean all the walls up.

It can be tough being an artist.

May

Two Doctors

Blinders is playing doctor. He pushes the toy syringe against his teddy bear's arm.

'Don't be afraid, Teddy,' says Blinders. 'There's no needle here.'

Blinders pretends to give Teddy his injection.

The bear looks at Blinders with a smile.

Then Blinders hears Mummy calling.

Oh no, it's his turn for an injection. He doesn't want that at all.

But if Mummy is calling, he'd better come.

A little later he's at the doctor's, sitting on a big table. The doctor takes a syringe and fills it with medicine. He wipes Blinders' arm clean with some cotton wool. Brrr, that feels cold.

Then the doctor tells Blinders a joke. Blinders laughs out loud!

'That's it,' says the doctor, 'you've had your injection.'

How can that be? Blinders didn't feel a thing.

It wasn't so bad. He didn't mind it since it was over so fast. Now he can tell Teddy the joke.

Maybe Teddy will laugh too.

Escaped

For weeks, Sam the policeman has been searching for that scoundrel, Roger Fox. Finally he's found his hideout. Sam hides himself behind a tree and waits for Roger to appear.

'Now I've got you!' he cries as Roger comes out.

'Come here, so I can take you to jail.'

'How did you find me?' asks Roger surprised.

'A policeman knows everything,' snorts Sam.

'Everything?' asks Roger.

Sam nods.

'Then do you know what will happen if I let go of this rope?'

Sam looks at the rope that's tied to a branch.

'Uh, no… I don't,' he has to admit.

'Perhaps you could give it a try. Then you'll know,' urges Roger.

'Hmmm,' sighs Sam, 'you have a point.'

Carefully he unties the rope. He barely has the knot undone when the heavy branch falls right on his head.

Sam sees stars.

Meanwhile the fox has escaped.

Poor Sam has become a little wiser today. Saying that you know everything isn't always a good idea.

Fire

3 MAY

My goodness, Nibbles has a sharp nose.

Today he was walking through the woods and suddenly he could smell smoke. Sniffing carefully, he followed the path of the scent. It led him right to Miss Hedgehog's house.

When Mister Sack, the postman, came by, Nibbles told him about the smoky smell. Mister Sack ran directly to Mister Owl and told him the news.

'Fire! Fire!' he cried, so loud that the whole village could hear him.

'There's a fire at Miss Hedgehog's house!' he announced breathlessly to the village.

Immediately everybody came running with buckets of water. They formed a long chain and handed the buckets along it. Mister Owl stands at the head of the chain. He throws water inside the open window. That should put the fire out.

Suddenly, Miss Hedgehog comes running out of her house furiously. She's totally soaked.

'What's this all about?' she asks angrily.

'Your house is on fire. Don't you know?' Mister Owl asks astonished.

Miss Hedgehog doesn't know what to make of this. 'I have been baking a cake. But there's no fire here.'

'Then you really need to take it out of the oven,' says Nibbles, coming up to them, 'because it's burning.'

Luckily everybody breaks out laughing.

Jogging

4 MAY

Mister Owl has his jogging shoes on. He's trying to lose some weight and thinks running will help.

After a few minutes of running he's puffing and sweating. He hasn't gone very far. He'd really like to stop.

Here comes Miss Hedgehog out for a walk.

Mister Owl doesn't want Miss Hedgehog to see him all tired out, so he tries to run a little faster.

'Hello, Miss Hedgehog,' he calls to her. 'Lovely – puff – lovely weather – puff, puff – for jogging, isn't it?'

'It certainly is,' she answers. 'But you can call me Helen, OK? That's what I prefer.'

Mister Owl doesn't hear her. He's turned the corner already. He looks back behind him. Luckily there's nobody to see him.

Panting and gasping, he drops to the ground. Sweat covers his face.

After a while, he catches his breath. From his resting place, he looks up and down the path. There's nobody to be seen.

Mister Owl begins to run again. This time he heads straight home.

He gets home and runs inside, closing the door behind him. He's so hungry now!

Losing weight will have to wait.

Sunrise

It's still dark when Mister Sack, the postman, leaves his home. His sack is pretty full.

Mister Sack walks along the path.

He arrives at the house on the edge of the woods. That's Mister Tie's house. As he comes to it, he sees Mister Tie standing outside.

'Good morning, Mister Sack.'

'Good morning, Mister Tie. Did you fall out of your bed?'

'No,' answers Mister Tie. 'I got up early on purpose. I heard yesterday on the radio that the weather will be gorgeous today. So I set my alarm extra early. I want to see the sunrise.'

'See the sunrise? I see that every day. What's so special about that?' asks Mister Sack.

'Don't you think it's lovely with all those colours?' asks Mister Tie surprised.

'Most of the time, I don't get a chance to watch. I have got to deliver the post.'

'Oh, but on such a lovely day as today, I don't think anyone will mind if the post arrives a little bit later. Why don't you come with me? We can watch it together. I've just made tea.'

Mister Sack thinks that's a fine idea. The two go and sit on a log. Sipping steaming cups of tea, they watch as the sun slowly rises.

Mister Sack has to admit that it's a really beautiful sight. And that's in spite of the fact that he sees it so often.

May

The Seesaw

Hopper has found an old board. He brings it with him to the Friendship Tree.

'Look,' he says, 'can't we do something with this?' Flopsy, Nibbles and Blinders are sitting outside, waiting for Hopper. They look curiously at the board.

'Let's make a seesaw,' suggests Flopsy.

'How do we do that?' asks Nibbles.

'Help me carry this log over here,' says Flopsy to Blinders. Together they lay the log on the grass. Flopsy lays the board across the log.

'Great!' cries Nibbles. 'We have a seesaw. Good thinking, Flopsy.'

First Flopsy and Hopper ride the seesaw, up and down, up and down. They laugh out loud.

Then it's Nibbles and Blinders' turn. They go fast.

'Maybe we could all ride at once,' suggests Hopper.

That's worth a try. Flopsy goes to sit with Nibbles and Hopper with Blinders.

'Ready?' asks Nibbles. 'Here we go!'

But he has barely said that when the board breaks in two with a loud crack. The four friends fall to the ground.

'What a shame. Now our seesaw is broken,' sighs Flopsy. 'I really liked it.'

The others are disappointed too.

Nibbles has an idea. His daddy is a carpenter. He'll ask Daddy to make them a real seesaw.

Daddy will certainly do that. Imagine: a real seesaw. One that won't break.

What the Carpenter Knows

Flopsy, Hopper, Blinders and Nibbles have met at Nibbles' daddy's workshop. Nibbles' daddy is a carpenter. He is going to make them a sturdy seesaw today.

First he looks for a strong board. He attaches four seats to it. That way all four of them can ride the seesaw. In front of each seat he also attaches a handle so they can hold on tightly.

He fastens the board to a big block of wood with some screws. That way the board can tip up and

88

down. In a few minutes, it's done.

They bring their seesaw to the Friendship Tree. The friends try it out. It works great!

'Thanks, Mister Mouse,' Flopsy and the others say. 'You've done a terrific job.'

'If we can ever do anything for you, just let us know,' says Hopper.

'Actually,' says Mister Mouse, 'there is something that you all can do. My workshop could do with a cleaning. Could you four do that for me?

At first the friends are grumpy. Why does he have to ask that now? They want to ride their new seesaw. But on the other hand, Mister Mouse took time to make it for them.

So in the end the friends are happy to clean up. In less than an hour the whole workshop is clean and tidy. How nice for kind Mister Mouse.

Swollen Finger

Nibbles is helping his father. His dad is going to make a chest today. Since it must be very strong, he needs to use a whole lot of nails. Nibbles gets a hammer and some nails. Then they begin to pound.

First Nibbles sets the nail where he wants it. Then he taps it lightly with his hammer so the nail stands up by itself.

'Look, Daddy,' says Nibbles proudly.

Daddy nods approvingly. But if he's going to keep up with Daddy, then Nibbles has to work quickly and do his best. Daddy has already pounded six nails into the chest.

Nibbles holds his nail straight with one hand. With the other he swings the hammer and aims at the nail. At least that is what he hopes to do. But guess what? The hammer hits Nibbles' finger instead.

'Ow!' he cries. Oh, it hurts so much! Nibbles quickly sticks his finger in his mouth.

Daddy knows exactly what's happened.

'Let me see it,' he says.

Nibbles takes his throbbing finger out of his mouth and shows it to Daddy. It's already red and swollen.

'You know what? That will happen less and less as you get to be a better carpenter.'

Luckily the pain is over now. Nibbles picks up the hammer and gets back to work.

That's what real carpenters do.

May

Flopsy and the Butterfly

Flopsy has just been told off by her mummy. That's why she's gone outside. Now she is feeling grumpy and sitting in a corner of the garden.

A butterfly lands softly beside Flopsy. It looks like he has two eyes painted on his wings. It seems like he is looking at her with them.

'Why are you staring at me, you silly butterfly,' says Flopsy angrily. But the butterfly stays there, resting peacefully. He flaps his wings once. It makes it seem like those eyes are winking.

Flopsy stamps a foot near the butterfly. She is so angry! But it just keeps sitting there. Flopsy glares at the friendly eyes on the insect's wings.

Suddenly the butterfly takes off. He makes a little circle around Flopsy, then comes slowly down and lands on Flopsy's nose!

First Flopsy wants to brush him away. But the butterfly just stays there resting.

Crossing her eyes, Flopsy tries to watch the butterfly. But then she realizes that she must look silly, with her eyes crossed and a butterfly on her nose. It's tickling her now too.

Flopsy starts to laugh.

The butterfly starts to fly in circles around Flopsy's head.

'Are you playing with me?' she asks, laughing at herself now too.

So that's how the butterfly cheers Flopsy up again.

Post for Misty and Nibbles

Nibbles opens the door.

'Hello, my friend,' says Mister Sack, the postman. 'I have a letter for your sister and you.'

'Really?' asks Nibbles. 'Who is it from?'

'It looks like it's from your Granddad and Grandma.'

Meanwhile Misty has come to see what's happening.

'Would you please read it for us? We can't read yet,'

she explains.

Of course Mister Sack will do that. He opens the envelope and pulls the letter out.

'They ask if you are doing well.'

Nibbles and Misty look at each other. Yes, everything is tip-top with them.

'And if you are still growing fast,' continues Mister Sack.

Nibbles looks at his trousers. They are too short, so he must be growing, he thinks. Or his trousers have shrunken in the wash.

'They ask if you eat everything on your plates at dinner.'

'Most of the time,' nods Nibbles. 'Except when we have Brussel sprouts.'

'What they'd like to know most is if you are being nice to each other.'

That's easy. Sometimes, not often, they get into a little fight. But almost all the time they are true friends.

'Finally, they are asking if you can come and stay with them next week.'

Misty and Nibbles jump up and down, clapping and laughing. To go and stay with Granddad and Grandma!

Hopper Wants to Fly

Today's the day when Hopper will become the first flying frog. That is why he's blown up fifty balloons and tied them to a stick. All Hopper has to do now is hold onto them while the balloons all take off into the sky.

Here goes. Slowly Hopper feels the balloons pulling him into the air. It is working so far. Hopper can't believe his eyes. The top of a small tree tickles his toes.

He drifts past a big oak tree. If he sticks out his hand he can touch the leaves. He can't wait until he flies higher than the oak.

But… what's that? The strings from the balloons are getting tangled around a branch that is sticking out. Hopper's going to get stuck…

'Oh, no!' he cries.

Swinging back and forth from a branch, Hopper feels the wind blowing through the leaves of the tree. Hopper doesn't mind that. He is more afraid of being so high. He looks down. Wow, is the ground far away!

Hopper looks around him, his fear growing. He calls out for help as loudly as he can. Luckily there is someone nearby who goes to get help. In a little while, Hopper is back on the ground, safe and sound.

But not before he promises himself he's going to give up on flying. For now.

May

Sweets

Flopsy is visiting Miss Crow. Miss Crow is very old, so Flopsy does her shopping for her. Most of the time Miss Crow has her shopping list ready, but not today. She forgot.

'I'll make it right now,' she says, taking out a piece of paper and pencil.

'Six eggs, two bottles of milk…'

She thinks it over.

'A chunk of cheese… what else?'

'Sweets?' jokes Flopsy.

Miss Crow looks at her in surprise.

'That's not a bad idea. I was still a child when I had my last sweet. Maybe it's time for another one. Let's give it a try.'

A little later Flopsy is standing in Miss Squirrel's shop with the list.

'And last of all, she wants the most delicious sweets you have,' she says.

Miss Squirrel takes a big bag and nearly fills it with sweets.

Flopsy hurries back to Miss Crow. She comes in triumphantly with the bags.

'Open it up,' cries Miss Crow, pointing to the sweets bag.

Flopsy spills all the sweets out on the table.

'My, my, my! Which one is the best?' asks Miss Crow.

Flopsy points to a few. Then they begin to sample all kinds of sweets, comparing them and commenting as they nibble away.

What a sweet old lady Miss Crow is!

The Puppet Play

Nibbles and Flopsy are visiting Mister Tie, the tailor. He's reading the newspaper.

'Oh, no, that can't be true!' he exclaims suddenly.

'What's wrong?' asks Flopsy worried.

'I wanted to surprise Miss Hedgehog. I bought tickets for a play tonight. But here it says the play is cancelled tonight. One of the actors is sick. What can I say to Miss Hedgehog?'

He heaves a huge sigh.

Nibbles looks at Flopsy. He has an idea. He explains it to Mister Tie, who thinks it's a great plan.

That evening Miss Hedgehog comes to Mister Tie's house. The whole place is lit with sparkling candles.

'Is this the surprise? It's lovely,' she says.

'No, this is just the beginning.'

Mister Tie takes Miss Hedgehog's jacket and hangs

it up. Flopsy brings them two glasses of berry juice.

'Ladies and gentlemen, please take your seats.' Flopsy points to two chairs that are lined up in a row in the middle of the room. Then she disappears behind a big board.

There is a loud drum-roll.

They hear Nibbles' voice say, 'Ladies and gentlemen, the show will begin.'

A bright light shines on a big red curtain. Slowly the curtain opens. It's a puppet theatre!

'Wonderful,' says Miss Hedgehog. 'I love puppet shows!'

The show begins. Miss Hedgehog and Mister Tie have a wonderful time.

So it still is a fine evening.

Granddad's Bike

Ring-ring! comes a sound from outside. Someone riding an old bicycle stops in front of Nibbles' house. A big basket on wheels, like bakers used to use, is attached to it.

As the biker comes to the door, he waves to Nibbles.

'Hello, Nibbles!' he calls loudly.

'Granddad! It's Granddad!' exclaims Nibbles.

Misty appears in a second at Granddad's side.

'So are you two coming to stay with us for a few days?'

'Yesss!' roar the brother and sister together.

'Great,' laughs Granddad. 'Let's get started. We have a long ride ahead of us.'

Together the three walk to the old bike. 'You two can ride in the basket,' he says.

Nibbles and Misty think this is really great. They jump in. Mummy gives each of them a big kiss.

Ring-ring! goes Granddad's bell as they take off. He begins to pedal away. Nibbles and Misty wave at Mummy until she disappears.

'I'm going to miss Mummy a little,' says Misty.

Nibbles gives Misty a hug. 'It's just for a few days.'

'That's true,' she says. 'And it's always so much fun at Granny and Granddad's.'

'I can't wait to see Granny again.'

'Me too,' says Misty.

'Faster, Granddad, faster!' exclaim the two. But he is already pedalling as fast as he can. And he has some busy days ahead with these two rascals.

short for him.

'Oh, no,' says Granny. 'You must be growing fast! Or else I made it too small.'

She helps Nibbles take the jumper off.

'What shall I do with this lovely jumper?' she asks herself.

'Maybe it will fit Misty,' suggests Nibbles.

'That's a good idea. Let's take a look.'

Granny helps Misty put the jumper on.

'Just look at that. It fits her perfectly, don't you think?'

Misty heaves a deep sigh.

'What's wrong, dear?' asks Granny.

'It's just… can you please take this off me? I'm melting!'

They all burst out laughing.

Nice and Warm

Nibbles and Misty are staying with their Grandparents for a few days.

'It's been quite a while,' says Granny when she sees them. 'I have a surprise for you.'

She takes two presents from a cupboard. She gives the first to Misty. A warm scarf and hat are inside.

'I knitted them myself,' says Granny proudly. She puts the hat on Misty's head and ties the scarf around Misty's neck. 'Do you like it?'

Misty nods. 'It is wonderful, Granny.'

Now it's Nibbles' turn to open his present.

Granny has made him a beautiful jumper. He puts it on – but what's the matter? The jumper is too

Waking Up to the Smell of …

Nibbles and Misty are lying in a huge bed. Nibbles wakes up first to the sound of birds singing.

When he opens his eyes, he's scared at first to find that he's not in his own bed. But in a second he knows where he is. He's in Granny and Granddad's spare room, staying with them for a few days.

'Misty…' he whispers. 'Hey, Misty, wake up.'

Blinking quickly, Misty opens her eyes. She wipes the sleep from them.

'Misty, I smell something. Do you too?'

Misty sits up straight in bed. First she breathes out hard, then she sticks her nose in the air and breathes the air in.

'I don't smell a thing,' she says.

Nibbles jumps out of the big bed. He puts on his slippers and opens the door carefully. A sweet, warm smell drifts into the room.

Now Misty can smell it too. She jumps out of bed and together they go to the top of the stairs. The smell gets stronger with every step as they go downstairs. When they get to the bottom, they walk to the kitchen door.

Nibbles can just reach the handle. Slowly he opens the door. The two stick their heads in. Granddad is busy in the kitchen. He has his baker's clothes on. He used to be a baker. Mummy told them that. And what was his specialty? You have already guessed, right?

Honey biscuits.

What fun it is to have a Granddad like that!

Attic Picnic

'How annoying. On this day of all days, it rains,' sighs Granddad. 'Just as we were leaving for our picnic in the park.'

Misty and Nibbles look sadly out of the window at the fat raindrops dripping down.

'And here I stand with our picnic basket,' says Granny. 'What are we going to do with our lovely honey biscuits that Granddad baked?'

'Eat them all up, naturally,' laughs Nibbles.

Everyone looks at Nibbles in surprise.

'If we can't picnic outside, let's do it inside.'

'That's a good idea,' laughs Granddad, 'but where should we do it?'

Nibbles thinks.

'In a place in the house where you don't go very often. Where would that be?'

'The attic, maybe?' asks Granny.

'Cool,' cries Nibbles. 'Let's have an attic picnic!'

Granddad and Granny look at each other smiling. An attic picnic? Why not?

They take the picnic basket and go to the attic. Granny lays a big cloth on the floor and sets the plates out on it. Granddad pours glasses full of berry juice while the youngsters put the honey biscuits on a platter. When everything is ready, they can begin to feast. Meanwhile the rain is pouring down outside. But they have their strange picnic anyway. It was great fun, even if it was strange!

May

Going Home

Nibbles and Misty are going home. They packed their suitcases this morning.

'Don't forget your toy animals,' reminds Granny.

'They are all packed,' says Nibbles confidently.

'You'd better look again,' she says. 'You can't be too careful.'

Nibbles looks one last time. The toy animals are sleeping softly in the suitcases.

Granddad picks up the suitcases and sets them in the basket in front of his bicycle.

'Make sure those suitcases can't fall out,' warns Granny. Granddad feels the suitcases.

'Only an earthquake could move those suitcases from their places,' he laughs.

'You can't be too careful,' says Granny.

Then the two youngsters get still another present from Granny.

For Misty, she has knitted a headband to keep her ears warm. For Nibbles, a new sweater, which this time is the right size. The last one was too small.

'Thank you! It looks really warm, Granny,' says Nibbles. 'This winter we aren't going to feel cold at all, with all these woollen clothes you have knitted for us.'

'I am glad you like them. You can't be too careful,' says Granny.

The youngsters climb into the baker's basket in front of the bicycle.

Granny waves to them and they wave back.

'Now stop waving and hold on,' she calls to them, 'because…'

'You can't be too careful!' the youngsters and Granddad call back, laughing as they go.

A Fight

Nibbles runs to the Friendship Tree. Hopper's sitting there.

'Where were you all this time?' asks Hopper angrily.

Nibbles looks at Hopper in surprise.

'With my Grannydparents,' he says. 'Didn't I tell you that?'

'No,' barks Hopper. 'I have just been sitting here.'

'What about Blinders and Flopsy? Couldn't you play with them?'

'They didn't have any time for me.'

'Hey, I am sorry, Hopper,' says Nibbles. 'Do you want to play a game?'

'No!' snorts Hopper. He crosses his arms and looks at Nibbles with a sour look.

Nibbles doesn't get it. He turns around and goes home, feeling awful.

Hopper laughs to himself. He's taught his best friend a good lesson. But a few seconds later he thinks, 'Hmm. There is something wrong. My best friend is back and I still feel bad.'

If two best friends are together, shouldn't they feel happy? Hopper jumps up. Maybe he has made a mistake sending Nibbles away. He runs after him.

'Nibbles…' he says. 'I'm sorry. That was silly of me.'

Slowly Nibbles turns and looks at Hopper. 'It's OK,' he says.

'Would you… would you like to play with me?' asks Hopper shyly.

'Yes!' smiles Nibbles. They walk on together.

Best friends shouldn't fight. No, they should play together and have fun.

The Advert

Mister Owl looks out of the window.

'Where is Mister Sack, anyway?' he asks himself. For the hundredth time he looks at the clock. Still no sign of Mister Sack.

Mister Owl takes a newspaper clipping out of his pocket and reads it. It is an advert for some powder that makes you thin. 'It works fast!' he reads.

Mister Owl wants to try it just once. So he ordered a box of the powder. He wants to look thin and cool. The box of powder should arrive today.

Finally. There is Mister Sack with his box. Mister Owl takes it and disappears inside.

Quickly he tears off the wrapping and pulls a big package out.

'The Wonder-Powder That Makes You Thin!' it says on the package.

Mister Owl opens it. He can't wait to start the treatment. He wets a finger and dabs it in the white powder, then puts his finger in his mouth.

'Yuk! Blugh! Bwah! It's awful!' he cries. 'It tastes like dish soap!'

Mister Owl closes the package and puts it away. He is never going to order anything like this again.

He is just going to have to stay his friendly, round self a while longer.

May

Snake

Today Nibbles is a snake. He hisses and slithers over the floor. This snake is hunting. Now and then he sticks his tongue out just like real snakes do. Not to be naughty, but because that is how snakes smell things.

Does he smell the lovely smell of his sweet mummy?

Slowly he slides up to his prey. She is standing in the kitchen, making soup.

'A yummy dish,' hisses Nibbles quietly.

He slides a little closer. Mummy has no idea he is around.

'Hiss! Hiss!' goes Nibbles. He gets even closer to Mummy. The snake is going to bite its prey!

Nibbles rears up and gets ready to bite Mummy on the leg.

Mummy turns around suddenly in surprise. Unfortunately, she steps on Nibbles' hand. Nibbles screams with pain.

'Nibbles, what on earth are you doing on the floor like that?' she asks really frightened.

She looks at Nibbles' hand. Luckily it isn't too bad. Sniffing, Nibbles explains to Mummy that he was a snake going after a meal.

'You poor little snake,' says Mummy tenderly, 'you were beaten by Mummy Mouse.'

Picking Berries

Miss Hedgehog and Mister Tie are strolling in the woods. They are going berry picking so that she can make a delicious berry tart for them. It's a pleasant task, but you do have to watch out. The berry bushes have sharp thorns.

'This bush is already picked bare,' she says proudly. 'My basket will be filled soon.'

As she goes to the next bush, her dress snags on one of the thorns and tears with a loud noise.

'Oh, no!' she cries, 'my beautiful dress!'

Mister Tie hurries over and helps her get free. 'It will be OK. It's just a little tear. I can fix that for you when we get home.'

They pick enough berries to fill both their baskets, and then walk home.

Mister Tie takes Miss Hedgehog's dress home with him to his workshop. With a needle and thread he fixes the tear so you can't see a thing any more.

He brings the dress back to her just as she takes the berry tart out of the oven.

Good timing and good eating!

A New Uniform for Sam

Sam, the police officer, goes to Mister Tie to have a new uniform made. It's not that his old one is worn out. Far from that. But he thinks that a cool police officer like himself should have a much fancier uniform.

He has drawn what he wants on a piece of paper. Dark blue cloth with gold decorations and silver buttons. On his hat, a silver badge. And a fancy belt with a silver buckle. If he wears that uniform, people will really be impressed.

Proudly he goes into Mister Tie's workshop.

'Good morning, tailor,' he says.

'Good morning, officer,' answers Mister Tie.

Sam shows him the drawing. 'That's the way it has to look. Can you make it like that for me?'

Mister Tie looks at the drawing.

'Yes, but it will be pretty expensive with all those silver and gold decorations.'

Sam looks at him in surprise. 'And… how much, exactly?'

Mister Tie does some calculations and shows Sam the total.

Sam turns completely red. He's never had that much money.

'Um, well…' he says flustered, 'actually I… I'm pretty happy with the uniform I'm wearing. Maybe I'll wait a while before I order my new one.'

He hurries out of the tailor's shop. He's going to have to save for a long, long time.

Flowers for Miss Hedgehog

This whole afternoon, Mister Tie has been wandering in the woods, looking for the most beautiful flowers he can find. Finally he has made a lovely bouquet. He goes to the house of Miss Hedgehog and rings the doorbell.

'Here is a bouquet for the sweetest creature in the woods,' he says proudly as he hands Miss Hedgehog his bouquet.

'Uh… thank you,' says Miss Hedgehog hesitatingly. 'But… uh…'

'What's wrong?' asks Mister Tie worried. 'Don't you like them?'

'Yes, but...'

'See these daisies? I really had doubts about them and almost left them out, but…'

'No, no,' interrupts Miss Hedgehog, 'the daisies are lovely, but...'

'You… you aren't in love with someone else, are you?' stammers Mister Tie.

'No, of course not, Mister Tie,' answers Miss Hedgehog. 'You are the sweetest fellow in the forest. It's just that I have hay fever, so I can't have flowers in my house. Just having them near makes me start sneezing.'

Mister Tie is actually relieved. If only he had known!

So they decide to put the flowers in a vase and set it on the garden table. That way Miss Hedgehog can look out of her window and enjoy the beautiful bouquet.

Without sneezing.

Zipping Cream

Nibbles is running an errand for Mummy. *Ding-a-ling!* sounds the bell as he opens the door to the shop.

'Hello, Nibbles,' Miss Squirrel says smiling. 'What can I do for you?'

'I need to get some zipping cream for Mummy.'

Miss Squirrel looks at him with her eyes wide open. 'What is it that you need?'

'Zipping cream,' repeats Nibbles confidently.

'Zipping cream? I am afraid I don't have any.'

'But Mummy said that she has just come from here. When she came home, she saw that she needed one more package of zipping cream than she bought. So she asked me to come and get one more.'

Miss Squirrel thinks hard. She's trying to remember what Mummy bought. Some vegetables, she's sure of that. And some potatoes and bread. Some soap, and a few packages of whipping cream.

'Of course,' she exclaims. 'That's it. I think you didn't hear her too well. Instead of *zipping* I think you mean *whipping* cream. That's what your mummy bought.'

'Oh, I see,' says Nibbles relieved.

Laughing, Miss Squirrel gets a package of whipping cream and gives it to Nibbles. He pays for it and runs back home.

Miss Squirrel watches him disappear down the path. She smiles and says to herself, 'Zipping cream – why not?'

'I think it must feel nice,' says Flopsy.

'Do you really think so?'

'We should try it sometime and see.'

Nibbles hesitates.

'Or don't you dare to?' teases Flopsy.

'Of course I dare to,' answers Nibbles bravely. He stands up and sticks out his lips. Flopsy stands and sticks hers out too. Then they move their lips closer together.

'You're supposed to close your eyes,' says Flopsy. Nibbles does.

Their lips touch. Then they sit down quickly.

'What did you think?' asks Flopsy after a moment.

'Nothing much,' says Nibbles, shrugging his shoulders.

'Me to!' says Flopsy disappointed. 'Do you want to play football? That's lots more fun.'

'Good idea!' laughs Nibbles.

They go and find the ball, laughing as they walk. That kissing stuff can wait until they are bigger.

Kisses

Flopsy and Nibbles are sitting on an old log.

'Nibbles,' asks Flopsy, 'have you ever kissed anyone?'

'Oh sure,' answers Nibbles, 'all the time.'

'Who have you kissed?'

'Mummy and Daddy before I go to bed. Granny, Granddad….'

'No, silly,' interrupts Flopsy. 'I mean *really* kissing. On the lips, like they do in the movies.'

Now Nibbles gets it.

'Isn't that kind of messy?' he asks Flopsy.

'How do I know?' answers Flopsy. 'If it isn't nice, why do people do it?'

Nibbles can't answer that.

Chicken Scratches

Mister Sack, the postman, has a problem. He holds an envelope in his hand. There is an address on it, but it's written so sloppily that he can hardly read it.

'What chicken scratches,' sighs Mister Sack. 'How in the world can I deliver this letter?'

Mister Owl wanders by.

'What's wrong, Mister Sack?'

Mister Sack shows him the envelope.

'Hmm,' says Mister Owl, thinking hard. 'I think that handwriting looks familiar. My goodness, what a messy writer. This letter must be from a really sloppy person.'

Nibbles comes wandering by.

'Nibbles,' asks Mister Sack, 'do you have any idea who this envelope could be from?'

Nibbles can't read yet. But the scribbles on the envelope look familiar right away. He runs to Mister Owl's house and picks up a piece of paper from the desk. He shows it to Mister Sack.

'Why, that is your handwriting, Mister Owl!' exclaims Mister Sack completely surprised. Mister Owl turns as red as a tomato.

'I… uh…' he stammers guiltily, '…will try to write more clearly next time I write a letter.'

'That will help a lot,' says Mister Sack smiling. 'Otherwise I can't deliver the post. And that would be a pity, wouldn't it?'

Mummy Mouse is Sick

One day, when Nibbles and Misty come in from playing outside, they find Mummy sleeping on the sofa.

'What is happening with Mummy?' Misty asks Nibbles.

Just then Mummy wakes up. She looks a little pale.

'I don't feel very well today,' says Mummy softly. 'I think I have flu.'

Misty and Nibbles look at each other.

'Just stay here and rest, Mummy,' Nibbles says gently. 'Misty and I will take care of you.'

A tiny smile lights up Mummy's face.

Nibbles and Misty go to the bedroom to get a blanket for Mummy. They start making some tea.

They carefully set some water to boil and find the teapot and some tea. When the water starts bubbling, they pour it into a teapot with the tea. They are very, very careful, because the water is so hot.

In a few minutes, the tea is ready. They fill a cup, add some honey, give it a stir and then bring the cup to Mummy.

Mummy takes a sip of the steaming tea.

'Delicious,' she sighs. Soon she's back asleep.

Nibbles and Misty cover her with the blanket they brought. Now she's cosy and warm.

With such good nurses, Mummy will get better quickly!

King Blinders

Blinders is king today. King of his bedroom. He has set a paper crown on his head and made a cape from his blanket. He has made a throne out of all the pillows, sheets and blankets on his bed.

Here and there he has set up his dolls and animals in front of him, ready to carry out his orders.

His kingdom looks messy, to tell the truth. But that isn't important now. He has to rule his kingdom.

Suddenly, there is a knock on his door.

'Who goes there?' he asks in a deep voice.

'It's me, your mummy,' he hears.

'Do you wish to enter my kingdom?'

'Yes, your Highness,' says Mummy. 'I have some clean clothes that I would like to put away.'

'Very well,' answers the king. 'You may enter.'

Mummy opens the door. When she sees what Blinders has done, she exclaims, 'What a mess!'

She looks around. 'I want you to clean this mess up right now. All the sheets and blankets that I folded so carefully! All these toys all over the floor! Get to work, Blinders.' She's really angry.

Blinders leaps of his throne in surprise and starts cleaning up as fast as he can. His time as a king was very, very short.

The Dam

When Hopper wakes up one morning, he can't believe his eyes. There's practically no water in the brook.

He quickly brings Mister Owl, the mayor, to see. They can't understand what has happened. They start to investigate together.

Suddenly they see the cause. There is a huge pile of wood at the top of the pool where Hopper lives. The wood makes a dam and it is holding the water back. They start cleaning up.

They have barely moved a few pieces of wood away when they hear an angry voice behind them.

'And just what do you think you are doing?'

Hopper and Mister Owl turn around in surprise.

An angry beaver is staring at them.

'Do you know how long I worked on this?'

'No, sorry. But it's blocking all the water from the rest of the brook,' explains Mister Owl.

'Really? Where do you live?'

'A bit below your dam,' explains Mister Owl.

'Oh, I didn't know that,' says the beaver apologetically. 'I will take my dam apart.'

'That's very good of you. If you like, you could make a new one further downstream, where nobody lives. That would bother no one.'

'Really? That would be great,' answers the beaver.

'Let me introduce myself. I am Bert Beaver, a professional dam builder.'

'I'm Mister Owl, mayor of our village, and this is Hopper. Welcome to our town.'

That's how Hopper met the newest resident of the village. Quite an interesting one. You'll soon see why.

Watch Out for Falling Trees

Nibbles and Flopsy are playing in the woods. Suddenly they hear a crack and then a loud, long bang.

'What was *that*?' asks Flopsy.

'I have no idea,' answers Nibbles.

They decide to go and check the sound out. They walk cautiously in the direction of the noise.

It's not hard to see. Not far away a tree lies fallen on the ground.

It's quiet now. Or almost quiet.

'Do you hear that?' asks Nibbles.

They hear a gnawing sound coming from close by. Then there's a long, slow cracking sound.

'Look out!' cries Flopsy. Nibbles and Flopsy barely get out of the way of a falling tree in time. With a huge groan it lands on the ground. Nibbles and Flopsy feel their hearts pounding in their throats. Suddenly a surprised face pokes out from behind the tree.

'What are you doing here?'

It's Bert Beaver. 'You almost got a knock on the head, you know. It is dangerous here.'

'What on earth are you doing?' Flopsy asks in a trembling voice.

'I need wood to build my new dam. It's going to be the most beautiful dam you have ever seen. Come and see it when it's done.'

'We certainly will do that,' says Nibbles with his knees still shaking. Then they run away as fast as they can. When Bert Beaver is busy working, they don't want to be anywhere near him.

Bert's Problem

1 JUNE

'Hello, children,' calls Bert Beaver when he spots Nibbles and Flopsy.

'My new dam is finished. Would you like to come and see it?'

Nibbles and Flopsy creep up close to the dam. They stop beside the giant wooden structure with their mouths open. Bert shows them all the special things about his dam.

'Aren't I something? There are more than two hundred tree branches in it. All of them cut to size by yours truly,' he says proudly.

Nibbles and Flopsy don't really know what to say. Nibbles glances behind him. Where there used to be a forest, he now sees lots of chewed-off stumps. Nibbles thinks it is sad to see all those trees destroyed.

'It certainly is a strong dam,' he says hesitatingly, 'but you also cut down a lot of trees. I don't like that part.'

'Yes,' says Flopsy beside him, 'if you keep on doing this, there will be no more forest for us to play and live in. And where will you find trees to repair your dam in the years to come?'

Bert doesn't know what to say. He scratches his head. How can he fix this problem? He is going to have to think this over, long and hard. But he will find a solution, or his name is not Bert Beaver.

Well, Bert, we're curious…

Operation Save the Forest

2 JUNE

This morning Nibbles and Flopsy are going to the brook. They walk to where Bert Beaver has cut down all the trees for his dam. Since Nibbles and Flopsy have told Bert they didn't like what he had done to the woods, Bert has been trying to find a solution. As Nibbles and Flopsy come to the open place, they hear Bert whistling happily.

'Hello, friends!' he calls excitedly. 'It's a beautiful day, isn't it?'

Nibbles and Flopsy look over the space. Bert

has stuck little branches of trees into the dirt all over the place.

'What are you doing?' they ask.

'Do you see that sack?' asks Bert. 'It's full of little twigs that I have cut off trees here and there.'

'So you have hurt even more trees?' asks Flopsy angrily.

'Absolutely not,' Bert assures her. 'The trees don't notice a thing. Look, when you stick this kind of twig in the ground, it will grow into a nice tall tree. All we have to do now is give them lots of water. Would you like to help?'

Of course Nibbles and Flopsy want to help! If it will help the forest, they are happy to do what they can.

While Bert goes on planting the little branches, Nibbles and Flopsy get water from the brook. They pour it over each of the twigs.

Much later they are finished, and they are really tired. But they are proud of what they have done for the forest.

He is curious, so he jumps up. He wants to know what the bee will do. It zooms around. And strange as it may seem, it holds a tiny golden thing between its two front feet.

Nibbles decides to follow the bee. He runs as fast as he can. The bee flies quickly over the flowers. Nibbles is barely able to keep up.

Beside a big tree he loses sight of the bee. It's just gone.

Suddenly Nibbles hears a buzzing above his head. Then he sees a bee flying out of a small hole in the tree trunk. Nibbles wants to know more about that. He climbs up the trunk. When he gets close to the hole, he carefully peeks inside.

He can't believe his eyes. The hole is filled with honey! Lovely, sweet, tasty honey.

'That's what the bee had between its feet. It was a piece of pollen that the bees use to make honey,' thinks Nibbles hungrily.

Clever little animals, those bees.

Honey Bees

It's a sunny summer day. Nibbles is lying on the grass, resting with his eyes shut.

Suddenly, he hears a zooming sound. He opens one eye. A fat honey bee is hovering over his leg. Nibbles watches as the bee goes to a big flower.

June

The Golden Treasure

4 JUNE

Nibbles has told Flopsy about a golden treasure. He is the only one who knows about it. If Flopsy likes, Nibbles will do his best to show her the treasure. On a piece of paper he has drawn a tree. They have to find that tree.

After a while they come to the big tree. Nibbles points to a hole in the trunk.

'There in that hole. That is where the treasure is,' he says.

'It is pretty high,' sighs Flopsy.

'Yes, but if you are careful, it's fine. And it is really worth the trouble.'

Flopsy agrees. Nibbles climbs up first and Flopsy follows. It's not easy.

Finally they get to the hole.

They sit on a branch close to the hole. Nibbles pulls a spoon out of his jacket pocket.

'What do you need that for?' asks Flopsy.

Carefully Nibbles sticks the spoon into the hole. When he pulls it out, it is filled with sticky, golden honey.

'This is my treasure,' says Nibbles proudly. He gives the spoon to Flopsy and she pops it in her mouth.

'Delicious!' she cries. 'This is the best treasure in the whole wide world.'

'I think so too,' laughs Nibbles. And then it is his turn to taste the wonderful treasure the bees have made.

The Flag

5 JUNE

Tomorrow is a holiday. In each house along the path through the forest, everybody is busy with preparations for the day.

Including Mister Owl. Since he is the mayor, he has written a speech. He is practising it for the first time.

'Dear fellow residents of our lovely village,' he begins seriously from behind his desk. 'It was exactly…'

Mister Owl needs to peek at his speech. 'It was exactly one hundred years ago today that the first resident of our village came to live here. Therefore…' He has to peek again.

'Therefore today is a holiday!'

'That's long enough,' thinks Mister Owl. 'Any longer and I won't be able to remember it at all.'

Mister Owl has just one more thing to do. He has to lay out the village's flag so that early tomorrow morning he can hang it from the flagpole in front of his house.

He goes to a big chest and opens a drawer. The flag lies there. It has a big tree in the centre. But what is that? There is a big hole in the flag, exactly in the middle of the tree. A moth has certainly been busy!

Now Mister Owl has a problem. He can't hang the flag up looking like this. What will the villagers say?

Tomorrow morning he will go and see Mister Tie, the tailor. Mister Tie will know what to do.

Mister Tie Saves the Day

Early in the morning Mister Owl hurries to Mister Tie's house. He knocks loudly on the door.

A moment later Mister Tie opens it.

'My goodness, Mister Owl. What are you doing here so early?' asks Mister Tie, who looks like he has come straight out of bed.

'Mister Tie, you have to help me,' whispers Mister Owl.

'What can I do for you?' asks Mister Tie worriedly.

Mister Owl shows the flag to Mister Tie then.

'It's our holiday today and I must hang our flag outside my house. But when I got it out yesterday, I found this hole.'

Mister Owl gives Mister Tie time to look at the hole carefully. He holds his breath and wonders what the news will be.

'Can you please fix it for me?'

Mister Tie shakes his head. 'It looks like a whole moth family had a picnic there,' he laughs. 'Sure, I can fix it. No problem.'

Mister Tie disappears into his workshop. He cuts and stitches many tiny pieces of cloth, whistling as he works. Soon the flag is as good as new.

Mister Owl thanks Mister Tie warmly and hurries home.

A few hours later, in their finest clothes, the villagers listen to Mister Owl's speech. Then he raises the village's flag. It looks wonderful. Thanks to Mister Tie's work!

June

The Trophy

It's morning. Blinders wakes up and wipes the sleep from his eyes. His hand automatically grabs for his glasses and sets them on his nose. Blinders opens his eyes and stares directly into the eyes of a lovely toy tiger, who looks back at him happily. It scares him for a second but then he's fine. The tiger is his trophy.

In the village holiday yesterday there was a ball toss stand. Blinders had a lot of fun there.

First it was Nibbles' turn. He picked up a ball and threw it hard. The three bottles still stood up.

'I can do better than that,' cried Hopper. And after Hopper's throw, only two bottles were standing.

'My turn!' called Flopsy eagerly. She took a ball and threw it. What a pity – the two bottles stayed stubbornly standing up.

'Your turn, Blinders,' says Nibbles.

'Be sure your glasses are on straight,' urged Flopsy.

'That won't help. He'll still see the bottles standing up,' teased Hopper.

Hesitantly, Blinders picked up a ball. Through his thick glasses, he peered at the bottles. His fingers tightened on the ball. Then he threw it as hard as he could in the direction of the bottles.

Both bottles fell down. It was very quiet.

No bottles left standing!

'I won!' cried Blinders. The lady who ran the stand gave him his lovely tiger.

Blinders felt like the village hero all evening.

Hopper's Big Secret

Beside the Friendship Tree stands a big, tall tent. Hopper has set it up there. He has hung a sign on it that says, 'Do Not Enter. Big Secret.'

Nobody knows what Hopper means by this. All day long the villagers talk and wonder about it. Nibbles, Flopsy and Blinders are sooo curious!

The tent flap opens and Hopper comes out.

'Hopper,' asks Flopsy, 'just what are you up to?'

'I am not ready yet. You have to wait until tomorrow morning,' says Hopper in an official sort of voice. 'Then I will reveal my secret.'

'Not until tomorrow? Can't you give give us a hint now?'

'Not until tomorrow,' repeats Hopper seriously.

Flopsy isn't so easily stopped.

'I know what you're up to,' she announces. 'It's a tree house.'

Hopper doesn't say anything.

'See? It is a tree house.'

Hopper shakes his head angrily.

'Yes it is!' crows Flopsy. 'It's a treehouse!'

110

'No it's not,' Hopper answers back, still angry. 'It is NOT a treehouse. It's a rocket!'

Oooh, Hopper has let his secret out by mistake. He glares at Flopsy. Then he runs into his tent. Flopsy, Nibbles and Blinders roll around on the ground, laughing and laughing.

Poor Hopper. It's hard to keep a secret from a stubborn friend like Flopsy.

The Green Tin

This morning Nibbles, Flopsy and Blinders run to the Friendship Tree. When they arrive, they see Hopper standing beside his home-made rocket. It looks more like a tin of orange juice with wings than a real rocket. But

Hopper is so proud of it that the three friends swallow their smiles.

'This is the *Green Tin*,' says Hopper proudly. 'What do you think of her?'

'Uh… cool!' says Nibbles after a second. 'How does it work?'

'Inside there are some pedals. When you pedal really fast, the rocket takes off and flies into space. Neat, huh?'

'That is how you are going to fly into space?' asks Flopsy surprised. 'Can we go with you?'

'Sorry,' says Hopper, 'there's only room for one. But when I land on a planet, I will pick up a rock to bring home for you.'

'That would be nice,' says Blinders doubtfully. 'Are you really sure that your rocket can fly?'

'Of course,' answers Hopper confidently. 'When I pedal, a propeller starts to spin. When it spins, the rocket takes off. All I have to do is keep pedalling until I get into space.'

'What if you get tired?' asks Flopsy.

'I have been practising and training all week. I think I could pedal in my sleep now.'

'When are you going to launch into space?' Nibbles asks.

'Tomorrow night. First, I need to get supplies. Do you want to come with me?'

'Sure!' cry the three friends. They want to help their brave explorer, Hopper. Hopefully his adventure will go well.

The Space Traveller

Hopper has stuffed his home-made rocket with biscuits and sweets. He needs to eat a lot to fly in space.

Tonight the friends come to see him take off. Hopper gets in, closes the door and sits on a sort of bicycle. He can watch the stars through a little window above his head.

'Let's go!' calls Hopper. He pedals as fast as he can. 'Outer space, here I come!'

After a while, Hopper wonders if he has arrived there yet. To see out of his window, he has to get off his bicycle. But he can't stop pedalling. If he does, the rocket will stop moving.

So Hopper keeps on pedalling. For hours. His legs are getting tired.

His eyes are beginning to close too.

'Keep on pedalling,' he urges himself.

'Keep pedalling, keep pedalling, keep…'

And Hopper falls asleep, exhausted, on his bicycle. The pedals stop. Hopper hangs over his bike snoring.

Filodophia

When Hopper wakes up, he opens the door of his rocket. He sticks his head out.

'I have landed on a planet!' he thinks excitedly.

Suddenly he sees three little creatures coming toward him. They are all covered in shiny silver foil.

'Space traveller, welcome to Filodofia,' says one of them.

'Space traveller, do you have any presents with you?' asks another.

'Presents? Of course!' replies Hopper pleased.

He grabs the biggest bag of sweets and throws it to the creatures. The creatures catch the bag and run away laughing.

'Hey, wait!' cries Hopper. He jumps out of his rocket and chases after them.

He can hear them laughing. Wait! It's Nibbles, Flopsy and Blinders, dressed up like space explorers.

'So you mean I am not in outer space?' asks Hopper sadly.

'You never left the ground, Hopper. When we came to see you this morning, you were sound asleep on your bike. So we dressed up to make you think you had landed on another planet.'

'Oh, bother,' sighs Hopper. 'I pedalled all night long for nothing.'

June

Shopping

Nibbles goes to the shop of Miss Squirrel with his mother.

'She is having a sale,' says Mummy.

'What is that?' Nibbles wants to know.

'Miss Squirrel is selling her things at a lower price. That way she can get the older things out of her shop and make room for new things.'

'Does Miss Squirrel do that a lot?'

'One or two times each year.'

'Is it fun?'

'You'll soon see,' says Mummy, opening the shop door. There are lots of customers shopping and it's very crowded. Nibbles doesn't like it.

'Hey,' Mummy says suddenly. 'Try this on.'

She pulls a t-shirt over Nibbles' head. Nibbles sticks his arms into the sleeves and pulls the shirt down. There is a picture of a big piece of cheese on the front. Nibbles thinks that is cool.

'Could I have this, Mummy?' he asks excitedly.

'Why not?' answers Mummy. 'It's on sale for half the normal price.'

They go to the queue of people waiting to pay for things. Miss Squirrel is really busy reading the prices and counting up what the shoppers must pay her. Finally it's their turn. Mummy pays for the t-shirt.

When they are standing outside a little later, Nibbles is really happy. First, because he is out of that crowded store and second because he has a cool new t-shirt. Mummy is happy too, because she saved so much money.

Play Dough

Nibbles passes by the house of Miss Hedgehog. Through the window he spots her inside making dough.

'She is going to make some kind of delicious cake,' thinks Nibbles hungrily. 'I think I will pay her a visit.'

Nibbles rings the door bell.

'Hello, Miss Hedgehog.'

'Hello Nibbles! Please come in.'

He follows Miss Hedgehog to the kitchen. There

is a big bowl with dough in it sitting on the table. When Miss Hedgehog isn't looking, Nibbles pinches a bit of the dough and pops it in his mouth.

'Bah!' he cries. 'This is too salty!'

Miss Hedgehog starts to laugh. 'Silly Nibbles, this isn't dough you eat. I thought you knew. I wondered why you stopped by.'

'It tastes awful,' says Nibbles with a sour look.

'That's because it's not meant to be eaten. It's play dough. You make it with flour and salt, and it is meant to get hard when it dries. I'm going to make a statue with it.'

Nibbles doesn't understand. So Miss Hedgehog lets him watch.

She takes a handful of dough and makes a little doll out of it. Then she bakes it until it is hard. Later she will paint it. Then it's done!

'So what do you think?' asks Miss Hedgehog.

'Nice, but…' answers Nibbles.

'Nice but what?' asks Miss Hedgehog.

'… but it would be nicer if I could eat it up!'

The Bat

It is pitch dark in Nibbles' bedroom. But Nibbles is up to something. He is hanging over the foot of his bed. His legs are on the bed but his head is over the side, almost on the floor. He is a bat today.

Bats sleep upside down in the dark.

Nibbles peers in the darkness. He can't even see his hand in front of his face.

Bats hunt for flying bugs in the dark without bumping into anything. They can do that because they send out high sounds. When the sounds bounce off a wall or tree, bats know where those things are and they fly around them.

Bat Nibbles is going hunting. He stands up and flaps his arms like wings. He makes high peeping sounds and moves around his bedroom without bumping into anything.

In his imagination, Nibbles sees a delicious snack flying by. Suddenly, he is a hungry bat. He runs through the room with his mouth wide open.

Then, there's a loud noise. This hungry bat has smacked into the toy chest. My, that really hurts! With one hand Nibbles rubs his knee and with the other he feels for the light switch.

When the light comes on, Nibbles sighs in relief. Being a bat is much harder than he thought.

The Thief-Catcher

Mister Sack, the postman, is delivering a big package to the police station in the village. It is really heavy. In big letters, you can see 'Sam Stork.'

'That's my automatic thief-catcher,' says Sam.

'How do you know that?' asks Mister Sack.

'I am a police officer, right? I know everything,' says Sam.

'Fine, then. See you later,' says Mister Sack and leaves.

Curious, Sam opens the package. There is a big machine in it. Sam pulls it out of the box. There's also a little book that tells how the machine works.

Sam puts the book aside.

'I am a police officer. I can figure out how this works. I don't need that book,' says Sam to himself.

On top of the machine there are two buttons, one red and one yellow. Which button should Sam push?

He tries the yellow button. He has barely pushed it when the machine springs open and a huge net shoots out. The net falls over Sam. He's been caught! With the tip of one wing he pushes on the red button. He hopes that it will take the net away. Instead, a loud alarm begins to sound.

'Thief! Call the police!' says a voice from the machine.

Oh bother! Everything's going wrong. Maybe Sam should read the instruction book first, next time?

The Escapee

Mister Sack, the postman, is making his deliveries when he sees somebody walk by. It's a weasel. He looks very tired. Since he is carrying two big suitcases, that makes sense.

'My goodness, you look exhausted,' says Mister Sack.

The weasel sets the suitcases down with a sigh. He takes a handkerchief out of his pocket and mops the sweat from his forehead.

'If you only knew,' he wheezes.

Mister Sack blinks in surprise.

'I used to have a nice office here, some time ago. Life went well. But then one day some people came to our woods. They had giant machines with them. They used them to cut down trees and dig deep holes in the ground. I barely had time to escape.

My nice office was flattened to the ground. I have nothing left except what I have in these two suitcases.'

'That's terrible!' cries Mister Sack. 'What are you going to do?'

'I am looking for a safe place to build a new office.'

'I think I know a good place for you. You are welcome to live in our village. I am Mister Sack, the postman.

'I am Walter Weasel. Do you really think I can fit in well in your village?

'I'm sure you can. When we can help someone, we love to do so.'

Walter heaves a big sigh of relief. Things are going to get better now.

The Village Courier

Yesterday Walter Weasel moved into the village. Mister Sack, Mister Tie, Bert Beaver and several others from the village helped him build a house. It is a special kind of house. On one side there is space to live, and on the other is an office. On that side Walter has hung up a big sign.

The Village Courier is written on it in nice, colourful letters.

'What is that? What kind of animal is a Village Courier?' Mister Sack wants to know.

'Haven't I told you? Look, I am a reporter. If anything happens in the village, then I write a little article about it. When I have some articles, then I put them all together in a newspaper: *The Village Courier.*'

'No kidding,' cries Mister Sack. 'You mean we have our own newspaper now? That's great.'

Bert Beaver, Mister Tie and the others think that it's a fine idea too. They nod happily.

'There's still a lot of work to do. I have to set up my office and buy a printing press.'

'We will help you get set up!' says Bert Beaver, excitedly. 'Then we will have our newspaper to read even faster.'

Everybody laughs. Then they go back to work, because they can't wait to see the first copy of *The Village Courier.*

say and then print it in the newspaper.'

'You work for a newspaper that doesn't exist?'

'The first edition hasn't come out yet, that's true. But if you can help me with this interview, then you will see a story about yourself tomorrow when the first edition comes out.'

'OK, that sounds good,' says Mister Owl.

Walter asks Mister Owl some questions and makes some notes. Then he takes a picture of him.

'So,' sighs Walter, when Mister Owl goes further up the path, 'there's my first interview. I hope the next ones go faster...'

The First Edition

This morning Walter puts a rack in front of his office.

Newspapers fill the rack. On the first page there is a picture of Mister Owl.

Now Walter starts calling out loudly, 'Read *The Village Courier!* Read *The Village Courier!* The first edition of *The Village Courier* is on sale now! Read the interview with Mister Owl!'

Suddenly several curious villagers come to see what's going on. They pay Walter and he gives them each a newspaper. The newspapers are almost all gone.

Then Mister Owl comes to have a look. When he sees his photo on the first page, he is really pleased.

'Mister Mayor,' says Walter proudly, 'I have a free

Interview with an Owl

It's morning. Walter Weasel is up early. He has packed a pencil, a notebook and a camera into his bag and is walking along the path. He sees Mister Owl walking nearby.

'Mister Mayor, may I interview you?'

'Inter-what? What do you mean?' asks Mister Owl puzzled.

'It's very simple. I ask you a couple of questions and you answer them. That's an interview.'

'Like a quiz?'

'Oh, no,' says Walter, 'it's easier than that. I can ask you about your work as the mayor of this village and you can tell me about it. I will write what you copy of *The Village Courier* for you as a thank-you for your interview.'

'That's very kind,' replies Mister Owl. 'I think I'll go right home to read your fine newspaper now.'

'Please do, Mister Owl,' smiles Walter Weasel. 'Tomorrow there will be a new edition to read.'

'Will you come and interview me again?' asks Mister Owl.

'No, not just now. Tomorrow I will write about other things.'

'That's too bad,' sighs Mister Owl. 'But in any case, thanks and see you soon.'

'Enjoy reading *The Village Courier*, Mister Owl.'

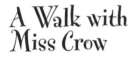

A Walk with Miss Crow

It's gorgeous weather. Flopsy invites Nibbles, Hopper and Blinders to visit Miss Crow with her.

'My, it's lovely outside,' sighs Miss Crow, smiling at the friends as they arrive at her house.

'It's so nice of you to come to visit me.'

'Won't you come out for a walk?' Flopsy asks.

'I would like to come outside, but my old wings don't hold me up any more.'

'I can fix that,' says Nibbles, and he runs home. He comes back with his cart. They make it comfortable and cosy with cushions and blankets. Hopper even puts a parasol on it.

'So,' says Nibbles, 'now you can come out for a walk and enjoy the fine weather with us.' They help Miss Crow get into the cart. Miss Crow thinks this is wonderful. They bring her to the bridge over the brook and set the cart in the shadow of a tree.

'Isn't it lovely here,' she sighs. 'I used to come here often with my grandmother.'

'Really?' asks Blinders.

'Yes, and we sat under this tree, looking at the water.'

'Just like we are now?'

'Yes. Do you know what my grandmother always brought along?' Miss Crow takes a small box out of her handbag.

'Honey biscuits!' she laughs. 'I brought enough for everyone.'

That's Miss Crow. She always knows how to make everybody happy.

119

June

What's Mister Mouse Making?

Mister Mouse has dragged a few boards into the garden. Nibbles and Misty have come for a look.

'Daddy,' asks Misty, 'what are you making?'

'I am not telling,' smiles Mister Mouse. 'You will have to wait and see.'

Daddy takes a spade and digs two holes.

Then he binds two boards together at one end. He sticks the other ends of the boards into the two holes. It begins to look a little like a tent.

Then he takes the other two boards and does the same thing with them, a little further away. It looks even more like a tent. But Nibbles and Misty have no idea what he's doing.

Now Daddy takes the last board and puts it across the two other sets of boards. He nails everything together. Then with his drill he makes four holes in the top board and puts in four strong hooks.

He ties heavy ropes to the hooks. He goes to his workshop and brings back two smaller boards, and attaches them to the ropes. The boards hang from the ropes now.

'I know what it is!' cries Misty excitedly. 'It's a swing!'

Daddy laughs. 'So you guessed it!' he says while he hangs the second swing up. 'One for each of you. Give them a try.'

Misty and Nibbles give Daddy big hugs and kisses. Are they ever happy with their swings!

Swinging

Misty and Nibbles are having so much fun! Daddy made swings for them in their garden.

Nibbles swings as high as he can.

'What's wrong, Misty? Don't you want to swing?'

'I can't,' she answers sadly.

'Do you want me to teach you? It's easy.'

Misty nods.

Nibbles jumps off his swing to stand behind Misty's.

'Hold tight to the two ropes with your hands. Then pull on the ropes and swing your legs forward.'

Misty does that. The swing moves a little. But when Nibbles gives her a push, she really starts to swing.

'Now just follow the swing's rhythm. When you go forward, swing your legs out. When you go backward, swing your legs back.'

Misty finds it a little hard, but it's working better and better.

Nibbles gives Misty a push from time to time. She swings higher and higher. She swings her legs like Nibbles taught her to do.

After a while Nibbles comes around to watch her.

'Do you like it?' he asks.

'Hey, don't stop!' begs Misty. 'You need to push me.'

'No I don't any more. You know how to swing yourself!'

Misty can't believe her ears. But even though Nibbles stops pushing, she can swing and swing. Is she ever proud of herself!

Nibbles has taught her well.

The Weather Report

The sun shines from a blue sky. There isn't a cloud to be seen.

Mister Mouse sits outside on a bench in the shade and reads *The Village Courier*.

Nibbles comes to sit beside him.

'What is in the paper, Daddy?' he asks.

'All sorts of news from our village, and a weather report.'

'What does the weather report say?'

'That tomorrow it will be sunny, and it will stay that way for a few days.'

Nibbles loves that. He wants to know more about the weather.

'It will be a little warmer tomorrow. You can wear your shorts, because long trousers will be too hot.'

'What about the day after tomorrow?'

Daddy reads further.

'Still sunny, and even warmer.'

'Warmer? How warm?'

'Swimming suit weather, and for another day after that too.'

'How do they know all that?' asks Nibbles.

'The weatherman uses special machines to track the clouds. If we don't have lots of clouds above us, that means we have nice weather coming. But if you see a thick pile of clouds and then some wind comes...'

'Then it's going to rain,' says Nibbles quickly.

'Right!' laughs Daddy.

Suddenly Nibbles jumps up.

'Where are you going?' asks Daddy.

'You said that I can wear my swimming trunks soon, right? I'm going to go find them so I will be ready when the warmer weather comes.'

Berry Juice

Mister Sack, the postman, is having trouble with his heavy bag today. Sweat stands out on his forehead.

'My goodness, it's warm,' he sighs.

What's that he sees over there?

In front of Nibbles' house there is a little stand. A sign in front of it says *Berry Juice*.

'Hello, Mister Sack,' say Nibbles and Misty welcoming him. 'Would you like a glass of berry juice? We made it ourselves.'

'Oh, yes,' says Mister Sack happily. 'With this warm weather that would be great.'

Misty gets a glass. Nibbles picks up a big jug, which makes nice sounds as the ice cubes inside

bump around. He fills the glass.

'Here you are,' he says politely. 'That's one coin.'

Mister Sack reaches into his pocket and finds a shiny coin, which he gives to them. 'Here you are.'

He takes a big sip of the berry juice. He sighs loudly. The cold juice cools him off and gives him a nice feeling.

'Great,' he says, smacking his lips. 'That was the best glass of berry juice I have ever had. I'd like another.'

Nibbles pours another glass full for him and Mister Sack pays another coin.

'No thanks,' smiles Nibbles. 'Our good customers get a second glass for free.'

'That's really nice of you,' smiles Mister Sack. 'I'd better get back to work. See you soon! 'Thanks.'

'You're welcome. See you soon, Mister Sack.'

The Ice Lolly Stand

Yesterday, Nibbles and Misty sold berry juice at their stand. They sold so much that their money bag is full.

Since it's still hot today, they have decided to sell something cold again. Nibbles found a whole box of ice lollies in the kitchen. They will sell these today. They set the box in their stand and wait for their first customer.

There is nobody in sight.

'Maybe we need to make some adverts?' wonders Misty.

Nibbles thinks that's a good idea.

'Ice-cold lollies for sale!' yells Nibbles into the empty street.

Here comes someone. It is Mister Owl. He wants an ice lolly.

Misty opens the box. But what's happened? All the ice lollies have melted. They should have put it into a cooler.

'I think you two have a problem,' smiles Mister Owl, when he sees the dripping mess.

The youngsters feel bad. Their dream is smashed.

Mister Owl wants to cheer them up. He takes them to Miss Squirrel's shop and buys three ice lollies. One for him and one for each of them. Frozen ones, this time.

The Good Gardener

Bert Beaver shakes his head. Recently he replanted a whole new forest. He had cut down a lot of trees to build a dam. Because he had seen how awful the bare space looked, he decided to plant new trees. So he planted more than two hundred little trees and has been taking good care of them since then.

Due to the warm weather over the last few days the little trees are really drooping. Bert gets busy. He runs to his garden, grabs his watering can, then runs to the river, fills the can up and waters the little trees. Then he runs back to the river to get more water.

Bert runs back and forth, back and forth, between the trees and the river. After a while all of the little trees have been watered.

Bert flops down on the ground. He's wet with sweat. That was a lot of work!

After his rest, Bert heads back to the river. He leaves his watering can on the edge and dives into the water.

'Oh, this is nice,' he sighs, closing his eyes and letting the water wash over him.

Rest well, Bert. The little trees are lucky to have you caring for them. Someday they will make a whole new forest.

June

The Fishing Frog

Nibbles, Flopsy and Blinders are visiting Hopper. As they come to the brook, they see him sitting on the bank with a fishing pole.

'Did you know Hopper likes to fish?' Nibbles asks the others.

'No, I never knew that,' answers Blinders. 'Has he caught anything?'

'Let's look.'

'Hello! It's warm today, isn't it?' smiles Hopper.

'Shhh,' hushes Nibbles, 'we don't want to scare the fish.'

'No problem,' says Hopper. 'I think I just had a bite.'

'Oh really? That's exciting!' the friends say. They watch as Hopper slowly pulls his line in.

But there is no fish on it.

Instead, there are four dripping bottles of berry juice hanging from his line.

'In the water it's nice and cool,' smiles Hopper, 'so I thought I'd cool the juice off. Would you like a bottle?'

Hopper is such a funny fellow. And often, he has such good ideas.

A Big Problem

Mister Owl has gone to his cellar to get some cool berry juice. Suddenly a wind blows through the house. The cellar door slams shut with a bang. Mister Owl tries to open the door but it won't budge. The door is stuck.

'There has to be a way out,' he says. 'How can I escape?'

He looks at the cellar window and gets an idea. He can climb out through it. Simple, huh?

Mister Owl opens the cellar window. He scrambles to get out through it. But what happens? Just as he wiggles his big tummy through, he gets stuck. He can't go in or out. He has a big problem.

Mister Owl starts calling for help.

Luckily some friendly villagers hear him and

come to help.

They pull him as hard as they can. It doesn't work, even though they do their best.

With a lot of pushing and pulling, they open the cellar door. Now they can see Mister Owl's bottom. After a lot of pulling, they get Mister Owl free.

He really needs to do something about that tummy of his.

Thunder and Lightning

Today the newspaper says that the heat wave is ending in the next few days. A big storm is coming.

When Nibbles looks outside, he sees dark clouds coming toward him. Oh no, his toys are all over the garden. They are going to get wet.

Nibbles runs outside. He gathers up his toys as fast as he can. In the distance he hears a roll of thunder. He is so scared that he drops everything. Now he has to start again. He gathers up his toys and runs inside.

He quickly runs out again. Zip! Was that a flash of lightning? Nibbles gathers up a second load of toys. Just one more load and his toys will all be inside, safe and dry. Here and there, drops of rain are starting to fall.

With his short legs, Nibbles runs inside with

his final load of toys. Just in time. The storm bursts out in full force.

'Ha-ha,' sighs Nibbles, 'to beat me, you're going to have to creep up on me a bit faster, Mister Weather.'

Hopscotch

After the storm yesterday there are puddles all over the street.

Flopsy and Nibbles are playing a special kind of hopscotch. Flopsy explains it.

'First you run, then you hop on one foot. Then you take another step with your other leg and you jump forward as far as you can.'

Flopsy draws a line on the ground.

'You can run up to here. Then you have to do the jumps. Whoever gets furthest wins.'

Nibbles goes first. He jumps pretty far.

Now here comes Flopsy. She lays her ears flat and starts her run. Then she starts her jumps. She makes a giant leap through the air. She jumps so far that she lands in a big puddle.

'Yikes!' she yells, 'I'm soaked!'

She springs out of the puddle dripping water. She is soaked, but she won!

July

The Advert

Miss Hedgehog walks into Walter Weasel's office one day.

'Good morning, Miss Hedgehog,' says Walter politely.

'Good morning. I would like to know if you can help me.'

'Of course,' says Walter. 'What can I do for you?'

'I would like to place an advert in *The Village Courier*,' says Miss Hedgehog.

'I'd be happy to help you with that. What would you like to say in your advert?'

'Well you see, I'd like to organise a play here in the village. I've written over half of it already myself. I'd like to ask Bert Beaver and Mister Mouse if they will help build the scenery. But at the moment I don't have any actors. So I thought maybe an advert would let people know about the play and they could act in it.'

'A play? How great! How many actors do you need?'

'Just five.'

'That's easy to arrange. I will put your advert into tomorrow's paper.'

Miss Hedgehog goes home satisfied with the plan. She's curious if anyone will read the ad and ask her about acting in the play. But she'll have to sleep one night before she knows.

Actors

Mister Sack, the postman, flops down on the sofa. He picks up a copy of *The Village Courier* and opens it up. First he reads the news. Then he spots Miss Hedgehog's advert.

'Miss Hedgehog is looking for actors for a play,' it says at the top of the page. 'Are you interested in acting in it? If so, please contact Miss Hedgehog.'

A play? Maybe Flopsy would like to act in it.

'Flopsy?' he calls. 'Could you come here?'

Mister Sack explains to Flopsy what the advert says, and tells her that if she wants to ask Miss Hedgehog about it, maybe she can act in the play.

Flopsy doesn't hesitate for a second. She runs out of the house, straight over to Miss Hedgehog's. When she arrives, it looks like half the village is standing outside the house.

'Are you also here about the play?' someone asks her. 'You'll have to queue up.'

'Goodness!' laughs Flopsy, 'if this play isn't a big success, I will be really surprised!'

The Audition

Flopsy stands among the villagers who have come to see about acting in Miss Hedgehog's play. They are waiting to do an audition.

'So,' says Miss Hedgehog when it's Flopsy's turn. 'What would you like to do in the play, Flopsy?'

'I want to act.'

'That might work. I need a princess for the play.'

'I could be a good princess,' says Flopsy excitedly. 'Could I show you?'

'Sure,' says Miss Hedgehog. 'That's what we call an audition. Go ahead, show me now.'

Flopsy walks around with tiny, graceful steps. Then she folds her hands together and says, 'Is that my charming prince that I see? Kiss me, my darling prince.' She closes her eyes and sticks out her lips.

'Kissing is icky,' says someone.

'Nibbles,' says Miss Hedgehog, 'where did you come from?'

'I came in the back door,' he laughs. 'I just wanted to see what was making the whole village go crazy.'

'We are in the middle of an audition. I am looking for actors for my play. Would you like to be in it? I need a prince.'

Nibbles doesn't know what to say. Then he sees the grin on Flopsy's face. 'Please do it,' she says.

'OK,' says Nibbles. 'I'll join the play. On one condition.'

'And that is?" asks Miss Hedgehog.

'That I don't have to do any kissing.'

'We'll see about that,' laughs Miss Hedgehog. 'Welcome to the acting club, Nibbles.'

The Prince

"How annoying,' grumbles Nibbles.

'That could be,' answers Mummy, 'but if you are going to play the prince in Miss Hedgehog's play, you need to learn your lines by heart.'

Nibbles crosses his arms and looks angry.

'Now, now, Nibbles,' soothes Mummy. 'Try it once more. It's not that long.'

'But what I have to say is boring,' says Nibbles.

'Wait,' says Mummy, 'maybe I have a solution for you.' She takes out an old sheet and a hat. She puts the hat on Nibble's head and wraps the sheet around his neck like a cape. Then she gets a wooden spoon from the kitchen and hands it to him.

'Now you look more like a prince. Shall we start again from the beginning?'

With his costume on, Nibbles feels different. It feels real now.

Nibbles goes out of the room and a second later comes storming in.

'Aha, you nasty dragon!' he yells loudly. 'Give me back the princess, or I'll cut you to pieces!'

Nibbles waves his wooden spoon around like a sword and starts to hack at the dragon. He gets so wild that Mummy tells him he has to calm down.

But he does know his lines by heart now, that's sure.

The Set-Builders

It's almost bedtime. The doorbell sounds.

'Hello, Bert,' Mister Mouse says to Bert Beaver. 'Let's get to work.' Together they leave the house.

'Why is Bert coming over so often? He has been here every night this week,' asks Misty.

'They are building the scenery for Miss Hedgehog's play. That's a whole lot of work,' says Mummy.

'What's scenery?' asks Misty.

'Scenery is the background that the actors act in during a play. Sometimes we call that scenery a set,' explains Mummy.

'Could we look at it?' asks Nibbles.

'Sure,' says Mummy.

She leads the two youngsters to the workshop.

When they get closer, they hear a lot of pounding and sawing. Mummy opens the door for them.

The youngsters go inside cautiously. It looks fantastic! They see a huge palace.

'Look, there's a treasure chest!' cries Nibbles.

'And there's a throne!' says Misty pointing.

It looks like a fairy tale. Everything is beautiful.

Daddy and Bert have noticed their visitors. They wave and blow kisses, and so do Nibbles and Flopsy.

'Come now, we should let them get back to work,' says Mummy.

The two youngsters are in bed in minutes. Just before the lights go off, Misty asks, 'When is the play, Mummy?'

'Just four nights of pleasant sleep away,' says Mummy. 'Because it's bedtime now. Sleep well, my darlings.'

'Sleep well too, Mummy.'

Posters

Mister Sack, the postman, has set out with Walter Weasel to hang up posters for Miss Hedgehog's play.
They stop by a big board and stick up a poster. Suddenly they hear a voice behind them.
'And what exactly do you gentlemen think you are doing?'
It's Sam Stork, the village's police officer.
'We are hanging up posters.'
'Do you think I didn't know that? I'm a police officer and I know everything. Why are you hanging these posters right here?'
'Because this is a poster board. It's for posters. Didn't you know that?'
'Uh, yes, of course,' Sam says, nodding his head. 'I'm a police officer, you know? I know everything. But what are these posters about?'
'They are about a play that Miss Hedgehog is putting on,' says Walter.
'Aha. A play by Miss Hedgehog, you say? Why does it say Dragon Slayer?'
'That's the name of the play. Are you going to come? The whole village will be there.'
'Is it a scary play?' asks Sam.
'No, it's for everybody, old and young,' explains Mister Sack.
'I don't know. It sounds scary,' worries Sam.
'Absolutely not,' Mister Sack reassures him.

'You're sure?'
'I'm sure,' promises Walter Weasel.
'OK then,' says Sam firmly. 'If you are sure.'
'Good to know you'll be there, sir.'
'Take care, gentlemen,' says Sam, back on patrol.

Mister Tie's Suit

Nibbles and Flopsy are on their way to Mister Tie, the tailor. They have to see him, because he is making the costumes for the actors in Miss Hedgehog's play.
First it's Nibbles' turn. Mister Tie has laid out a fancy costume for him. He looks amazed. There is even a sword. Nibbles is thrilled.

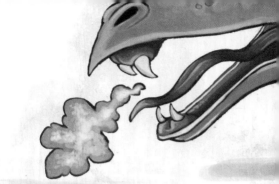

Mister Tie checks to make sure the costume fits well.

'Perfect,' he says. 'Next, please?'

Flopsy is super-curious to see her outfit. Mister Tie takes a pink gown that is covered with glitter out of the wardrobe. Flopsy can't believe her eyes as Mister Tie holds the gown out.

'It's lovely,' she breathes.

'Try it on. I think it should fit fine.'

You don't need to ask Flopsy twice. A moment later she is twirling around in her dress. A beautiful cape goes with it.

Flopsy and Nibbles are so happy with their costumes! Mister Tie is a super tailor.

They look at each other in disappointment as Mister Tie puts the costumes away.

'You still have two nights to sleep before the play. Then you can put the costumes on again. You'll have your make-up on then too. You will look like real stars.'

Nibbles and Flopsy can't believe it. It's all so exciting!

The Final Rehearsal

8 JULY

Today is the final rehearsal before the play opens tomorrow.

All the actors seem a little nervous. Tomorrow they have to perform in front of all the villagers.

'We'll go through the play one last time,' says Miss Hedgehog. 'Is everyone in place? Let's go.'

Slowly the curtain rises.

Mister Owl plays the role of the old king. He sits on a throne. He is very serious.

'Ahhh,' he sighs, 'where has my poor daughter gone? I can't find her anywhere.'

Behind the curtains Nibbles is watching carefully. Will he be able to remember his lines? Will everything go well?

'Is there anyone in my kingdom who can help me find my darling daughter?' asks Mister Owl.

Nibbles takes a deep breath and then steps on the stage.

'I can, sir. I'm Prince Dragon Slayer. By my sword I swear that I will find your daughter.'

Nibbles knows his lines by heart now. He's no longer Nibbles, but instead, the courageous dragon slayer.

When he finishes, a couple of actors come up to him and say, 'Good job! You were great!'

Nibbles feels super. It was hard to learn his lines, but now he's glad that he did.

Well done, Nibbles.

July

The Show

9 JULY

Today the play opens. The whole village has gathered on the village square. After everyone has found a place, the lights go out and the curtain opens.

The scenery and costumes are wonderful. Nibbles steals the show in his role of Prince Dragon Slayer. He has to search for the missing princess.

Flopsy plays the princess. She has been captured by a dragon. Not a real one, of course, but a dragon made from cardboard.

'Help!' cries Flopsy from her prison.

'Go away, you ugly dragon,' cries Nibbles.

Grrr, growls the dragon. Smoke comes out of his mouth from between his sharp teeth.

Nibbles takes out his sword. 'OK,' he says bravely, 'you will feel the point of my sword.'

Nibbles starts to hack at the dragon as it claws and roars. The audience holds its breath. What an exciting fight!

Then Nibbles hits the dragon hard on its snout with his sword. Oh no! The sword breaks in two! Nibbles stands there with just the handle in his hand. That wasn't supposed to happen.

Luckily Mister Tie provided for that. He stands behind the curtain, ready to help. Fast as lightening, he picks up a new sword and throws it to Nibbles. Nibbles catches it and gives the dragon another blow on his snout. Groaning and moaning, the dragon falls to the floor. That was really exciting. For the audience as well as the actors.

The Newspaper

10 JULY

'Nibbles, could you run over to Walter Weasel's shop to buy me a copy of *The Village Courier*?' asks Nibbles' father.

Nibbles sighs. He really doesn't want to.

'Come on, Nibbles,' presses Daddy. 'If you are quick, you can be back in five minutes.'

'But Daddy, can't someone else do it? I don't feel like it.'

'Don't complain, Nibbles. Just go, please. It's worth doing.'

Sighing, Nibbles gets up and goes outside.

'Why do I have to do all the bad jobs?' he grumbles to himself as he walks down the path. He kicks a small stone as he goes.

A little later, Nibbles wanders into the newspaper office and finds Walter Weasel there. He picks up a copy of the paper and puts a coin on the desk.

Then he looks at the paper. What in the world? A huge photo of him almost covers the front page. Nibbles doesn't know what to say.

'Hey, Nibbles,' laughs Walter, 'you are the star of the village, ever since the play last night. We've never had such a fine actor. Congratulations!'

Nibbles begins to blush. He's proud as a peacock. That's why Daddy wanted him to get that newspaper!

Plaster

Flopsy rides her bicycle through the village. She is wearing her pink dress. She picked it out on purpose. It matches her pink bike perfectly.

Flopsy can ride her bike without her stabilisers now. She loves that and feels happy as she rides along the path. She rings her bell as she sees Miss Hedgehog. Miss Hedgehog waves to Flopsy.

Flopsy waves back. Then she loses control of her bike. She falls hard on the ground. Her knee hurts. Flopsy cries.

Miss Hedgehog runs over to her.

'Poor you!' she says. 'Have you hurt your knee?'

Flopsy nods. Thick tears run down her cheeks.

'Let's see how bad this is,' says Miss Hedgehog. Flopsy takes her hands away from her knee. It's just a small cut, but it's bleeding a lot.

'Come with me, Flopsy,' says Miss Hedgehog. She takes Flopsy to her house. She cleans the cut with water and then dabs it with some disinfectant. Flopsy feels a stinging pain, but she knows it is a good idea.

Then Miss Hedgehog gets a box of plasters of all sorts of colours.

'Pick your favourite colour, Flopsy,' says Miss Hedgehog.

Flopsy picks a pink one.

A little later Flopsy rides on through the forest with her pink plaster on her knee. She doesn't mind, because it matches her dress perfectly. Nice, isn't it?

133

July

Doctor

Nibbles, Hopper, Flopsy and Blinders are playing doctor in the Friendship Tree. Blinders is the doctor.

Flopsy is his first patient. Doctor Blinders picks up a thermometer to check Flopsy's fever.

'Hmm,' says Doctor Blinders, 'you are quite sick. I'll write you a prescription.'

He writes something on a piece of paper and hands it to her.

'Thank you, doctor.'

After Flopsy leaves, the next patient comes in. It's Nibbles.

When he sees Blinders, he thinks Blinders looks a little pale.

'Doctor Blinders,' says Nibbles, 'are you feeling OK?'

'Sure,' says Blinders a little slowly.

'Doctor, I think my arm is broken. Can you please take a look at it?'

But Blinders doesn't react. He looks even paler now.

'Blinders, you don't look very good,' Nibbles says.

Doctor Blinders puts his hand on his own forehead.

'I… don't feel so good,' he says faintly.

Nibbles takes the thermometer and puts it under Blinders' tongue.

'This doesn't look good,' he says, as he watches the temperature rise. 'I think we'd better take Blinders home.'

'I… think that's a good idea,' Blinders says in a weak voice. 'I'm a little dizzy.'

The friends bring Blinders home quickly.

Now the friends aren't playing doctor any more.

Doctors get sick too, now and then.

Red Spots

Yesterday Blinders got sick. Today Flopsy is visiting him. Blinders is covered in red spots. He has measles, says his doctor.

'I think your spots are cute,' laughs Flopsy.

'Maybe they are to you, but I would like to get rid of them,' grumbles Blinders.

'How long do you have to stay in bed?'

'Two days.'

'Oh, two days of lazy time in bed isn't so bad,' jokes Flopsy. But Blinders doesn't agree. He'd rather be outside playing.

'Is it catching?' Flopsy wants to know.

Blinders looks at Flopsy, thinking it over.

'I think so,' he says.

'Why are you looking at me like that?' Flopsy asks nervously.

'I think I see some red spots on your face.'

Flopsy jumps up and runs to the mirror. She looks at her face. There are no spots to be seen.

'I was just joking,' says Blinders.

'Luckily,' sighs Flopsy.

'I sort of wish I had found some spots,' Blinders says. 'Then we could rest and enjoy the measles together.'

'Don't worry, we are still enjoying our visit now,' says Flopsy. 'I brought some games we could play.'

'That's nice of you,' replies Blinders.

'But what if I get sick?' Flopsy wonders.

'Then I'd come and visit you,' says Blinders. 'That's what friends are for.'

That's true, Blinders. That's what friends are for.

Grunt-Grunt!

It's nice and warm outside. Nibbles plays in his sandpit in his swimming trunks. He has poured a few buckets of water into the sandpit so that the whole thing is a big, wet mess.

Nibbles lies in the wet sand. Why?

Today Nibbles is a pig. Pigs love lying in the mud. Nibbles rolls around in the mess, grunting happily. He puts his face into the wet sand and soon it's covered, just like a pig's with mud.

'Grunt-grunt,' says the little pig. 'My stomach is grumbling. I'm hungry.' He crawls into the house on his hands and knees to get a honey biscuit. Just as he starts to open the biscuit jar, he hears someone behind him.

It's Mummy. She looks really angry. She points to the floor, which is covered with wet sand. Then she points at Nibbles, who's all sandy too. She points to the bathroom. Nibbles had better get in there fast. He puts the biscuit jar down and goes there right away.

Mummy fills the bath and Nibbles climbs in. Mummy washes his snout, then shampoos the sand out of his hair. She keeps on washing until pretty soon, Nibbles is all clean.

Mummy wraps Nibbles in a big towel and gives him a hug.

'So that's that,' she says, happily. 'My little piglet is as clean as can be.'

Grunt-grunt!

135

key, and with a click, he gets them to open.

'Here's what you do,' he says, while he carefully puts one around Sam's left wingtip. 'Then you click it and it locks shut. See?'

Sam looks at the handcuff doubtfully.

'Shall I show you again?' asks Roger.

Sam watches extra carefully as Roger shows him, using the other wingtip. Click! The second handcuff is shut.

'Now you use the little key to open them?' asks Sam hopefully.

'That's the idea, but I don't think I'll do that now,' grins Roger. The fox tosses the key into the grass and runs away.

There stands Sam, handcuffed, looking like a thief. Meanwhile the real thief is laughing as he escapes.

Handcuffs

Sam Stork, the police officer for the village, has just trapped the thief, Roger Fox.

'I've caught you at last!' he says, as he grabs his handcuffs.

'How did you find me?' Roger wants to know.

'I'm a police officer. I know everything,' says Sam, fumbling with the handcuffs. But he is having trouble and can't get them to open.

'Shall I show you how they work?' asks Roger Fox helpfully.

'OK, but don't try any funny stuff,' says Sam.

'Of course,' replies Roger. 'Let me take a look.'

Sam hands the handcuffs to Roger. He turns the

Ninety

Who's that coming along in the early morning light? It's Mister Sack, the postman. His sack is full to the top with letters. He carries a huge envelope under his arm. It's so big that it won't fit in his sack.

In big letters it says who this envelope is for: Miss Crow. When Mister Sack arrives at her house, he knocks on her door.

'Come in,' calls Miss Crow from inside. She's very old, and not at her best any more.

When Mister Sack comes in, she spots the big envelope.

'Good morning! This is for you, Miss Crow.'

'For me?' asks Miss Crow. 'Such a big envelope? Would you mind opening it for me, Mister Sack?'

'Of course.'

Quickly, Mister Sack opens it. He takes out the card and hands it to Miss Crow.

The card is covered with drawings of candles. 'Happy 90th Birthday!' is written in the centre. At the bottom, Flopsy, Nibbles, Blinders and Hopper have signed their names.

'Look at that! They found out it's my birthday. How sweet,' Miss Crow exclaims with a huge smile.

'Not just an ordinary birthday, but your 90th!' says Mister Sack, and he gives her a birthday kiss.

Now he knows why the envelope was so big: you need one when you have to draw 90 candles on the card inside.

Crash Pilot

Finally it has happened: Hopper can fly like a bird.

Not really, though. No, Hopper is dreaming he can fly. He is fast asleep in his bed with a big smile on his face. He is dreaming that he is flying over the forest village.

He finds that if he flaps his arms, he can fly higher. Then he stops flapping and glides along with the wind.

Below he can see his friends walking along. He waves to them and they wave back, watching while he soars over their heads. They laugh and call to Hopper. But Hopper can't hear them. He's flying further on, with the wind blowing gently in his face.

But what's that? Suddenly a big pole appears in front of him. He tries to avoid it, but he's flying too fast. He tries to slow down by waving his arms, but it doesn't help. In the end, he does not hit the pole, but he lands on the ground with a hard smack.

'Ow,' Hopper cries. When he opens his eyes, it's totally dark…

Of course it's dark. It's the middle of the night. Hopper knows that he has been dreaming. Not a perfect dream, maybe, because he's on the floor beside his bed. He must have fallen out when he tried to miss that pole.

A real crash pilot, that Hopper.

Romantic Evening

Miss Hedgehog has been invited for a special outing by Mister Tie.

They go to the stream together. Bert Beaver is waiting for them. He is wearing a fancy outfit. He takes a deep bow.

'Good evening, madam and sir. Welcome. Please take your places on my boat so we can take an evening cruise on the stream.'

'How romantic,' says Miss Hedgehog while they take their seats.

With a long pole, Bert pushes the boat off the shore.

'O sole mio,' Bert begins to sing loudly.

'Ahem,' says Mister Tie, 'must you do that?'

'Yes!' laughs Bert. 'You always hear Italian love songs on evening boat rides.' He starts again, 'O sole mio!' and Mister Tie looks at him crossly.

'The boat!' cries Miss Hedgehog suddenly in alarm. She points to the bottom, where there's a big hole. 'We're sinking!'

Oh, no! The boat is filling with water. Bert can barely steer it to the shore before it sinks to the bottom. They all jump out just in time.

'So much for a romantic boat ride,' sighs Miss Hedgehog disappointed.

But then Bert reaches into the grass and pulls out a picnic basket and some candles.

'The boat ride was not a great success, but here's all you need for a romantic picnic.'

And so the evening was a success. Without any more Italian love songs.

Instrument

"What's wrong, Nibbles? You look sad," says Daddy as he comes into the workshop.

'I'm feeling a bit blue,' says Nibbles with a shake of his head.

'Let's make something,' Daddy says. 'That will cheer you up.'

'What can we make?'

Daddy thinks about it. 'How about an instrument?'

There is an empty paint tin on Daddy's

workbench. He takes the lid off. 'We can use this,' he says.

'Let's put an elastic band over the opening,' says Daddy.

He takes some elastic bands out of a drawer. He stretches one over the opening. Then he puts some tape on it to keep it in place.

Nibbles plucks the band with his finger.

Ploing! goes the band.

That's fun. It's a bit like a guitar.

Nibbles and Daddy add some more bands. Each one has its own tone. Nibbles tries them all. It's neat.

Quickly, Nibbles makes up a little song. He practises it until he can play it perfectly. Then he runs outside to find his friends so he can play it for them.

Daddy smiles as Nibbles runs out of the workshop.

'I think Nibbles won't feel blue any more today, now that he can make music.'

The Thief

Mealtime. Mister Owl hears his stomach rumble. It's time to find something to eat. He goes to his garden to pick some juicy lettuce leaves so he can make a delicious salad.

But when he gets there, he sees something that bothers him: all the lettuce plants are gone! Here and there a leaf or two is left, but almost all of it has disappeared. There goes his meal.

'Who stole my lettuce plants?' he asks himself. Mister Owl looks all over his garden for clues, but he can't find any.

'It's time to put a real detective on this case,' he finally decides. He goes to the police station.

'Sam,' he says to Sam Stork, 'I've had some thieves in my garden. You have to help me find the no-good rascals.'

'Thieves?' asks Sam, who has just put his soup pot on the stove. 'I'll get right on it. But first I need to eat. A police officer can't work on an empty stomach.'

While Sam serves himself, Mister Owl watches with hungry eyes.

'Would you like to have some?' asks Sam.

Mister Owl laughs happily and sits down. 'Yes, thanks.'

Sam serves him some delicious soup.

'Mmm, that's great,' says Mister Owl. 'I love this.'

And so Mister Owl gets a lunch anyway.

July

The Snail

Sam Stork, the police officer, is searching Mister Owl's garden. Somebody has stolen most of Mister Owl's lettuce plants. Now Sam has to find out who did it.

Sam has dug a hiding hole at the edge of the garden. He is sitting in it now, with just his head sticking out. He has put a few lettuce leaves on his head. He looks a bit like a salad. Now all he has to do is wait until the thieves return to steal more lettuce plants.

After a while he feels something crawling along his beak. It's a snail. He sees the snail start to nibble on the lettuce on Sam's head.

'Wow, you can really eat a lot,' he says to the snail after it eats the whole leaf.

Mister Owl wanders into the garden just then. 'And so? Have you found the thief?' he asks.

Sam shows him the snail. 'Here he is.'

Mister Owl bends over to see the snail better. 'Have you eaten all my lettuce plants, little one?' The snail starts peacefully chewing on a new leaf.

It seems it's so delicious that nobody can resist it!

Raisin Bread

Miss Hedgehog comes into the shop of Miss Squirrel. She spots Nibbles there.

'Hi Nibbles, are you shopping for your mother today?'

'No, I'm not. I'm here to buy some raisins,' says Nibbles.

'Raisins? That's nice,' says Miss Hedgehog.

'They are for you.'

'For me? Really?'

Nibbles nods and hands a box of raisins to her.

'No, really Nibbles, you don't need to give me anything. It's a nice thought, though.'

Nibbles keeps on looking at her.

'Is there anything else you need, Nibbles?' asks Miss Hedgehog, who's feeling a little uncomfortable now.

Suddenly a big smile spreads across Nibbles' face.

Then Miss Hedgehog gets it. Nibbles is giving her raisins so she can make him some raisin bread.

'You are really clever, Nibbles,' she laughs. 'Just wait. I'll get the other things I need to make you some bread.'

Miss Hedgehog buys flour, yeast and some other things. She doesn't need more raisins, since she has some at home. She and Nibbles leave the shop and go home to start baking.

Nibbles is a lucky fellow, for sure.

The Helpers

'Whew!' sighs Mister Sack as he sees his post bag, filled to the top. 'It's going to be a long day. Just when there's a good football game on telly at the end of the day.'

Bending under the weight of his sack, he starts on his way.

After he has walked for a while he needs to rest. That sack is really heavy!

Here come Flopsy and Nibbles. They see Mister Sack sitting there.

'Are you tired, Daddy?' asks Flopsy.

'A bit. This sack is very heavy,' sighs Mister Sack. 'So many letters! I don't know if I can deliver them all today.'

'Can we help you?' asks Nibbles.

'How can you do that? You both can't read yet. How would you know which letter goes to which address?'

'That's a problem,' says Nibbles. 'But if you tell us which letters go to which house, then we can remember and help you out.'

'That's a good idea,' smiles Mister Sack, relieved. 'Let's do it.'

He gives several letters to Nibbles and tells him which houses they should go to. He does the same for Flopsy. The two youngsters run off to do their jobs.

Now Mister Sack has to carry a lot less. Cheerfully, he starts out again. He has only delivered a few letters before Flopsy and Nibbles are back. They get more letters to deliver and are off again. Mister Sack looks at them as they run off. This way he's sure to get back home in time to see that football game on telly.

Darkness

"Flopsy,' calls Mummy angrily, 'would you please go and get your doll from the garden? I've asked you twice already.'

'But Mummy,' protests Flopsy, 'it's dark outside.'

'You should have thought about that earlier,' Mummy says sternly.

'Go on, run out and get it. There aren't any monsters in our garden.'

Reluctantly Flopsy opens the door and goes slowly outside. It's really dark out there. Some light comes through a window and helps her see a bit.

It feels like hundreds of eyes are watching her as she goes toward her doll.

Then Flopsy remembers what Mummy just said: 'There aren't any monsters in our garden.'

Flopsy listens. She doesn't hear anything moving around. She spots her doll in the darkness. Holding her breath, she goes over to it. She picks her doll up and walks back through the garden. Though she really wants to run as fast as she can, she keeps walking slowly.

'There aren't any monsters in our garden,' she repeats to herself as loudly as she can. When she's back inside, she closes the door behind her. She sighs in relief. It's true, there aren't any monsters out there. But she's not completely sure about that.

A Sweltering Night

Nibbles is lying awake tonight. It's really hot.

He has tossed his sheet off. But he is still far too hot, sweating and uncomfortable. No matter how he tosses and turns, he can't sleep. He decides to open his window wider. It's not very wide open now.

He gets out of bed and opens it. A hot breeze rolls in.

'Ahhh,' says Nibble as he crawls back into bed. 'That's better.'

He soon falls fast asleep.

When Nibbles wakes up the next morning to the sound of twittering birds, he wipes his eyes. What is that on his snout? There's a little bump. It itches. On his arm he spots another bump, then another, and then several more. Oh, these bumps are all itchy!

Nibbles runs to Mummy to show her his bumps.

'Those are mosquito bites,' she explains. 'I will put some cream on them.'

After Mummy does that, they don't itch as much.

'How did you get those mosquito bites?' Mummy wants to know.

Nibbles explains how he opened his window wide open.

'We need to put a screen on your window. That way the breeze can come in but the mosquitoes will stay out.'

Mummy is right. That will help a lot.

July

A Night in the Tent

Whoopee! Mister Mouse has set up the tent in the garden. Nibbles and his friends can sleep outside tonight. They will have a great time. Daddy and Mummy Mouse wish them all a good night.

'Don't talk too long, OK? When you wake up tomorrow we'll make you a lovely breakfast. You will see it on the garden table when you all wake up.'

'Great!' the youngsters answer.

But these rascals are not planning to sleep right away. They have so much to say!

After a while, Blinders starts to fall asleep.

'Hey, you!' Hopper laughs at him. 'We are staying up late, right?'

'We aren't tired yet,' says Nibbles loudly.

But Blinders doesn't hear them. He sleeps peacefully on.

Some time later the sun begins to rise. Blinders wakes up.

'It's going to be a beautiful day. I'm hungry. Do you want to have breakfast?' he asks the rest.

The others have talked too long into the night. They want to keep on sleeping. So now it's Blinders' turn to laugh. Especially because he will have all the lovely breakfast he wants. Enjoy it, Blinders!

Locked Up

Nibbles and Misty are playing in the garden. Nibbles, the policeman, has just arrested Misty, the burglar. She must go to jail. He puts her into the garden shed and locks the door with a rusty key. Then he puts the key in his pocket.

After a while Misty asks to be let out.

'If you promise never to steal again,' says Nibbles sternly.

'I promise,' says Misty, the burglar.

'OK then.' Nibbles takes the key and puts it into the keyhole. He tries to turn it, but it just won't. Nibbles tries his hardest, but he can't make it turn.

He gives it one more try. It's stuck.

'I can't open the door,' he says uneasily.

Little Misty doesn't like that at all. 'Try again,' she says.

Nibbles does, but the lock stays stubbornly stuck.

144

Uh-oh. Misty starts to cry.

Nibbles runs as fast as he can to Mummy.

'You've locked Misty in the garden shed?' cries Mummy in shock. 'That old key is terribly rusty.' Mummy runs to the shed and tries to turn the key. It won't move. She tries again. Luckily, this time she manages to open the lock. Misty comes running out and jumps into Mummy's arms crying.

'Never do that again,' says Mummy sternly to Nibbles. Nibbles has learned his lesson. Locking someone up, even in a game, is a bad idea.

The Mysterious Letter

28 JULY

This morning Nibbles has received a letter. Mummy asks him to open it and then she reads it out loud.

'Come as quickly as you can to the Friendship Tree. A surprise is waiting for you there.'

Nibbles can't believe his ears.

'I would run over there right away,' urges Mummy, and moments later, he runs out of the house.

He spots Blinders and Flopsy. They also have letters like his. The three run to the Friendship Tree. On the way they meet Hopper, who is reading a letter just like theirs. He has no idea who sent his either.

'So let's get going now,' calls Nibbles.

All four are really curious about what could be waiting for them. Finally they get to the tree. One by one they go inside. It looks like there's nothing to see. Then Flopsy sees a package in a corner. They run to it.

Nibbles opens the package. There are fresh honey biscuits inside! They smell wonderful. Who could have left them? Then they hear footsteps outside. They run out to see who it is. It's Miss Hedgehog.

'So you found your package,' she says when she sees them.

'I wanted to surprise you because you have been so kind to me. What better way could I say thanks than with a package of honey biscuits?'

Isn't Miss Hedgehog a sweetheart?

July

Bert Beaver's Order

Miss Squirrel has just received a huge delivery in her shop. Two packages have arrived, addressed to Bert Beaver. Here he comes now.

'I see that my order has come,' he smiles.

'Indeed,' says Miss Squirrel. 'Those two packages are heavy. What's inside?'

'That's a secret, Miss Squirrel. You will find out soon.'

'But how are you going to get those heavy packages to the stream?'

Bert Beaver has arranged for that. He has made a sturdy cart. With the help of two strong customers, he loads the two packages into his cart. Then he starts up the path. His cart creaks and groans under the heavy load.

'I hope it holds together,' thinks Bert anxiously. After a while he comes to his place by the stream. Using a rope, he pulls the packages from the cart. Now he can finally open them.

Bert opens them and laughs happily.

'Ah-hah! This is just what I had hoped for. I'm going to have lots of fun with these.'

Bert runs to his garden shed and takes out a spade and a hoe. Whistling happily, he begins to dig. He makes hundreds of little holes. What is crazy Bert up to?

You know what? We will find out tomorrow.

Bert Beaver's Plan

'Hurry!' calls Nibbles. He runs to the stream with Flopsy. They want to know what's in the packages that Bert Beaver received.

'Shhh,' hushes Nibbles. 'There he is.'

They see Bert walking along, carrying a bucket toward the packages. He fills his bucket. With what? Flopsy and Nibbles can't see. With the full bucket he goes to a bare spot. He takes something from the bucket and puts it in a little hole. Then he takes something else from the bucket and puts that in another hole.

'What is he doing?' asks Flopsy burning with curiosity.

'I have an idea…' answers Nibbles.

Suddenly Flopsy jumps up and runs over to Bert. Nibbles runs after her.

'Hello, Mister Beaver,' calls Flopsy. 'What are you doing?'

Bert Beaver hides the bucket behind his back. But when he sees how curious the youngsters are, he decides to tell them what he's up to.

'I've bought those two big packages of flower bulbs. I want to plant them in this open space in the forest so it will become a flower patch. I wanted to surprise everyone.'

'Cool!' exclaim Flopsy and Nibbles together.

'Actually, I could use a little help now. Would you mind?'

Nibbles and Flopsy are thrilled to help. Planting a new flower patch will be lots of fun.

Headphones

Mummy has let Nibbles use her headphones to listen to music.

'Don't turn them up too loud,' Mummy says, 'because I want to be sure you can hear me.'

'OK, Mummy,' says Nibbles. But after a while he turns the music up louder. He closes his eyes and sings as loud as he can.

When the song is over, he opens his eyes again. The first thing he sees is his sister Misty, who is eating a honey biscuit.

'How did you get that?' he wants to know.

'I got it from Mummy,' says Misty.

'How come I didn't get one?' he asks Mummy.

'Would you like a biscuit? Why didn't you answer before?'

'Did you ask me?' Nibbles wonders.

'Yes, of course,' says Mummy. 'But you didn't answer. So I thought you didn't want one. Didn't you hear me?'

Nibbles knows the answer.

'Of course you didn't hear me,' continues Mummy, 'because your music was too loud. You couldn't hear me and so you didn't answer. I don't think that was nice.'

Nibbles lowers his head.

'May I please have a biscuit now?' he asks softly.

'No, because you turned the music up loud after I told you not to. So no biscuit for you just now. Listening to loud music is bad for your ears. Remember that.'

Nibbles will remember that. No biscuit. Through his own fault.

August

Craftwork

Nibbles and Flopsy have collected some coloured papers, paints and other things because they want to do some craftwork today.

'What should we make?' asks Flopsy.

'No idea,' says Nibbles. 'We can do anything. I am going to make a big circle of paper.'

'I don't like cutting very much. I like painting better,' says Flopsy. She takes a piece of paper and a paintbrush. Then she opens the paint box.

She starts to paint some flowers. She can do that really well. She soon fills the whole page.

Nibbles has an idea. He cuts a hole in his paper circle so it looks like a big donut.

When Flopsy is done with her painting, Nibbles asks her if he can use it.

'Sure,' says Flopsy.

Nibbles rolls her painting into a tube with the flowers on the outside and tapes it so it stays that way.

'What are you doing?' asks Flopsy.

'Just watch,' Nibbles says.

He takes the tube and slips it inside the hole in his circle.

'I get it!' exclaims Flopsy. 'You're making a top hat!'

'Yes indeed,' laughs Nibbles. He puts the hat on Flopsy's head. 'It looks great on you.'

Flopsy runs to the mirror. It is a really nice hat!

'Now let's make one for you,' says Flopsy. 'Then let's go for a walk through the village.'

Nibbles thinks that is a super idea. Craftwork can be so much fun.

Painting

Mister Tie is really busy today. He is going to paint a room for Miss Hedgehog. It won't be easy. But Mister Tie is happy to help Miss Hedgehog, because meanwhile she is going to bake him a cake.

It goes pretty fast.

Mister Tie only has the last corner to do. How annoying, though. From where he stands on his ladder he just can't reach that last spot. He doesn't

want to move the ladder, so he leans way over. He shouldn't have done that! Suddenly the ladder tips over. Mister Tie lands on the floor with a thud. The tin of paint lands on his head.

When Miss Hedgehog hears the noise, she runs to the room. She finds Mister Tie on the floor, covered in paint.

'Oh my! Have you hurt yourself?' she asks anxiously.

'No, no,' says Mister Tie, 'I'm just a little shaken up.'

'And you're completely covered with paint,' laughs Miss Hedgehog. 'You'd better take a shower before the paint dries. I'll clean the floor up.'

'That sounds like a good idea,' says Mister Tie while he stands up. He wipes off as much paint as he can and goes to the bathroom.

After half an hour of scrubbing, he's all clean. Mister Tie puts on clean clothes and goes to the living room. Miss Hedgehog has a slice of her delicious cake and a cup of hot tea waiting for him. That's a nice reward for an unlucky painter.

The Contest Prize

When Walter Weasel opens his newspaper shop this morning, someone is already waiting at the door. It's Mister Owl.

'Good morning, Mister Owl,' says Walter. 'What can I do for you?'

'Am I right that *The Village Courier* is holding a contest?'

'Yes indeed. The readers must guess how many copies of *The Village Courier* are sold today.'

'OK,' says Mister Owl. 'That's why I'm at your door. That way I can count all the customers who buy *The Village Courier* and I will know the right answer for sure.'

'Is that so?' asks Walter. 'You know, anybody can enter the contest.'

Mister Owl keeps an eye on the door of the shop all day long. Each time someone goes in, he marks a line on a piece of paper.

As Walter is shutting the shop at the end of the day, Mister Owl springs up in front of him.

'I have the answer for the contest,' he says smiling.

'You need to fill in your answer in the contest form that's in today's paper and put it in our postbox.'

'OK, could I buy a copy of the paper now, please?'

Walter looks over at the newspaper rack. Oh no, there aren't any copies left. They've all been sold. How silly of Mister Owl. He could have bought his paper this morning. Then he would have had a contest form.

That's just plain bad luck.

August

The Winner

'Blinders!' calls Mummy Mole.

Blinders is looking at a book about knights. It's his favourite book.

'What, Mummy?' he asks.

'Come and look at this,' she replies.

Slowly Blinders puts his favourite book down.

'Remember how you entered the contest in *The Village Courier*? Look who won!'

Blinders can't read yet. He only knows the letters in his own name. He looks where Mummy points and reads the letters one by one: BLINDERS.

Astonished, he looks at Mummy.

'Yes, you won! You can get your prize from Walter Weasel.'

Blinders can't believe his ears. It's his lucky day. He runs as fast as he can on his short legs to the newspaper shop. He goes in, panting hard.

'Here's the lucky winner,' Walter greets him. 'I'll go and get your prize.'

Walter goes behind the counter and brings a package out.

'For you,' he says beaming.

Blinders tears the wrapping paper off excitedly.

'Oh, wow!' he cries when he sees what's inside. 'Thank you so much!'

Blinders hurries home. He runs to his bedroom with his prize. And what is it, you ask? It's a book about knights! Now he has two, but that's no problem. Blinders can never have enough stuff that has to do with knights. He's really happy now.

The Chinese Dragon

Flopsy has taken one of Mummy's old sheets. She already knows what she is going to do with it. She meets her friends at the Friendship Tree.

They paint coloured circles on the sheet. Then Flopsy takes an ugly old mask and sets it on top. Nibbles, Blinders and Hopper have to stand behind

her in a line. They each have to bend over and hold on to the shoulders of the friend in front of them. Now Flopsy covers them with the sheet. She puts the mask on and stands at the front of the line. Together they make a Chinese dragon.

'Come on, let's go outside with our dragon,' says Nibbles.

'Yes! Outside,' yell the others.

Flopsy peers through the eye holes in her mask. She can only see little slices of things. But she sees well enough to get through the door. The dragon moves outside. They are having so much fun!

'Let's go to the village!' they cry. 'Yes, the village!' Flopsy really can't see well. But the others push her along. Where is the village? Over there? Yes, she sees it…!

Suddenly there's a loud thud. The Chinese dragon has crashed into a tree. All four of them are on the ground with the old sheet over them. Flopsy's mask is a mess. Luckily, nobody was hurt.

This Chinese dragon really needs a pair of glasses.

The Magical Postbox

When Mister Sack comes to the Mouse family's house, he stops by the red postbox that stands near the street. It's a big red box with a slot in it. While Mister Sack stands there, he looks in his postsack. He takes out several letters. He'll stick them in the slot.

'What?' mumbles Mister Sack. 'Where has the postbox gone?'

Then he sees it. It has moved several steps away from him. That's weird. It was here just a moment ago.

'Oh, well,' thinks Mister Sack, 'I must have seen it wrong.'

But as Mister Sack starts to put the letters into the slot, the postbox slides a little further away.

Mister Sack's eyes are wide open. 'I think I must need glasses,' he says completely amazed.

With a couple of careful steps he walks up to the postbox. Very slowly he brings the letters to the slot. The box stands still.

Mister Sack puts them quickly into the box.

'Aha!' he laughs. 'I thought I was going crazy.'

But just as Mister Sack says that, the letters flip out of the slot and flutter to the grass below.

'Oh, my whiskers! This really is crazy!' he cries.

Suddenly the postbox begins to laugh. Mister Sack peers in through the slot. He sees two blinking eyes. It's Nibbles. He has hidden himself in a fake postbox that Nibbles made to play a trick on Mister Sack.

Did it work? For sure!

August

Bert Beaver's Idea

It was in the newspaper: the weather would stay warm and sunny all week.

Two friends walk under the beaming sun toward the stream. It's Nibbles and Flopsy. They're going there to cool off. When they get there, they see Bert Beaver, floating on his back in the stream.

'Hello, little friends,' he calls to them. 'Come on in. The water's fine.'

'We'd better not, because we can't swim yet,' Flopsy calls back.

'That's a pity, says Bert. 'With such warm weather, the cool water is the best place to be.'

'We know,' says Nibbles. 'We really envy you.' Bert feels sorry for them. But then he gets an idea. He climbs out of the water. As he does, he shakes his fur dry. Then he runs home. Nibbles and Flopsy run after him, but Bert closes his door.

'Sorry, but you have to stay outside while I get a surprise ready for you.'

What a disappointment. He doesn't come back for a long time.

They run to look in through the window. Inside they see Bert, at his work table, drawing lots of lines with a pencil. But they are too far away to see what exactly he's drawing.

They go home disappointed. They will come back tomorrow for sure. Will you too?

The Hard Worker

Bert Beaver is busy again. He has dug a large hole next to the stream.

He doesn't know that four pairs of eyes are watching him from the high grass nearby. Those eyes belong to Nibbles, Flopsy, Blinders and Hopper.

'What in the world is he doing?' asks Nibbles. Bert takes a big sail and lays it in the hole. Then he lays stones around the hole to make a terrace.

Finally he takes several pipes and puts them side by side. He puts one end in the stream. The other end is in the hole. The water begins to flow through the pipes from the stream into Bert's strange construction.

Suddenly Blinders gets it.

'I know what it'll be,' he cries. 'It's going to be a swimming pool!'

'Shhh,' hush the others. 'He'll hear you. Bert wants this to be a surprise until tomorrow. He won't like it that we spied on him.'

'Do you really think that it will be a swimming pool?' asks Flopsy. 'Maybe it will be something completely different.'

'Look!' calls Nibbles. 'Bert Beaver is running home.'

But Bert is back before long. He has his swimming trunks on, and he jumps into the swimming pool, laughing out loud.

The youngsters now know for sure it's a swimming pool. Tomorrow morning they can spend the whole day playing in Bert's pool. What a super idea he had!

open the swimming pool. That means he will cut an official ribbon and then everybody can jump in the pool.

But first Mister Owl will make a speech. That is, he wants to, but he can't find the paper he wrote his speech on.

'Hmmm,' says Mister Owl embarrassed, 'then I'll go right ahead and cut the ribbon.'

He holds the ribbon in one hand. Now he needs the scissors. He put them in his jacket pocket, but now he is wearing just his swimming trunks. His jacket is back at home.

Oh, no! How can he cut the ribbon?

While Mister Owl stands helplessly with his ribbon, Bert Beaver comes forward.

'Maybe I can help?' he asks Mister Owl.

'Do you have scissors with you?'

'No,' says Bert, 'but I do have these.' Bert points to his strong teeth. With one bite he cuts through the ribbon. 'The swimming pool is officially open!' he cries.

Old and young, big and small jump into the water. It's a fantastic afternoon. Everyone agrees: Bert Beaver's swimming pool is a great success.

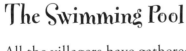

The Swimming Pool

9 AUGUST

All the villagers have gathered at the swimming pool that Bert Beaver has built. Everyone is set for a swim. Even Mister Owl is here. He has come to officially

153

August

The Thing

10 AUGUST

Nibbles, Flopsy, Hopper and Blinders are playing in the swimming pool that Bert Beaver has built. They splash around and have a wonderful time.

'Hey,' says Hopper suddenly. 'Do you hear that?'

They hear sawing and hammering noises coming from Bert's garden shed. Suddenly the door swings open. Mister Mouse and Bert Beaver carry a big thing toward the swimming pool. They have their swimming trunks on.

'A water slide!' exclaim the youngsters excitedly. They get out of the water as fast as they can.

'Stop!' says Mister Mouse. 'The heroes who made this slide get to try it out first.' The youngsters get that.

Daddy slides down the water slide, followed by Bert Beaver. They land in the swimming pool with lots of whooping and splashing.

'What do you think?' Daddy asks Bert as they come out of the water.

'It's great,' laughs Bert.

The youngsters think so too. Now it's their turn. They run to the water slide. What a super thing.

Splash!

11 AUGUST

It's dark outside.

Somebody in swimming trunks slips into the swimming pool that Bert Beaver has built. He goes to the water slide. Holding on to the ladder, he climbs to the top. Then he stands still, as if frozen.

It's Mister Sack, the postman. Mister Sack is afraid of heights. If he ever has to be in a high spot, his body freezes and he feels scared as can be.

But Mister Sack wants to try the water slide just one time. Since he can't do that during the day, with all the villagers around, he has decided to try it in the evening.

'Go for it,' he says to himself. Sweating with fear, his knees shaking, he sits on the water slide. He pushes off and slides down…

Suddenly a loud splash breaks the silence of the village.

A moment later, a voice cries, 'I did it! I did it!'

Nobody sees a dripping wet but happy rabbit walking home in the darkness.

August

Diving

Sam Stork, the police officer, has planned a new way to catch Roger Fox. Since he is a stork, he can fly. So he is going to fly to the top of a tall tree and stand watch. 'Fantastic,' says Sam as he settles down at the top of an oak. 'I can see the whole area from here.'

The sun sets in the distance. This is the moment that Roger Fox likes to go out, looking for things to steal.

Sam peers through the gathering darkness.

Over there he sees something moving. It's Roger Fox!

Like a hawk, Sam dives below after Roger. The wind races through his feathers.

'Go ahead and run, foxie, I'm on your trail,' laughs Sam to himself.

Suddenly Roger looks behind him and sees the huge stork zooming after him. He starts to run as fast as he can. Through the growing darkness, Sam keeps following. His prey can't escape again.

His eyes have closed down to tiny slits and his claws stretch out, ready to grab Roger.

Suddenly Roger ducks behind a huge tree. Sam can't follow him and he smacks hard into it.

Sam sees stars. That rascal, Roger Fox, is always too clever for him!

The Hot Air Balloon

Hopper has found a huge plastic shopping bag in the woods.

Suddenly he gets a great idea. He can make a hot air balloon from it.

He runs home with the plastic bag. Under some of his toys he finds an old basket and some rope.

He ties one end of the rope to the plastic bag. He ties the other end to the basket. Then he gathers some pieces of wood, puts them into a tin, then sets them on fire. Smoke comes out of the can. He puts it into the basket.

He holds the plastic bag over the smoke. It catches the warm, smoky air and fills up like a balloon.

Hopper jumps quickly into the basket. The plastic bag is now filled with hot air. It lifts the basket with Hopper in it off the ground.

'It works!' cries Hopper thrilled to be flying. Slowly Hopper rises higher and higher. Suddenly the fire goes out. His fuel has burned up. The balloon starts to drift lower and lower. It gets tangled in a tree and stops, hanging from a branch.

And there also hangs Hopper, high and dry. But that doesn't disappoint him. His dream has come true: he has flown.

A Secret Rascal

The weather is wonderful again. Mister Sack, the postman, is heading home after making his rounds. As he goes by Miss Crow's home, he feels a splash of water on his neck. Angrily, Mister Sack looks around him, but there's nothing to be seen. He goes on walking.

A little later Miss Hedgehog walks by Miss Crow's house. She feels a splash of water on her nose. Miss Hedgehog jumps in surprise. She is angry, but when she looks around, there's nobody to be seen.

'Rascals!' she cries, and she walks on.

Now Mister Owl comes walking by the house of Miss Crow. Whistling happily, he strolls along. But the whistling stops when he feels a splash of water on his beak.

'What's going on here?' he roars. 'Where did that water come from?'

He peers around, but there is nobody to be seen.

'Nasty coward,' he calls. 'Come out if you dare.'

He's barely said that when he feels another splash of water on his head. He turns red as a tomato and quickly walks away.

Inside Miss Crow's house you can hear giggling. Behind her window she's sitting there with her water pistol, waiting for the next villager to pass by. She may be old, but she has a sense of humour and she's quite a rascal.

August

Hanging Up the Washing

Nibbles feels like eating a honey biscuit. He knows that if he helps Mummy, he will get a biscuit as a thank-you. So Nibbles is watching Mummy carefully.

She's going to the washing machine. A load of washing has just finished. Mummy takes the wet clothes and puts them in a basket, then takes them outside to hang up on the washing line so they can dry.

Nibbles can certainly help her with that. He runs after her.

'Would you like some help, Mummy?' he asks.

'Sure,' says Mummy, smiling with surprise. 'Are your hands clean?'

Nibbles looks at his hands. They are really dirty.

'Go and wash them first,' says Mummy, 'otherwise you will get the clothes dirty again.'

Nibbles runs fast as he can to the bathroom. He soaps up his hands, rinses them clean and dries them off. Then he runs back outside and shows Mummy.

'That's great,' she says. 'Can you hand me the wet clothes? Then I can hang them up.' Nibbles does that. Before long, all the things are on the washing line and the basket is empty.

'Since you helped me so nicely, I'd like to give you a honey biscuit,' says Mummy.

'Yippee!' cries Nibbles. 'My plan worked!'

'What plan?' asks Mummy.

'Uh… nothing,' smiles Nibbles, and he hurries away with his biscuit. Nibbles is such a rascal. But he did help Mummy a lot!

Sun Bathing

What a beautiful summer day! Nibbles and his friends are playing in the swimming pool that Bert Beaver built. Suddenly he asks, 'Where is Flopsy?'

'I'm here,' she calls. Flopsy is lying on a big towel, wearing black sunglasses. 'I'm sunbathing, and it's wonderful.'

'You're doing what?'

'Sunbathing. That gives you a nice brown colour.'

'I want to do that too,' laughs Nibbles as he jumps

out of the water.

'You'd better put on some sun screen first,' says Flopsy. She shows him a bottle with a picture of a sun on it. 'Turn around and I'll do your back.' Flopsy squeezes the bottle and some white cream comes out on Nibbles' back.

'Oooh, that's cold,' he cries.

'Sit still,' says Flopsy, 'I'll rub it in now.'

When that's done, Flopsy lies down again.

'What do I do now?'

'Just lie there and enjoy it.'

Nibbles lies down a bit unsure. He shuts his eyes, like Flopsy has done. He waits. Goodness, it's hot. Nibbles sighs. He feels like ice cream that's melting in the sun.

He has had enough of this. Nibbles opens his eyes. The strong sunlight blinds him. Then he looks at his body, but there's no change in colour.

'This sunbathing stuff is silly,' he says. 'I know what's lots more fun.' And he jumps back into the swimming pool with a splash.

Mister Sack's Trousers

Mister Sack hurries to the tailor shop of Mister Tie. He has his hands over his bottom and looks around anxiously to see if anyone can see him. Luckily, it's early in the morning and most of the villagers are still at home.

'Mister Tie,' calls Mister Sack when he finally arrives at the shop's door. 'You must help me.'

Mister Tie comes to the door, curious. When he sees Mister Sack, he quickly opens the door.

'My friend, you have to help me,' pleads Mister Sack.

'Easy there, friend,' Mister Tie says, trying to calm him. 'Whatever is wrong?'

'Just now as I was on my rounds, I dropped a letter on the ground. When I tried to pick it up, I heard a ripping noise. I looked around and saw that…'

Mister Sack turns and lets Mister Tie take a look. There's a big hole in his trousers. You can see Mister Sack's red-and-white striped underwear. Mister Tie finds it pretty funny.

'Can you fix it?' asks Mister Sack.

'Of course. Come in,' laughs Mister Tie.

Mister Sack is really happy to be inside. At least that way nobody can see him. He gives his trousers to Mister Tie, who goes to his sewing machine right away.

In a short while Mister Sack is back on the street delivering the post. Nobody can see the tear in his trousers. Thanks, Mister Tie!

August

Grown Up

When Nibbles comes home from a great time with his friends, he hears hammering in the house. The noise comes from his bedroom. He opens the door and sees Mister Mouse, who is taking Nibbles' bed apart.

'Daddy, what are you doing?' asks Nibbles anxiously.

'Relax, Nibbles,' says Daddy calmly. 'I've made you a new bed.'

'What was wrong with my old one?'

'Absolutely nothing. It was just getting a bit small, though, don't you think?'

'Uh, yes,' Nibbles agrees hesitantly.

'We'll give your bed to your sister. She needs a bigger bed too, since you're both growing like crazy.'

A new bed? Nibbles thinks that's exciting. What will it look like?

'Wait downstairs while I put your new bed together,' says Daddy to Nibbles. 'That way the surprise will be a lot more fun.'

Excitedly, Nibbles waits until Daddy calls him. He could climb the walls, he's so curious. Finally he hears Daddy's voice: 'Nibbles, your new bed is ready.'

In a flash, Nibbles runs upstairs to his room. His new bed is incredible! The sides look like a pirate ship. At the foot end, there's a big rudder and at the head end there's a little mast with a pirate flag. Nibbles can't believe his eyes. It's the coolest bed he has ever seen.

Picnic at the Friendship Tree

Nibbles, Flopsy, Hopper and Blinders are each carrying a basket. They are going picnicking at the Friendship Tree. They have agreed that whatever is in each one's basket will be a secret until they get there. It makes the picnic a lot more fun.

Finally, they arrive. Nibbles and Hopper spread a cloth on the ground so they can all sit down. Now it's time to see what is in those baskets.

Flopsy begins. She dumps her basket out on the cloth. All sorts of sweets and biscuits. Now it's Hopper's turn. With a grin he spills out his basket. Again, sweets and biscuits.

Blinders shakes his basket out. Still more sweets and biscuits! Now it's Nibbles' turn.

'Oh my! Even more sweets and biscuits! What a wonderful picnic,' cries Flopsy.

They start eating all the goodies as quickly as they can. But as the piles get smaller, the friends grow quieter.

After the last sweet disappears into Flopsy's mouth, she says, 'My stomach hurts.'

'Mine too,' groans Blinders.

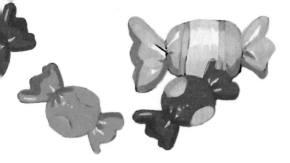

'And mine,' whinges Hopper.

Nibbles doesn't say anything. His painful expression says it all.

Our friends have learned a hard lesson today: Too many sweets can make you sick.

Horse

Click-clack! Click-clack! sounds through the house. A horse is running through the house of the Mouse family. Not a real one. No, it's Nibbles. Today, he is a horse. He gallops through the kitchen and out of the door.

'Don't go too far. Lunch is almost ready,' Mummy calls.

Nibbles whinnies in reply.

Mummy has to laugh at him. He is always thinking up such funny games.

When the table is set, Mummy calls everyone to come and eat. She has made chips.

Neighing loudly, Nibbles sits down.

'Isn't that horse supposed to be in his stable?' asks Mummy.

Nibbles neighs no. She spoons out some dry oatmeal into a bowl and sets it in front of Nibbles.

'This is a special surprise for our horse,' she smiles. Nibbles looks at the bowl with huge eyes.

'I thought that horses loved oats,' says Mummy thoughtfully.

'That could be,' thinks Nibbles, 'but I'd much rather have chips.' He shakes his head no.

'Maybe the horse would rather have grass,' says Daddy.

Nibbles is fed up with this. 'I'm not a horse. I'm Nibbles and I would like some chips.'

'Oh, now we can hear you speak,' says Mummy. 'But you've forgotten something. What do we say when we ask for something?'

'Please,' says Nibbles politely.

'Very good,' says Mummy, serving Nibbles some delicious golden chips.

August

Chocolates

21 AUGUST

Mister Tie is visiting Miss Hedgehog. Since the weather is so beautiful, they are sitting outside in her garden. Mister Tie has brought a special gift for Miss Hedgehog. It's a big, red heart that's filled with special chocolates. Mister Tie wants to give it to Miss Hedgehog at a special moment. But she's chattering away so fast that he can't get a word in. He listens, enchanted, as she tells him about all the things that happened last week. Meanwhile the box of chocolates sits beside him.

Finally Miss Hedgehog finishes her story. Mister Tie picks up the box and gives it to her.

'A little present for you,' he smiles.

'Oh, Mister Tie, thank you so much,' she exclaims in surprise. She takes the box and unwraps it. It feels warm because it's been lying in the sun. When Miss Hedgehog takes off the top, she finds a box full of… melted chocolates.

'Oh, no,' groans Mister Tie. 'I've left the box in the sun too long.'

'That's OK,' says Miss Hedgehog. 'I'll just put them in the fridge for a while.'

And indeed, within an hour they are solid again.

'They aren't as beautiful now, but they taste even better,' she jokes. And when Mister Tie tastes one, he has to agree.

That Miss Hedgehog is such a sweet, smart lady.

The Fork in the Path

22 AUGUST

Nibbles and his friends are going to take a long hike today. They have filled their backpacks with sandwiches and bottles of water. With their sturdy boots, they look like real hikers. Now they're off.

But they've not gone very far before they come to a fork in the path. Which way should they take?

'I want to take that way,' says Hopper.

Flopsy doesn't agree. She would rather take the other fork. Blinders agrees with Hopper, while Nibbles agrees with Flopsy.

'Don't be silly, just come along with us,' says Hopper.

Flopsy and Nibbles don't want that. 'This fork looks nice to us. Let's follow this way.'

'Why would you want to pick that one? There is nothing there,' says Blinders.

'Nothing there? What about your path? There's really nothing there.'

They stand there for a while, arguing back and forth, until Hopper has had enough.

'I'm going home,' he grumbles.

'If that's the way you feel, then I'm out too,' snarls Flopsy.

'If that's the way you two feel, I'm ready to go home too. What about you, Nibbles?' asks Blinders gently.

Nibbles answers sadly, 'Let's give up.'
Thanks to this squabble, the great hike doesn't happen. It's true: when you squabble, you go nowhere.

Heads and Tails

Today our friends have agreed to start their big hike again. With heavy backpacks and sturdy boots, they are set to go.

Yesterday they wanted to do this too. But because they had a fight about a fork in the path, they blew up the whole plan.

Nibbles has found a solution, though. A coin can decide which fork they will take.

Nibbles gets ready. He tosses the coin in the air. It lands beside his foot. 'If the coin lands with its face up, then we'll go to the left. If it lands with the other side up, we'll go to the right.'

The others think that's a great idea. Whistling happily, they start off. When they come to the fork in the path, they toss the coin. It falls with its face up, so they go to the left.

After a while they come to another fork. Again they toss the coin and it sends them to the left. After they have walked for some distance, Flopsy asks, 'Isn't that our village?'

'Yes, it is!' exclaims Nibbles. 'That's our village. The coin has led us in a circle around our own village.'

They have a good laugh. Oh well, at least this time they didn't have a fight about which path to take.

August

Sunset

Nibbles looks through the window at the setting sun. The light is orange, and here and there he sees pink clouds. It's so beautiful. Mummy comes into his room.

'Come on, Nibbles, it's time to get ready for bed.'

Nibbles hasn't had enough of the beautiful sunset.

'Mummy?' he asks. 'Where does the sun go when it sets?'

'Just like you, it goes to sleep.'

'Where does it sleep, then?'

'In a huge bed, one that's a thousand times bigger than yours.'

'So big?' asks Nibbles sleepy.

'Uh-huh,' nods Mummy. 'Sleep well. It's late.'

But before Mummy can turn the light out, Nibbles has one more question for her.

'Is the sun's bed far from here?'

'It's beyond the horizon. You can't see it from here.'

'You have to travel far to get there?'

'Very far. So far that nobody has ever been there.'

'When I'm big, then I want to be an explorer. I'll go looking for the sun's bed.'

'That would be nice, dear. But to be an explorer you need to sleep now. Then you will get big and strong so you can hike for day after day. So close your eyes.'

She gives Nibbles a big good-night kiss and tucks him in.

Nibbles' eyes fall shut and he dreams about how someday he'll discover the sun's bed...

Miss Squirrel Has a Birthday

'This is the nicest day of the year,' say Nibbles, Hopper, Flopsy and Blinders as they walk to Miss Squirrel's shop. Each of them has a big drawing. It's

for Miss Squirrel, because it's her birthday today. She has told the villagers that each youngster who brings her a birthday drawing will get a big bag of sweets.

The youngsters have worked hard to make the best drawings they could.

Here they come, storming into the shop. They stand in a row. Nibbles counts to three. 'Happy Birthday to You, Happy Birthday to You…' they sing happily.

When the song is over, Miss Squirrel claps for joy.

'Happy Birthday, Miss Squirrel,' the youngsters say again. They give her their drawings.

'My, what lovely drawings,' she says. 'These will have a place of honour in my shop. And here are your sweets,' she laughs. The youngsters take their bags, which are so big that they can't believe their eyes.

They thank Miss Squirrel and run outside. They all hope Miss Squirrel has many more birthdays!

The Band

Nibbles has a toy trumpet. He's sitting on a bench in the garden, practising. Suddenly he hears some tootling. It is Flopsy with her little flute.

'I heard you making music, so I came over with my flute. Can I play with you?' she asks.

Of course she can. They start up again and make quite a lot of noise. Then Blinders wanders into the garden with a big drum.

'Cool,' cry Nibbles and Flopsy. 'Where did you get that?'

'It's my granddad's. He plays it in a band.'

'Hey, let's make our own band,' suggests Nibbles.

'Can I join?' asks Hopper, who's just come into the garden.

'Do you have an instrument?' asks Blinders.

'No,' sighs Hopper.

Oooh, that's a problem. Because if you want to play in a band, you need an instrument. At least…

'I have an idea,' says Nibbles. 'You can be our director and keep us on the beat. OK?'

That's a great idea, they all agree.

A little later a new band marches through the village. First comes a frog with a director's baton. Then comes a fluting bunny and a trumpeting mouse. At the end there's a small mole with a huge drum. It's the nicest band the village has ever had.

August

The Village Champions

It's early morning and Walter Weasel is standing in front of his counter. He woke up with an idea: he wants to organise a sports contest. Anybody who wants to can join in. It should be lots of fun. He picks up his pen and thinks long and hard about what to call the competition.

'The Village Champions! That sounds good,' he thinks.

But what kinds of contests should there be? A foot race is always exciting. But maybe a bicycle race would be good. Or a swimming race?

'Hmmm,' thinks Walter. 'Why not mix all three together in one race? First some swimming, then some biking and then some running as a big finish. Yes, that would be great.'

Walter writes an announcement and puts it into *The Village Courier*.

When he sees that he has sold all of his newspapers that evening, he knows the competition will be a success.

The next day he sees Mister Sack, the postman, jogging with Mister Tie, the tailor. 'Hello Walter,' they call. 'We're training for the competition.' But not only the grown-ups are training for the event.

Nibbles, Hopper, Flopsy and Blinders come jogging along the path. And there is Miss Hedgehog and Miss Squirrel on their bikes. Everybody seems to be training for the competition.

Happily, Walter thinks, 'I wonder who the Village Champion will be…'

Exciting, isn't it?

The Athlete

He stands in front of the mirror in the bathroom and splashes ice-cold water on his face and chest. He doesn't mind a bit. He is as hard as steel.

Then he goes into his bedroom and pulls on his yellow t-shirt. There is a picture of a bolt of lightning on it. He smoothes his t-shirt down, then pulls on his tracksuit. Next he puts on his white sports socks, wiggling his toes happily. Then he puts on his trainers. He stands up, bends his knees and takes a deep breath. It's time to get outside and begin the real work of the day: serious training. He starts jogging. Before long, Miss Hedgehog and Mister Tie, who are out jogging this morning too, pass him by.

'Good morning, Mister Owl. Are you training too? Good luck with your programme to slim down,' they call to him as they speed ahead.

Nibbles and Flopsy jog by him too. 'Keep at it, Mister Owl,' they call back encouragingly.

But our athlete doesn't need help. Puffing and sweating, he jogs on at his own, peaceful tempo. After all, isn't just doing it more important than winning?

after her. Luckily, Nibbles isn't a strong swimmer. But Hopper is. With a beautiful dive he springs into the water and passes Nibbles. Then he swims like crazy after Flopsy. She swims as fast as she can, but Hopper is catching up.

Here comes the finish line. Flopsy gives it her best. With a last burst, she crosses the finish line just before Hopper. Cheering and clapping ring out from the villagers.

The Village Champion has been found: It's Flopsy!

The Competition

29 AUGUST

Craaack! goes the starting gun.

A pack of runners spill over the starting line. They are taking part in the Village Champions' competition that Walter Weasel started. They are all doing their best to win the race.

Already there is someone leading. It's Flopsy. She is running as fast as she can. It's natural, because she is a bunny. She already has a big lead.

Now she comes to the second part of the race: biking. She jumps on her bike and pedals hard. Along the path some villagers cheer her on. Flopsy looks behind her.

Oh-oh, here comes Nibbles. Flopsy knows he is a fast biker, so she really goes for it. It's really exciting.

Flopsy finishes the second stage of the race just before Nibbles. Now comes the swimming. With a splash she jumps in the water, with Nibbles right

167

August

The Prize-Winners

The entire front page of *The Village Courier* tells about just one thing today. In big, fat letters, the headline shouts, 'The Village Champion is Flopsy!'

A big picture shows Flopsy making her final run for the finish line, just barely ahead of Nibbles, Hopper and Blinders. She's running for her life. Everybody else is doing their best to win too.

But of course, there can only be one winner, and that was Flopsy. She was the fastest at running, biking and swimming. She really deserved to get the golden trophy.

Hopper came in second. He proudly received the big box of honey biscuits and a bottle of berry juice. 'Mmm,' he exclaimed, smacking his lips.

Nibbles came in third. He got a box of honey biscuits as well and started munching them happily right away.

Mister Owl finished last. Almost everybody was on their way home when he puffed his way across the finish line. The few spectators still there clapped and gave him a cheer as a well-deserved reward for his hard work.

Everyone agreed that it was a wonderful day. It was great to see the racers doing all that running, biking and swimming. Walter Weasel said that he could hardly wait to organise next year's race.

Way to go, Walter!

Miss Hedgehog Makes Pancakes

Nibbles is wandering through the village with his friends. Suddenly he stops and freezes.

'Nibbles, what is it?' asks Hopper. Nibbles sniffs with his nose in the air. Yes, there it is again…

'Come on, follow me,' says Nibbles, as he leads them ahead, sniffing the breeze. The others follow, curious about where they will end up.

'What's he up to?' asks Flopsy.

'I have no idea,' answers Blinders.

Nibbles leads them straight to Miss Hedgehog's house.

'See? My nose never misleads me,' says Nibbles confidently.

'What do you mean?' ask the others.

Nibbles points to the kitchen window. There they can see Miss Hedgehog standing in the kitchen making pancakes.

Suddenly she looks outside. When she sees them, she waves.

'I wondered where you were, Nibbles. I don't have to call you when I'm cooking or baking. Sit down and have some pancakes, youngsters!'

That's Miss Hedgehog all the way.

September

Robin Hood

Blinders has a new book. It's about Robin Hood. Robin is a thief who steals from the rich Prince John. He gives the gold he steals to the poor people. So Prince John wants to put Robin in prison. But it never works, because Robin always gets away.

'What a hero Robin is!' thinks Blinders to himself dreamily.

Blinders jumps up and runs to his toy chest. He pulls out a bow and some arrows. Exactly what he needs to be Robin Hood.

Robin was a master bowman. Blinders wants to practise so he can shoot an arrow as well as Robin Hood, his hero.

He holds his bow steady and gets an arrow ready. Then he pulls the bow-string back, aims at the wall, and lets fly. *Zip!*

But Blinders doesn't aim very well and the arrow goes in a different direction. It hits a photo in a picture frame. The frame falls to the floor and the glass inside it breaks with a crash.

It's not long before Blinder's mummy arrives. When she sees Blinders standing there with his bow, she knows exactly what has happened. She is angry about the broken glass. Blinders is being punished and he has to stand in the corner.

The next time Blinders wants to practise with his bow and arrows, he'd better do it outside.

BlinHopNibFlop

As Blinders ducks into the Friendship Tree, he finds his friends are there waiting for him.

'So tell us: what's so important that we had to run here?'

'Because I want to tell you about Robin Hood,' says Blinders.

He tells them about how Robin steals from the rich to give to the poor.

'That's what I want to do,' says Blinders heroically. 'We can make our own merry band of thieves.'

'Hey, yeah, that's cool,' say the others.

'What will we do?' Nibbles wants to know.

'We attack... uh...' stammers Blinders.

Yes, just who should they attack? In the village there's no nasty, rich prince like Prince John they can steal from. That's a real problem for them.

'I have it! Anyone carrying treats!' crows Blinders.

'Yesss!' the others cry. They think it's a super idea.

'And who are we going to give the treats to, Robin Hood?' asks Flopsy a bit crossly.

'To… to ourselves!' Blinders decides.

'Yeee-haaa!' the band of thieves cries.

'And what should we call our band?' asks Hopper.

Blinders thinks deeply. 'What do you think of "The Blinders Hood Band"?'

'That's not very good,' complains Flopsy. 'What about BlinHopNibFlop? From the first letters of our names?'

The villagers better watch out. Anyone who carries treats on the public paths will have to reckon with BlinHopNibFlop!

Thieves!

Miss Hedgehog is walking slowly through the village with a basket full of honey biscuits. She is a little scared, because she has heard there is a band of thieves called BlinHopNibFlop that attacks anyone who is carrying treats.

Suddenly somebody springs onto the path in front of her. He's masked and carries a bow and arrow. He reminds her of Blinders.

'Stop! This is an attack!' he cries.

Miss Hedgehog stops, terrified, and sets her basket on the ground. She puts her hands in the air.

Three thieves jump out of the bushes. They are the same size as the youngsters that Miss Hedgehog knows so well. Miss Hedgehog picks up her basket and opens it.

'See? My nose was right! Her basket is full of honey biscuits.'

'Great. Bring it here. That basket is ours.'

'Please don't do that,' pleads Miss Hedgehog. 'I baked these biscuits for four wonderful youngsters. Their names are Flopsy, Nibbles, Hopper and Blinders. Do you know them?'

'Uh… no, we don't,' says the leader. 'Just tell them that BlinHopNibFlop thanks them for the biscuits. Have a good day.'

Then the thieves disappear into the bushes as suddenly as they came. Miss Hedgehog stays behind. If the thieves think that she is going to let this happen, they are very much mistaken!

September

Lessons Learned

Yesterday the band of thieves made their first attack. They took a basket of honey biscuits from Miss Hedgehog. The next day, in the safety of the Friendship Tree, they open the basket, and each one takes a delicious biscuit out. At that very moment, a dark figure springs into the Friendship Tree. It's wrapped in a black cape and wears a mask.

'Stop,' it cries, shaking its head. They do as their told, in shock.

'Aren't you forgetting something?' asks the intruder sternly.

The youngsters look at each other in fear. They have no idea who this is. Then the intruder takes two big bottles of berry juice out from under its cape. 'Like this, for instance?' The intruder takes its mask off. It's Miss Hedgehog!

'Lessons learned,' she laughs. 'You wouldn't want to eat your honey biscuits without some berry juice, would you?'

The youngsters sigh in relief. Miss Hedgehog has really scared them. While she opens the bottles, Nibbles arranges five glasses.

'Mmm,' says Blinders, 'honey biscuits and berry juice.'

There's going to be a big feast in the Friendship Tree.

Blowing Up

While Nibbles, Hopper and Blinders splash around happily in Bert Beaver's swimming pool, Flopsy sits on the edge. She has a big plastic thing beside her. It has a valve on it. She opens the valve and blows into it with little puffs.

After a while she has the thing half blown up.

'Flopsy, what are you up to?' the others ask. 'Come and play with us.'

But Flopsy keeps on puffing. She is getting a little dizzy, but she won't give up. While the others play in the water, she is filling it with air.

Finally it's ready. As fast as she can, she pushes the top into the valve so the air can't escape.

Flopsy picks up the thing and throws it into the water. She jumps in after it.

'Hey, it's an air bed!' exclaim the others.

'Yes,' says Flopsy, 'but since I blew it up, I will lie on it first. I really need a rest after that job. You can have it in a minute.'

Flopsy pulls herself up on the air bed and lies on it. At first it wobbles a bit. But if she lies still, the wobbling slowly stops.

'Oh, this is wonderful,' she sighs.

Nibbles takes the air bed and pushes it around like a boat. Flopsy loves it. It's like she is on a ride at an amusement park. All that blowing and puffing was worth it.

Urgent Needs

Nibbles wakes up in the middle of the night. He needs to go to the bathroom. Reaching out, he turns on his bedside lamp. He slips out of his warm bed. Now he really needs to go!

He walks down the hall, hearing crickets chirping in the darkness outside.

Nibbles doesn't feel too easy in the darkness. He walks towards the end of the hall. What's that? Light shines from under the bathroom door!

Somebody must have forgotten to turn the light off. As he reaches for the bathroom door handle, he hears a weird sound inside: Yaaaw!

Nibbles stands like his feet are nailed to the floor, his knees shaking with fear.

What made that sound? What should he do? What if it's a burglar who has come to steal his sister?

But Nibbles' curiosity is finally greater than his fear. Very quietly and slowly, he turns the door handle and opens the door a crack.

Through the opening he sees… Daddy!

'Hey there, Nibbles,' whispers Daddy smiling. 'Do you have to go to the bathroom too?'

Nibbles nods.

'What made that strange noise? I got scared.'

'Noise? Oh, that was me. I just yawned,' laughs Daddy, and he yawns again. Then he gives Nibbles a hug and starts back to bed.

'What a relief,' sighs Nibbles as Daddy disappears. 'I was so scared for a moment.'

Now he can do what he really needs to do.

September

Auntie Sniffle

7 SEPTEMBER

Oh, no! Today Auntie Sniffle is coming to visit. She is an annoying old aunt of Mister Mouse's. When she comes, she spends the whole time cuddling and stuffing Nibbles with awful sweets that she always brings. Nibbles really doesn't like it. He needs to come up with a plan. But what can he do? He thinks long and hard about it. There's one thing he can do… but Nibbles keeps that a secret.

Ding-dong sounds the door bell. Auntie Sniffle has arrived. As soon as Nibbles hears her shrill voice down the hall, he runs outside.

'Where is my little Nibbles?' asks Auntie Sniffle. 'I have some yummy sweets for him.'

'Nibbles,' calls Mummy. 'Where are you? Auntie Sniffle is here!'

'I'm here,' calls Nibbles back. 'Hello, Auntie Sniffle.' He walks right up to Auntie Sniffle and gives her a big hug.

'Eeek!' cries Auntie Sniffle. 'You're covered with mud! You've made my dress all dirty! Look at that! I'm not coming back, ever!'

After Auntie Sniffle bustles out of the house, Mummy asks angrily, 'Where have you been, Nibbles?'

'I was outside playing and I fell in a puddle,' he answers.

Later Nibbles is in the bath. He gets a scrubbing from Mummy. But he doesn't mind that. As long as Auntie Sniffle doesn't turn up again.

Sam and Auntie Sniffle

8 SEPTEMBER

Yesterday Auntie Sniffle visited Nibbles. She wanted to give him a big hug. Nibbles, who dislikes her, rolled in a mud puddle first. Then he gave Auntie Sniffle a big hug, making sure he got her dress all dirty. Auntie Sniffle got mad and left.

Today Sam Stork, the police officer, is walking through the village when he spots a fat lady coming toward him. It's Auntie Sniffle.

'Where are you going in such a hurry today?' he

174

asks her.

'My dress. My dress is a complete mess!' she stammers.

'Easy now, young lady,' he says, trying to calm her. 'Tell me all about it.'

Auntie Sniffle tells him her story in bits and pieces. Sam doesn't understand it at all.

'But miss, he says, 'there's nothing really wrong with your dress, is there?'

'Oh, no?' cries Auntie Sniffle. 'Take a good look.'

'OK, young lady. I don't see anything wrong. In fact, it looks lovely. I like… brown a lot.'

'That's just the point!' she says, waving her arms around. 'It was blue with pink flowers, and now it's brown all over from the mud.'

She stomps away furiously.

'Uh-oh,' Sam thinks to himself, 'maybe I'd better get new glasses.'

The Painter

For weeks Flopsy's mummy has been asking Flopsy's daddy, Mister Sack, to paint the garden bench. Mister Sack hates painting, so he's been putting it off. But today he has his paint and a brush in his hands.

He opens the paint tin and stirs the paint. Then he dips the brush into the paint and starts working.

'What an annoying kind of task,' sighs Mister Sack. Nibbles, Flopsy, Hopper and Blinders walk by him. They are going for a swim at Bert Beaver's swimming pool.

'You'll have a lot more fun than I will,' sulks Mister Sack. 'I'll be here painting.'

He dips his brush in the paint and goes on working. Why does he hate painting so much?

After lots more sighing and grumbling, the bench is painted.

'Finally,' he sighs. He lays his brush down and looks at the bench. It really does look good with its new coat of paint. Mister Sack is tired from the work.

He stretches out. His back hurts. Mister Sack needs to sit down. With a plop he settles down on the bench. Immediately he realises what he has done. He has just sat down on the wet paint! Mister Sack jumps up. There's a big spot where he was sitting.

'Oh, no,' wails Mister Sack, 'now I have to start all over again.'

Poor Mister Sack!

September

Water Balloons

Mummy has given Nibbles a great present: water balloons. He fills them with water and ties knots in the tops. Then he lays the filled balloons in a bucket. He hides with it in the bushes.

Here comes Flopsy, not suspecting a thing, walking by the bushes.

Nibbles tosses one of the water balloons at her. 'Pssst!' it goes as it lands in front of her, soaking her through.

Nibbles bursts out laughing. Flopsy storms away angrily.

Nibbles doesn't have to wait long before his next victim arrives. Here come Blinders and Hopper.

He can get them both at once.

'Pssst! Pssst!' go the balloons. His friends stand dripping and laughing, looking at Nibbles and then they go on.

Nibbles waits for his next victim. He has only one balloon left. He will have to make very good use of it.

Aha! Here comes Flopsy again. Hopper and Blinders are also coming, from the other side. But what's that? Each of them is carrying a bucket. The buckets are filled with water balloons.

When Flopsy, Blinders and Hopper each pick up a balloon, Nibbles realises what's up. They're going to get him back! Under a rain of water balloons, Nibbles runs home. When he gets there, he's wet from tip to toe.

See, Nibbles? What goes around comes around.

In the Attic

Today Nibbles is helping Daddy. They are going to clean out the attic. That is going to be a fun task for Nibbles. But after he moves piles of boxes from one side to the other, he has had enough of it. What a silly job this is.

And after one pile of boxes is cleaned up, Daddy makes another pile appear. He won't stop. Except when Daddy finds an unusual box in the last pile.

'Well, look at this!' he cries.

Curious, Nibbles comes over to look.

'This is my old magician's box. I haven't seen it in years.'

Daddy first blows the dust off the cover and then opens it.

Inside are balls, flowers, pieces of string, cards, and of course, a magic wand and magician's hat.

'Wow!' exclaims Nibbles amazed. He has never seen a magic box like this.

'Here, you can have it,' says Daddy. 'It's for you.'

Nibbles can't believe his ears.

'Because you helped me so much.' Daddy puts the box in Nibbles' hands. He is grinning and laughing.

So a silly job can lead to a surprising ending.

The Magician's Apprentice

Yesterday Nibbles received an old magician's box from his daddy. It's a beautifully decorated box. When Nibbles opens the lid, he holds his breath. He can't believe that this wonderful thing, which used to belong to Daddy, is now his.

The box is loaded with all sorts of magic stuff. Nibbles puts on the magician's hat. He waves the magic wand around and says *Abracadabra*,

but nothing happens…

'What's wrong, Nibbles?' asks Daddy. 'Isn't it working?'

'No,' answers Nibbles.

'Shall I teach you some tricks?'

Nibbles is all set to learn! Daddy takes a little ball and hides it in his hand. Nibbles has to tap Daddy's hand lightly with the magic wand. When Daddy opens his hand, the ball has disappeared!

'How do you do that?' asks Nibbles amazed.

Daddy shows him how the trick works. It's really not hard.

'You need to practise the trick a lot so you can do it without making any mistakes,' explains Daddy. 'Because there's nothing so annoying for a magician as a trick that doesn't work.'

But Nibbles doesn't hear. Waving the magic wand and casting spells, he can practise tomorrow. He'll be a good magician soon.

September

The Magic Show

Nibbles has called his friends to the Friendship Tree. He has prepared a big magic show for them. Flopsy, Blinders and Hopper are really curious.

As the audience arrives, Nibbles stands there waiting for them. He wears a high, black magician's hat, a red cape and white gloves. The audience sits down and the show begins.

Nibbles is a little nervous. His hands shake a little, but everything seems to be going well.

'Welcome, ladies and gentlemen,' says Nibbles officially. 'I'm going to do a very difficult trick for you first.'

He takes a ball and shows it to the audience. 'Now watch closely.' He hides the ball in his hand. He shows his closed fist to the audience, then he takes his magic wand and says *Abracadabra* three times. Flopsy, Blinders and Hopper watch with wide eyes.

Slowly Nibbles opens his fist again. The ball is gone!

'Oooh!' breathes the audience totally astonished. They start clapping and stamping their feet. The magician bows formally to the audience. That was a really good show!

My, my, Nibbles is proud that he can finally do magic.

Wax

Mummy has collected a whole lot of candle stumps. The table is covered with them.

She breaks the candles into pieces and pulls the old wicks out. She puts the stumps into an old pan.

'What are you doing?' Nibbles wants to know.

'I'm going to make new candles from these old ones.'

'How do you do that?' asks Nibbles surprised.

'Just watch,' says Mummy. She takes the pan and sets it on the cooker over a tiny flame. Before long the wax is all melted. It looks a bit like pudding. Mummy has a bunch of toilet paper roll centres set up. She has closed one end of each one with tape. In the middle of each she also has put a new wick. Now she takes the melted wax and fills one after another.

After about an hour the new candles have cooled. Mummy uses a knife to cut through the toilet paper roll centres. Beautiful candles come into view. Nibbles looks them over carefully. They look just like they came from Miss Squirrel's shop.

Mummy did a good job! Now they will have lots of new candles to burn in the evenings. That will be lovely.

It's nice when you can turn old things into new ones, and sometimes it's not even hard to do.

The Pie Thief

Miss Hedgehog is really busy with her baking today, because she is having a big party. She has already baked four berry tarts. To let them cool, she has opened the kitchen window and put them on the window sill. The last five tarts are in the oven.

Suddenly Miss Hedgehog hears a noise by the window. She sees a hand reaching for one of the tarts. She stands still, then she slips outside really quietly. She's going to catch that thief!

It's probably Nibbles. That little rascal can always smell when she's baking. Then he comes by, just 'by chance.' But Miss Hedgehog doesn't mind, because she thinks Nibbles is a sweet youngster.

But what if he has come to steal a tart? That's not very sweet at all.

Now Miss Hedgehog is close to the window. She is going to teach this little thief a lesson.

With a quick movement she pounces on the thief and grabs his jacket.

'Ow! Ow!' But it's not Nibbles! It's… Mister Owl.

'I was hungry. When I left my shop, I could smell the tarts coming out of the oven. I couldn't resist coming here.'

Miss Hedgehog is really angry at Mister Owl. He wants to make it up to her. She appreciates that. For starters, he can wash up all the pots and pans that are piled in her kitchen.

Poor Mister Owl.

September

The Birthday Gift

Walter Weasel opens the door to his newspaper shop.

He is barely back behind the counter when his first customer arrives. It's Mister Tie. But Mister Tie doesn't come in. He stays outside.

'Why won't he come in?' Walter asks himself.

A little later, Mister Owl and Bert the Beaver come by, but they don't come in.

Walter can't understand it. Alas, if they don't want to come in, he can't do anything about it.

Before long there's a whole troop of villagers in front of the shop. He hears them cheering as Miss Hedgehog comes along. Then the whole group comes inside the shop, led by Miss Hedgehog.

'A very happy birthday to you, Walter,' she says.

'We have brought something for you.'

She gives Walter a big box with a ribbon around it. Walter is surprised, but he happily unties the ribbon and looks inside. He sees five berry tarts.

'Oh, thank you so much!' he cries excitedly. 'But five tarts is too much for me alone.'

Miss Hedgehog coughs to attract Walter's attention. She points to all the smiling villagers around her.

'Oh, I get it! Please help yourselves!'

That was why so many villagers came to the shop this morning. They are happy to share a bit of Miss Hedgehog's famous berry tarts. It's a nice day for them all.

Hopper Flies

It's storming outside. Everybody who doesn't have to be outside is staying safely indoors. Except Hopper. He's figured out a new way to fly. He has a huge old kite tied to his back. He can hardly walk. But with it on his back, he climbs onto his bike.

He tries to keep the wind at his back. It pushes hard on the kite. Hopper holds tight to the handlebars of his bike while the storm begins to move him slowly ahead. Bit by bit he speeds up until he's going pretty fast. That's why he's pedalling as fast as he can. He races through

the village. It won't be long before he takes off and flies.

Oh, no, there's a branch lying across the path! Hopper's wheel bangs into it really hard. He flies over the handlebars. But just before Hopper hits the ground, a blast of wind from the storm roars through the village and carries him through the air!

'I'm flying! I'm flying!' yells Hopper. Just at that moment, though, the wind drops. Hopper drops like a rock – right into the brook.

Soaking wet and covered in mud, Hopper crawls out. The kite is still on his back and he hurts all over. But he certainly did go flying!

The Ghost

It's late in the evening and high time to go to bed. Mister Owl climbs upstairs, yawning. As he comes into his bedroom, he's startled: right in front of him flutters a thin, white thing.

Whooo! Whooo! it goes.

'A ghost,' screams Mister Owl, and he runs out of the room.

What was that? Mister Owl can feel his heart pounding. What do you do if you have a ghost in your house?

As Mister Owl recovers from his shock, he decides something. He's going to get rid of that ghost.

In the kitchen, Mister Owl finds a big frying pan. He carries it upstairs as quietly as he can. He carefully opens the bedroom door. The white thing is still there.

With a loud shout, Mister Owl charges into the room. He swings the pan and knocks the white thing to the ground. Then he jumps up and down on it until he can't jump any more.

Exhausted, Mister Owl turns the light on.

The white thing was no ghost at all. It was his shirt that he washed this morning and hung there to dry. But he forgot it. Now his shirt is totally dirty.

Whooo! Whooo! Now Mister Owl gets it. The howling sound was the wind outside.

He was wrong in many ways tonight.

181

September

Tiger

A dangerous animal sneaks through the Mouse family's garden. It's a tiger. Not a real one, of course. No, it's another one of Nibbles' funny games.

The tiger is hunting. He has just spotted some prey. The tiger is ready for anything…

Not aware of danger, his prey comes wandering down the path. It's Miss Hedgehog. She has a basket on her arm.

Roarrr! she hears. The tiger jumps at his prey. With his claws he grabs Miss Hedgehog's jacket while he growls loudly.

'Help!' cries Miss Hedgehog. 'I'm being attacked by a tiger!'

'I'm going to eat you up!' growls the tiger.

'But I have such delicious honey biscuits for you, tiger,' cries Miss Hedgehog.

Suddenly, the wild tiger changes into a tiny, sweet kitty.

'For me?' it purrs.

'And for your sister,' says Miss Hedgehog.

Nibbles lets Miss Hedgehog go and goes inside with her.

That Miss Hedgehog is really something. She can bake so well, as we know. But who would know she could tame tigers?

Ballerina

'I want to do that too,' says Flopsy. She's watching ballet on telly. Girls in pink tutus are dancing gracefully to piano music.

Flopsy runs to her bedroom and puts on a dress that looks a lot like a tutu. Then she turns on some music.

A little later Flopsy is twirling around her bedroom like a real ballerina. She makes a leap just like they did on telly. Her arms swing from left to right.

Then Flopsy comes to the highpoint of the dance, the pirouette. That's where the ballerinas turn round and round really fast.

Flopsy begins to twirl. She goes faster and faster, until she feels dizzy. She stops. But even though she has stopped, it seems like her room is spinning around her. She has to hold on to something or else she will fall down.

After a while the dancing goes better. When the music stops, she steps forward to make a deep curtsy. You've never seen a lovelier ballerina.

September

Mister Mouse Makes…

Mister Mouse has been hammering and sawing in his workshop.

'What's Daddy making?' Nibbles asks Mummy.

'I don't know,' she answers, 'but he says he needed to make it right away.'

Nibbles can't imagine what it could be. He plays some more with his toy soldiers, which are scattered all over his bedroom floor.

That evening Daddy is done. He brings a lot of wooden panels into the house. Then he sets them up together.

Nibbles looks at it curiously. What has Daddy made?

All of a sudden he knows: it's a chest. But Nibbles doesn't say anything yet. What if it's really something else? Then he might get laughed at, and he doesn't want that.

A short while later Daddy is nearly finished. He screws doors onto the chest. He attaches a bunch of latches. When all of that is done, Daddy pushes the chest against the wall.

'OK!' he exclaims at last. 'What do you think of your new toy chest?'

'Toy chest?' asks Nibbles in surprise.

'Yes. Now you can finally put away all your things instead of leaving them scattered all over,' laughs Daddy, while he picks up some of the toy soldiers in the living room.

Nibbles isn't sure what he thinks of the toy chest. But he knows that he won't be leaving his toys around any more. Nibbles helps out. Before long, the room is clean.

Rag Doll

Old Miss Crow and Flopsy are busy working on a project together. They are making a rag doll out of left-over pieces of cloth. While Flopsy cuts pieces of cloth, Miss Crow sews them together. Slowly a lovely rag doll begins to take shape.

'She needs hair,' says Miss Crow. She takes some pieces of yellow yarn and cuts them to the same length. Then she sews them to the doll's head. She ties a ribbon around the ends so the doll has two plaits. They look great.

Now they give the doll a face. Miss Crow takes two buttons out of her sewing box. They will become eyes. Flopsy thinks that's nice. Miss Crow sews them in place.

What about a mouth and a nose? Miss Crow

has no ideas. But Flopsy does. She picks up a pen and draws the mouth and nose.

Now the doll is done. Almost. Flopsy has another idea. She takes the pen again and gives the doll eyelashes and a some smile lines.

'Isn't that nice?' laughs Miss Crow. 'Now your doll looks just like a little girl.'

'My doll? We made her together, so she belongs to us both.'

'That's true, dear, but you may have her. I'm a little too old to play with dolls.'

And so Flopsy gets a nice new doll.

Protector

Misty, Nibbles' sister, wants a honey biscuit. But it's not biscuit time.

'If I take one for myself, nobody will notice,' she thinks.

Mummy keeps them high up in the kitchen cupboard. That's where Misty is heading. She takes a chair and puts it near the cupboard. Then she climbs up on the chair.

'Oh, bother,' grumbles Misty. 'I still can't reach them.'

Misty is disappointed and she walks away from the chair. But wait: What if she puts a stool on top of the chair? Maybe then she can reach the biscuits.

Misty picks the stool up and puts it on the chair. It wiggles a bit. But Misty isn't worried. She crawls up on the chair and then on the stool. If she can reach out her hand now, she can touch the cupboard where the biscuits are.

Suddenly, the stool starts to fall. Misty loses her balance. The stool lands on the floor with a crash. She closes her eyes and waits until she lands on the floor too.

But she doesn't hit the floor. It's too soft. What's going on?

When she opens her eyes, she sees that Nibbles has caught her in his arms.

'I just barely caught you, Misty. You almost had a very bad fall.'

What a nice brother. He really is her protector.

Miss Squirrel Has a Visitor

24 SEPTEMBER

Nibbles is going to the shop of Miss Squirrel for Mummy. In his hand he has a list of the things he needs.

When he goes into the shop, he says hello to Miss Squirrel, who's standing behind the counter. Miss Squirrel says hello back.

Nibbles gives her the list and Miss Squirrel reads it over.

'A bag of hazelnuts, a package of flour and six eggs.' Miss Squirrel goes looking for them.

'Hazelnuts. I wonder where they are?'

She looks all over the shelves but she doesn't see them.

'There, on the left,' helps Nibbles.

'Oh, yes. Now the flour…' mumbles Miss Squirrel.

Nibbles thinks to himself, 'Miss Squirrel seems a little confused today. She didn't spot those hazelnuts.'

At that moment, Miss Squirrel comes into the shop.

'Are you finding everything, sister?' she asks.

'No, I can't find the flour,' says the first Miss Squirrel.

'Behind the bread,' says the other.

'Nibbles,' says the second Miss Squirrel, 'I'd like you to meet my twin sister, Bitsy. She's visiting me for a while.'

Nibbles can't believe his eyes. They look exactly like each other!

'Pleased to meet you,' says Bitsy, handing him his

things.

Boy, twins can make life confusing.

The Bridge

25 SEPTEMBER

The bridge over the stream is old and wobbly. When you walk over it, it creaks and groans as if it could fall apart at any second. One day, after a storm, Mister Sack starts his postal rounds, but he can't cross the bridge. It isn't there any more.

'It must have fallen apart last night during the storm and washed away,' thinks Mister Sack. 'How annoying.'

There's nothing to do but to go and report it at the city hall.

A while later, he is back at the stream with Mister Owl.

'This is a real disaster,' mutters Mister Owl. 'How can we reach our friends on the other side of the stream?'

'Can we help?' a voice asks suddenly. When Mister Owl looks around, he sees Bert Beaver and Mister Mouse with their carpentry tools beside them.

'You are just in time and most welcome,' laughs Mister Owl.

'At your service,' says Mister Mouse. 'Come on, Bert, let's not waste time. Here we go!'

The two woodworkers hammer and saw with lots of noise and laughing.

By midday they have set six posts into the stream. The bridge will rest on them. By sunset the bridge is done. The new one is much prettier than the old one. Everyone agrees on that.

Mister Mouse and Bert are exhausted. The villagers give them a round of applause. As a reward Miss Hedgehog brings them slices of berry tart. They really earned them, didn't they?

Full Moon

'Tonight we have a full moon,' says Hopper to his friends.

'What does that mean?' asks Blinders.

'Some people turn into werewolves!' says Hopper with a scary look.

'Where-whats?' asks Flopsy.

'Werewolves. They are half man, half wolf. They eat you up.'

'Yucky,' say the others.

'Wait!' says Nibbles. 'You said half man, half wolf?'

'Yes,' answers Hopper.

'Well, we aren't people, we're animals.'

'Oh, yeah, so then we can't turn into werewolves,' says Flopsy.

'Maybe so,' says Hopper.

'It would be weird to see your face, if you turned into a werewolf. You'd be a were-frog.'

'And I'd be a were-mole,' laughs Blinders.

'Or a were-mouse,' says Flopsy, pointing to Nibbles with a giggle.

'And you, Flopsy? You'd be a were-rabbit. Watch out, you carrots, the were-rabbit is loose.'

The friends laugh until tears run down their faces. They have so much fun.

But that night, as Nibbles lies in bed, he wakes up hearing a noise outside. He perks up his ears and sits up. 'Maybe that's the were-rabbit, who's just murdered a carrot,' laughs Nibbles. He lies back down and goes to sleep.

September

The Idea

Nibbles and his friends are going to see Mister Tie, the tailor. They enjoy visiting him because Mister Tie is a nice fellow.

In his workshop hang all sorts of nice clothes. The youngsters like to look at them.

'Mister Tie?' calls Flopsy. 'Have you thought of giving a fashion show, so everyone can see your work?'

Mister Tie looks up from his sewing. He strokes his chin and thinks about it.

'That's not a bad idea,' he says. 'That would be nice to do.'

'Yes, let's have a fashion show!' says Nibbles.

'But I think that's going to take a lot of work,' says Mister Tie. 'I'll need your help. Can I count on you?'

'Just tell us what to do!' smiles Nibbles. 'We'll do all we can.'

Mister Tie takes a pen and paper and writes a message.

'Please take this to Walter Weasel at *The Village Courier*. He should put this invitation to the show in the paper.'

'OK, I'll do that,' says Hopper, and he's gone in a flash.

'We'll need to build a stage, find models and fit clothing. It's going to be a lot of work,' sighs Mister Tie.

'Don't worry, Mister Tie,' says Nibbles. 'You can count on us.'

The Models

It's in today's *Village Courier*: 'Tomorrow Mister Tie is holding a fashion show. Everyone is welcome.'

In his shop, Mister Tie is the centre of a storm of activity.

While he sews, Nibbles and Flopsy hang the finished clothing on hangers.

Hopper and Blinders are working outside with Mister Mouse and Bert Beaver. They are building a stage. It will be a long, narrow platform where the models will walk to show off Mister Tie's clothes. Daddy and Bert are hammering and sawing like crazy.

Suddenly, two customers enter the shop. They look exactly like each other. It's Miss Squirrel and her sister Bitsy.

'We hear that you're looking for models for your fashion show, Mister Tie,' they say.

'Yes, and I'm glad to see you,' says Mister Tie. 'To have twins in the show would be wonderful. Miss Hedgehog and the youngsters are also going to model. Now I just need a few fellows.'

'Why don't you ask the two outside?' asks Bitsy.

'Super idea,' says Mister Tie. 'I wouldn't have thought of them.'
Mister Tie goes outside and asks Mister Mouse and Bert Beaver.

'It will certainly be different from hammering and sawing,' laughs Bert. 'Sure, we'll model for you.'
'That's great,' says Mister Tie. 'Thanks. I'd better get back to work now.'

September

29 SEPTEMBER

The Collection

Mister Tie and the youngsters stand in front of a long rack. It's filled with clothing that Mister Tie has made. Today they will see who will wear what. That's why Mister Tie has brought his models together. They stand in a row: Miss Hedgehog, Nibbles, Hopper, Flopsy, Blinders, the Squirrel sisters, Mister Mouse, Bert Beaver and Mister Owl. Despite his tummy, he wants to model. There

is just one problem: there's nothing big enough for him. That's annoying.

'Can we let him do something else?' asks Mister Tie.

It gets quiet. Nibbles has an idea: 'We could let him present the show. As mayor, he's used to speaking.'

'Why of course,' exclaims Mister Tie. 'Brilliant idea. What do you think, Mister Owl?'

'Sounds good to me. But just one thing.'

'And that is?' asks Mister Tie.

'Could you make me a new outfit for the show? I really want to wear something you made.'

'Of course. I'll get started measuring you now,' says Mister Tie.

While Mister Tie makes a suit for Mister Owl, the rest go home. Because tomorrow is the big day. Tomorrow is the fashion show!

Fashion Show

It's a perfect day, with warm sunshine, a gentle breeze and happy chatter filling the air. The villagers have arrived and settled in their chairs. They know they are going to see something really special.

'Ladies and gentlemen, welcome to Mister Tie's Fashion Show!' cries Mister Owl. 'You will see the finest clothing from his collection today. Therefore please welcome our models.'

A hush falls over the crowd as they wait for the show to start. How exciting!

Miss Hedgehog and Flopsy walk hand in hand. The villagers clap and cheer, twisting their heads to see better.

Miss Hedgehog wears a white dress and Flopsy a pink glittering dress. They look lovely.

Then Bert Beaver and Mister Mouse come to the stage. They wear sturdy workmen's clothes that have been turned into elegant suits. They look very cool.

Then Nibbles, Blinders and Hopper come to the stage. They wear funny pyjamas.

Everyone blinks as the Squirrel sisters walk to the stage. They wear exactly the same beautiful red flowered dresses and look exactly alike. And they move exactly alike, as if they were mirror images. Everyone holds their breaths because they look so lovely.

The Squirrel sisters smile and nod at the villagers. It is a magic moment.

'So, ladies and gentlemen,' cries Mister Owl at the end, 'that was our fashion show. Before we say goodbye, I'd like to ask for your applause for the designer of these wonderful clothes. Your warm applause for Mister Tie!'

While the villagers cheer, Mister Tie comes to the stage a little shyly. 'Bravo!' cry the villagers. Mister Tie begins to blush. He's such a sweet fellow.

October

bed, for sure.

Then Mister Sack sees something on the ground. It's a plump acorn.

'That's what it was! An acorn falling from this oak tree,' says Mister Sack. He looks up in amazement at the tree. Then he notices that the trees aren't green any more. They have turned a beautiful shade of brown, with some green and orange leaves mixed in. Just then a few leaves drift down and one lands at Mister Sack's feet. A light goes on in his head.

'It's autumn!' he cries in surprise. That's why the acorn fell. It won't be long before all the leaves fall too. That's the way it is in the autumn.

Autumn in the Countryside

Early in the morning, Mister Sack, the postman, is on his rounds. He walks along the path, whistling cheerfully. Sometime later he comes to a big oak tree, which is Mister Owl's home. Suddenly Mister Sack feels something hit his head hard.

'Ow!' he cries. That hurt! He sees stars. He feels his head. A bump is growing up there.

'If this is some kind of joke Mister Owl is playing, I'm going to have a word with him,' thinks Mister Sack. But when he sees that all the curtains in Mister Owl's house are still drawn shut, he decides Mister Owl isn't playing with him. He's still in

Mister Tie is Befuddled

Mister Tie is wearing his finest suit and he is adjusting his tie in front of the mirror. He brushes his hair and then goes to his bedroom. Suddenly he sees he doesn't have his shoes on. He hurries to the shoe rack and picks out his best pair. He polishes them with a shoe brush until they shine like a mirror. Then he puts them on and ties his laces so their loops are exactly the same size.

'Fine,' says Mister Tie, 'that's how I want to look tomorrow.'

Now he takes the clothes off. He hangs things up and puts them away carefully, then dresses in normal clothes.

Sighing, he sinks down on the sofa in the living room. But just as he thinks everything is ready, he slaps his forehead. Mister Tie goes back to his bedroom. He puts a letter in his jacket.

'Finally, everything really is ready,' he murmurs. But he has the feeling that he has still forgotten something. What could it be?

'Of course, the flowers!' he exclaims.

Mister Tie rushes out to order flowers. He's certainly very befuddled today. As he passes by Miss Hedgehog's house, he smiles. Could the flowers be for her? Is he so befuddled because of Miss Hedgehog? We'll have to wait until tomorrow to see.

The Conversation

As Flopsy walks through the village, she goes by Miss Hedgehog's house. What does she see? It's Mister Tie. He is wearing his finest suit and has a beautiful bouquet in his hands.

'Hello, Mister Tie,' she calls to him.

Mister Tie looks like he's daydreaming and barely sees Flopsy. That's not like him.

'Are you OK?' she asks concerned.

Mister Tie jumps a little. When he sees Flopsy, he waves to her. She quickly comes over to him.

'My, don't you look chic, Mister Tie,' she says. 'Do you have special plans today?'

'Yes, very special,' he replies nervously, 'with Miss Hedgehog.'

'Are those flowers for her?'

Mister Tie nods. 'I like her a lot. That's why I brought them.'

'She'll love them,' smiles Flopsy. 'Why don't you ring the bell?'

Mister Tie blushes. 'I… I don't dare,' he says.

'But you visit her almost every day. Why can't you today?'

'I want to ask her something very important. That's why I'm so nervous.'

Flopsy doesn't get it.

'You know what,' asks Flopsy. 'I'll ring the bell for you. Then it's done.'

She stands on tiptoes to reach the button.

Ding-dong! it sounds. Flopsy hurries away. Miss Hedgehog opens the door and lets Mister Tie inside.

Flopsy wonders what Mister Tie could want to ask Miss Hedgehog. She's really curious!

October

In the Newspaper

Nibbles plays in the living room while Daddy Mouse reads the paper, sitting on the sofa.

Suddenly, Daddy cries out to Mummy, who's in the kitchen, 'Guess what!'

Mummy comes quickly and looks at Daddy with a question on her face.

'Miss Hedgehog and Mister Tie are going to get married.'

'How lovely,' smiles Mummy. 'They make a fine couple. When will they marry?'

'In a few days,' says Daddy. 'The whole village is invited.'

'Aha!' thinks Nibbles. 'Now I get what Flopsy told me yesterday.'

Nibbles saw Flopsy yesterday and she told him about what happened when she saw Mister Tie. She told him about the nice suit, the bouquet and how nervous he was. She said he wanted to ask Miss Hedgehog something important, but she didn't know what it was.

'So he asked her to marry him,' grins Nibbles. He runs outside. The whole village is in a stir about the wonderful news. The twin Squirrel sisters are talking with Walter Weasel about how to decorate the village. Daddy Mouse and Bert Beaver are planning to build a giant table for the wedding feast. Mister Owl runs to his house so he can write a fine speech. 'My goodness, if this isn't going to be a big party, I don't know anything,' laughs Nibbles.

Washing Up

Just as every night, the dishes need washing up. But Nibbles hates it. Still, the youngsters must help Mummy every night.

'It's a good lesson for the rest of your life,' Mummy always says. 'Could you help me clean up?' she asks, while she fills the sink with water.

Misty and Nibbles stack the plates and put the forks and knives on top. While Nibbles takes them to Mummy, Misty collects the glasses.

194

Now the washing starts. Mummy washes the dishes and puts them on the drying rack. Misty picks up a tea towel. And Nibbles? He sneaks away…

'Be careful not to drop anything,' smiles Mummy at Misty. Misty is so helpful. She holds the dish and wipes it dry. She sets it aside and picks up the next one.

'Well done!' encourages Mummy.

Meanwhile Nibbles is hiding in the living room.

Suddenly, Mummy is standing beside him.

'Nibbles?' she asks angrily, 'why aren't you helping with the dishes?'

Nibbles doesn't know what to say.

'You aren't doing your best to share our work. That is not nice. So tomorrow, you will help me with the dishes. Misty doesn't have to, because she's done her best today.'

Silly Nibbles. That's the last time he'll sneak out from work, that's for sure.

The Artist

Flopsy decides it's time to visit old Miss Crow again. It's been a while. She knocks on the door. A friendly voice calls out, 'Come in!'

She sees Miss Crow sitting on a chair in front of an easel that holds a painter's canvas. Beside her is a box full of tubes of paint. She holds a brush in one hand and a painter's palette in the other.

'Hello, Flopsy,' she smiles, 'you're just in time. I need someone to pose for me.'

'Pose?'

'Yes,' laughs Miss Crow. 'Painting is my new hobby. If you don't mind sitting still for a while, I'll paint your portrait.'

Flopsy is delighted. Miss Crow carries on with her work. She looks carefully at Flopsy and gets busy with her brush.

Flopsy must sit still for some time before Miss Crow is done. Finally she can take a look. She has been so curious!

It looks great.

'I didn't know you could paint so well,' says Flopsy very impressed.

'Thanks, dear,' says Miss Crow. 'You may have this. You sat long enough to earn it.'

Flopsy gives Miss Crow a big hug. What a lovely present.

October

Wood Gathering

'Hey, Hopper, do you want to go wood gathering?' asks Nibbles.

'Wood gathering? What's that?' Hopper wants to know.

'Collecting branches. Daddy uses the branches to start our fires in the fireplace,' explains Nibbles.

'OK,' says Hopper. They walk into the woods. Nibbles has a huge basket to hold the branches they find on the ground.

A sharp wind starts blowing, bending the branches here and there. The leaves fly off the trees and swirl around.

'I always wonder how this wood gets on the ground,' Hopper says.

Just at that moment a blast of wind shakes the trees. In one tall tree, a branch breaks off. It lands with a crash right at Hopper's feet. He jumps and yells.

'That's the answer to your question,' laughs Nibbles.

'You said it,' answers Hopper still startled. 'The basket's full, so can we get out of here?'

They take the basket and go home quickly. When there's a strong wind, it's better to stay out of the woods.

Nut Gathering

Miss Hedgehog is walking in the woods with a basket on her arm.

Autumn is a wonderful time to go collecting nuts. She looks forward to cooking with them and eating them in the months to come.

While she searches, she has the strange feeling that someone is watching her. Then she hears a branch break and she turns around.

'Nibbles! What are you doing here?'

'I saw you over here and I wondered what you were doing,' answers Nibbles.

'I'm gathering nuts. I do this every autumn. I bring them home and use them in my baking and cooking all winter long. And they are nice snacks too,' she explains.

'I like nuts in my breakfast cereal,' Nibbles smiles.

'Me too,' agrees Miss Hedgehog. 'In the winter there are no berries or nuts in the woods, so this is our chance.'

'Would you like some help?' asks Nibbles.

'Sure,' laughs Miss Hedgehog, 'as long as you don't eat too many.'

Nibbles promises that he won't and together they get to work.

Nuts for the Winter

9 OCTOBER

Flopsy and Nibbles are going to visit Miss Hedgehog. They can't wait to help her with a nice job. Yesterday, she collected nuts from the woods. Today, she will prepare them for her food cupboard and winter treats.

As they arrive at Miss Hedgehog's kitchen, they are welcomed by the lovely scent of toasted nuts.

'I toasted them last night,' says Miss Hedgehog. 'Would you like to try some?'

She gives them each a handful and they eat them up in no time.

They taste wonderful.

'Can you help me put them into the jars?' asks Miss Hedgehog. Flopsy and Nibbles are happy to do that.

Nibbles holds a jar while Flopsy pours the toasted nuts into it. When it's full Flopsy puts a lid on it. Before long, the whole table is covered with jars.

Miss Hedgehog takes some labels and writes what's in each jar. On two of the jars, she writes something else. She shows Nibbles and Flopsy. They can't read, but they know how to read their names and they see them on the labels.

'Why did you write our names?'

'Because you helped me so much. I wanted to give you each a jar of toasted nuts.'

The youngsters are thrilled. They give Miss Hedgehog big hugs and run home with their gifts.

Riddle

10 OCTOBER

Just before bedtime, Mummy tells Nibbles a riddle. He listens carefully.

'What runs around with a question now and sleeps with an answer?'

Nibbles stares at Mummy, thinking hard. What a hard riddle.

'Think it over while you brush your teeth.'

Nibbles goes to the bathroom, thinking. While he brushes his teeth, he repeats the riddle once more.

He tries to figure it out. He forgets about time.

'Nibbles, it's bedtime, OK?'

He rinses his mouth and runs to bed.

'Have you figured it out?' asks Mummy eagerly while she tucks him in.

'No,' sighs Nibbles disappointed. But as he lies there, the answer flashes through his mind.

'The answer is that it's me!' he crows. 'I run around asking what the answer to the riddle is. Now I go to sleep with the answer: me!'

'Good for you,' laughs Mummy. 'I thought you'd figure it out.' She gives Nibbles a good-night kiss.

'Sleep well, you clever boy,' she smiles as she turns out the light.

Then Nibbles falls asleep. With the answer.

A Pile of Leaves

Nibbles and Misty are in the garden. Somebody has raked all their fallen leaves into a pile.

'Hey, look!' cries Misty.

They run over to it and look at all the colourful leaves, admiring the golds, browns and greens.

Flopsy throws an armful of leaves into the air. They float down, filling the air with wonderful smells.

Nibbles has other ideas. He walks away from the pile, takes a run and jumps into the middle of it. The dry, soft leaves make it seem like he is jumping into bed.

They take turns jumping until they are exhausted. Nibbles picks up a leaf, turns it over and looks at it carefully.

'Isn't this a beauty?' he says showing Misty.

'I want one too,' says Misty.

'Let's look together for one for you,' says Nibbles. They begin to dig in the pile. Suddenly, Misty holds one up. Alas, that one has a hole in it. She doesn't want that. She throws it away and digs further. The leaves fly around. Nibbles has found one that seems nice.

'No, not that one either,' says Misty. They keep diving into the pile, scattering leaves all over as they do.

At that moment, Daddy Mouse comes into the garden.

'Who said you youngsters could do this?' he asks angrily.

'We're looking for a leaf for Misty,' explains Nibbles meekly.

'That may be, but I worked hard to rake all those leaves into this pile. Now you've scattered them all over again. That's not nice.'

'Uh-oh,' say Misty and Nibbles.

'Would you please help me clean them up again?' Daddy asks.

The youngsters are happy to. Together they get the leaves back into a pile.

Suddenly, Misty gasps. She has just found a perfect leaf! Now everybody is happy.

Bath Time

'Nibbles, Misty,' calls Mummy. 'It's bath time!'

She's filled the bath with warm water. It's full when the youngsters climb in. Now the fun can begin.

In no time, they are splashing, laughing and having a ball. Mummy goes to the kitchen.

Misty flutters her feet in the water so it flies around. Nibbles says, 'Hey, I can do that too,' and he starts flutter-kicking too.

'I've got a better idea,' squeals Misty. She stands up, then flops down to sit in the water. A wave of water washes over the edge of the bath.

'Watch this,' roars Nibbles. He sits on the edge of the tub, then slides into the water, sending another wave over the side.

Mummy comes back. The floor is flooded with water.

'What has got into your heads?' she asks angrily. 'The floor looks like a swimming pool.'

Misty and Nibbles look cautiously over the edge of the bath. They certainly have made a mess. While Mummy mops up the flood, the youngsters begin to play again. But they play a little more quietly this time, since they don't want to make Mummy angry again.

Pink

Flopsy loves pink. It's her favourite colour. Her whole bedroom is pink. Pink walls, pink curtains, a pink bed and a pink wardrobe.

It's time that the walls get a new coat of paint, thinks Daddy. He's brought a brochure along that shows various colours of paint.

There are soft greens, like spring leaves. There are bright yellows, like the centres of daisies. There are calm, peaceful blues, like the most beautiful sky you ever saw. And there are even different kinds of white: creamy white, sparkling white and a sort of greyish white.

Flopsy and Daddy look at all the different colours and then look all around the room.

'Maybe you'd like to try another colour,' he suggests. Flopsy has no interest in that. The walls will stay pink.

'What if I paint just one wall white? White goes well with pink. If you don't like it, then I'll make it pink again. You can choose.'

Flopsy isn't so sure. She decides to let Daddy try it, though.

Daddy gets a tin of white and a tin of pink paint and gets to work. He paints the biggest wall of her room white. The others will stay pink.

When he's done, he calls to Flopsy. 'Come take a look.'

Flopsy comes slowly into the room. She's pleasantly surprised. The white wall is bright and it makes the pink walls seem pinker. She loves it.

'See?' laughs Daddy. 'Sometimes it's good to try something new. That's how you discover nice things.'

Daddy's right.

Hedgehog would love to get a glimpse of that drawing. But Mister Tie has put a book over it so she can't see it.

While he measures her waist, Miss Hedgehog notices that Mister Tie has forgotten to put the book back over the drawing. If she can just bend over a little, she can see the drawing! Carefully she leans forward. She almost can see it now…

Mister Tie is done. He walks over to the work table and writes a number on the drawing. Then he picks up the book and covers the drawing again. Too bad for Miss Hedgehog. She still didn't get to see it.

The Wedding Dress

Mister Tie is making a wedding dress for Miss Hedgehog, because the day after tomorrow they are getting married.

Miss Hedgehog is not allowed to see the dress yet, though. It's going to be a secret. She can only see it on their wedding day. Miss Hedgehog doesn't mind. She's sure that Mister Tie will make a lovely gown for her. Still, she'd like to see it just once…

Mister Tie takes Miss Hedgehog's measurements. That way he knows how big to make her dress. After he measures how long her arm is, he writes it down on his drawing of the gown. Miss

October

Picking Flowers

15 OCTOBER

Nibbles, Flopsy, Hopper and Blinders are going flower picking in the woods. They need flowers for Miss Hedgehog and Mister Tie's wedding. They want to decorate the village for the big day tomorrow.

They look and look for flowers, but don't find any. They walk further, along narrow paths. After a while, when they are almost ready to give up, they come to the edge of the woods and see a field of flowers.

'Ooof,' sighs Hopper, 'I thought we'd never get here.'

'There are plenty of flowers here!' cry the others.

They quickly get to work. Their baskets are nearly full of flowers when they hear an angry voice.

'Who has ruined my flower patch?'

The youngsters look at each other in fear. A dark shape comes straight toward them. It's Bert Beaver. If he sees their baskets full of flowers, he's going to be mad.

'You have ruined my whole garden.'

'We didn't know it was yours,' stammers Nibbles.

'The flowers are for Miss Hedgehog and Mister Tie's wedding,' offers Flopsy.

Bert's angry face changes suddenly and he smiles. 'Oh! For the wedding? Oh, that will be nice for Miss Hedgehog and Mister Tie.'

The youngsters breathe a sigh of relief. If they ever go flower picking again, they will make sure that they ask permission first.

The Wedding

16 OCTOBER

The big day has finally arrived. Miss Hedgehog and Mister Tie are getting married. The whole village has gathered in front of Miss Hedgehog's house. They have decorated it with flowers and ribbons. Now they are waiting for Miss Hedgehog and Mister Tie to come out in their wedding outfits. The villagers can't wait to see them.

Suddenly the door opens. Everyone holds their breaths as Miss Hedgehog and Mister Tie step outside. Oh, they look lovely. Miss Hedgehog's lacy dress is a dream. The villagers clap and cheer.

They go up the path, followed by the villagers. Nibbles, Hopper, Flopsy and Blinders scatter flowers ahead of them on the path. At the village square Mister Owl awaits them. Miss Hedgehog and Mister Tie can sit down in front of him. Then the ceremony

202

begins.

At least…

Mister Owl feels around in his trouser pockets. 'Where did I put the wedding rings?' he mumbles to himself anxiously.

Mister Tie coughs and Mister Owl looks up at him. Mister Tie points to the little box that's on Mister Owl's chair.

'Ah, yes, of course,' laughs Mister Owl.

Then he asks Miss Hedgehog if she wants to marry Mister Tie. She answers, 'Yes.' He asks Mister Tie the same question. He also says yes with a smile.

'Then I declare you to be married to each other!' says Mister Owl in an official voice.

Miss Hedgehog and Mister Tie give each other a big kiss. What a lovely wedding.

The Wedding Feast

It's still quiet in the village, because it's barely morning.

That's because the party is finally over. Miss Hedgehog and Mister Tie are married now. Last night the whole village was invited to the wedding feast. There was music and dancing. Nibbles and his friends had a wonderful time twirling and jumping around to the music. After a while Nibbles slipped away.

The music ended a little later. A drum roll rumbled in the distance. The villagers looked around in surprise. Nobody knew what it was. They looked toward where the drum sound came from.

Here they came. Nibbles was first, as the drummer. Behind him you could see some lights in the darkness, coming closer and closer. Miss Hedgehog, Mister Tie and the rest of the villagers held their breaths.

From out of the darkness the Squirrel sisters appeared, carrying an enormous wedding cake that was decorated with countless candles. Those were the lights they saw coming.

Loud applause and cheers greeted them and soon the cake was eaten up. And then? Then the party continued until the early morning.

October

Stomach Ache

18 OCTOBER

Mister Owl has a stomach ache – a bad one. He can't get out of bed. When Miss Squirrel hears that, she comes to see him.

'How are you feeling?' she asks concerned.

'It hurts! It hurts!' he groans.

'Let me take a look,' says Miss Squirrel. Mister Owl shows her his tummy. Carefully she touches it.

'Ow!' cries Mister Owl. 'That hurts!'

Miss Squirrel pulls her finger back. She thinks: what has Mister Owl been doing in the last few days? Of course there was the big wedding feast…

'How many pieces of wedding cake did you eat at the feast?'

'Uh… three,' answers Mister Owl.

'Three? No more?'

'Well, maybe four…'

'Four? And after those four?'

'Uh… another two…'

'Another two?' cries Miss Squirrel in surprise. 'You had six pieces of cake? You should be ashamed of yourself. What a greedy little…'

'Ow, it hurts,' Mister Owl whimpers.

'That's because you ate too much. There's only one cure,' says Miss Squirrel.

'You need to stop eating for a day and only drink water. Will you promise to do that?'

'Yes, yes,' moans Mister Owl, 'I promise.'

Poor Mister Owl. Of course you get a stomach ache if you eat so much wedding cake!

Big Fish, Little Fish

19 OCTOBER

Nibbles is lying on his tummy in the bath. All around him are little toy fish. They are his prey. He is a shark today. He imagines he has a big, grey fin on his back. His baby teeth are horrible, sharp shark's teeth.

Out of the corner of his eye, Nibbles sees one of the toy fish drifting toward him. 'That's a delicious snack for a hungry shark,' he thinks. Very slowly, the fish drifts closer to Nibbles' mouth. Nibbles is ready to strike. He lowers his face a bit more in the water. The little fish is close now.

Nibbles strikes! He snaps at the fish. Because he opens his mouth under water, he takes some water inside. It floods into his nose too. Nibbles gulps and snorts and sprays water out.

'Cough-cough-cough!' he splutters, while he sits up straight.

Mummy comes running into the bathroom. 'Are you choking?' she asks worried.

'Cough!' answers Nibbles.

Mummy takes his arms and holds them over his head. That helps you if you are choking. Suddenly, his coughing stops.

'That was a tasty snack, wasn't it?' smiles Mummy. 'Are you OK now?'

Nibbles nods. He turns back on his stomach and becomes a shark again. Because he still wants that little fish. But he won't try to swallow it again.

Daddy Mouse Makes…

Daddy Mouse is hard at work in his workshop. Nibbles and Misty, playing in the garden nearby, hear him sawing and hammering again. What could Daddy be making now?

After a while they see Mummy go into the workshop with a big roll of wrapping paper. What's going on?

Mummy and Daddy come out a while later with a big package. The youngsters spring up. What's in that package?

'Happy Birthday to You, Happy Birthday to You…' sing Mummy and Daddy. It's Misty's birthday! They didn't realise that.

Misty takes the package and tears the wrapping paper off. It's a lovely doll's house.

'I made it all myself,' says Daddy. 'See the chairs and tables? And the beds and chests? Downstairs is the kitchen and living room. And upstairs is a bathroom and two bedrooms. What do you think of it?'

Misty stands open-mouthed, looking at her present. She has never seen anything like this and she is thrilled. But that's not all.

Mummy has made a birthday girl's crown for Misty. She sets it carefully on her little head.

'Now everybody will know it's your birthday,' smiles Mummy.

Misty goes back to marvelling at her new doll house. My, Daddy has done a wonderful job. What a daddy he is!

October

On a Beautiful Autumn Day…

21 OCTOBER

'What a lovely autumn day,' the twin Squirrel sisters say to each other. They each pick up a basket and walk down the path.

'I'll take this wild rose bush,' says Miss Squirrel, 'so would you like to take that one, further down the path?'

'Sure,' her sister Bitsy replies.

Sam Stork, the police officer, comes walking by.

'Good afternoon, Miss Squirrel,' he says politely. 'My, that's a nice dress.'

'Thanks, Sam,' answers Miss Squirrel busy picking.

Sam walks further. But what does he see? Here's Miss Squirrel again. And she has changed her dress. How could she do that so fast?

He walks back a few steps and looks back.

Now Miss Squirrel is back where she was and amazingly, she's changed back to her first dress. Sam doesn't get it.

Miss Squirrel notices Sam staring at her in amazement.

'Oh, Sam, have you met my twin sister Bitsy? She's just down the path a bit.'

Now Sam gets it: it wasn't Miss Squirrel he saw down the path, but her twin sister. Sam heaves a deep sigh. He thought he needed new glasses.

Coming Home

22 OCTOBER

All the villagers have gathered together. Something special is happening. Nibbles and Flopsy are there too. They are peering up into the blue sky.

'Do you see anything yet?' Nibbles asks Flopsy.

Flopsy shakes her head.

Somebody cries, 'There they are!'

They all look in the same direction. They watch a white dot in the blue sky that slowly gets closer. It's a swan. She's flying toward the village.

'Make room, make room!' orders Sam Stork, the police officer. Everyone moves to make a free space in the centre of the village square.

The swan flies slowly to the middle of the space. Around its neck is a basket. She lands gently and

sets the basket on the ground. She taps on the basket. A little door opens and Miss Hedgehog and Mister Tie look out.

'How was your honeymoon?' everyone asks.

'Fantastic,' smiles Miss Hedgehog, while she helps Mister Tie out of the basket.

'We saw marvellous places and had some wonderful meals,' says Mister Tie.

'Yes,' Miss Hedgehog continues, 'and I collected a whole new set of cake and biscuit recipes.'

That's music to Nibbles' ears. He will visit the couple soon.

The Advertising Stunt

Miss Squirrel has an idea. She has lots of tins of tomatoes in her storeroom. She wants to sell them as fast as possible.

So she decides to build a huge tower of tins in the middle of her shop.

She goes to the storeroom and takes out a big, heavy box full of tins, putting it on the floor of the shop. Then she gets another box and then another.

She gets to work. She stacks the tins on each other.

She works the whole evening so the tower is ready for the next day. She puts a sign on top that says, 'Two for the price of one!' She's sure that with such a stunt, she will sell a lot of tomatoes.

The next morning Mister Owl comes in with his shopping basket. When he sees the tower of tinned tomatoes he stops. He looks at the sign.

'What a bargain,' he thinks. He bends over and takes a tin from the bottom of the tower. Oh no, he shouldn't have done that! The tower begins to wobble and then falls apart with a crash.

Mister Owl stands there in shock, with the tin of tomatoes in his hand. He looks at Miss Squirrel in astonishment.

'Here,' stammers Miss Squirrel, while she picks up a second tin from the floor. 'The second one is free.'

'That was quite a stunt,' puffs Mister Owl.

Miss Squirrel smiles a bit sadly, 'That's true. It was.'

Poor Miss Squirrel. Now she has to build the tower all over again.

October

fast too. He gnaws on the trunk as if it were a giant sweet.

It's a very exciting competition. They both do their very best.

Suddenly there's a cracking sound. Daddy Mouse's tree begins to sway. Then another crack from Bert's tree. Then both trees fall to the ground with an enormous crash. But who won?

'I think it's a tie,' says Daddy Mouse.

'Me too,' sighs Bert, while he wipes sweat from his forehead.

'It doesn't matter,' laughs Daddy Mouse. 'It's clear we are both champions!' They laugh and clap each other on the shoulder. Such good friends!

The Challenge

In the woods stand two old trees. They don't have any leaves any more. That's why Daddy Mouse and Bert Beaver want to cut them down and use them for firewood.

'Hey, should we have a contest?' asks Bert. 'Whoever cuts his tree down first wins, OK?'

'OK! I'm up for the challenge,' laughs Daddy Mouse. He picks up his axe and walks over to one of the trees.

Bert Beaver doesn't need an axe. He will cut his tree down with his teeth. That will be a show, for sure.

'1-2-3 Go!' yells Daddy and the two get started. Daddy chops as hard as he can. But Bert works

What an Idea

Nibbles is going to visit Miss Hedgehog. She's always baking something: cakes, tarts, biscuits. But she also bakes bread. Today, as she takes a fragrant, golden-brown loaf of bread out of the oven, Nibbles watches with his mouth watering.

'Since you bake so well,' says Nibbles, 'why don't you open a bakery? We don't have one in the village.'

She looks at him in surprise.

'Nibbles, that's a great idea!' she exclaims.

Actually, Nibbles was joking, but she is serious. She thinks it's a fantastic idea. That way she can spend all day doing what she loves to do and get paid for it too.

She takes a piece of paper and begins to draw her bakery - where the oven and counter must go and where the bread racks stand.

'My dear husband can make the curtains, too. He's so clever.'

But then Nibbles has some doubts. If she opens a bakery, then he won't get any more free biscuits and tarts, will he?

'Oh, Nibbles, of course you will. First, because we are friends and then to thank you for your good idea.'

Nibbles sighs in happiness and relief.

'From now you must call me Helen, because we are real friends,' she smiles, handing him a slice of bread.

'OK… Thanks… Helen.'

As Nibbles walks home, he has a big smile on his face. He has a good friend and he had a good idea.

The Bakery

Daddy Mouse and Bert Beaver are busy building Helen Hedgehog's bakery. It's a lot of work. They need to make a glass case, a counter, bread racks and lots more.

Helen has drawn everything very clearly. She knows exactly how it should be.

Nibbles, Flopsy, Hopper and Blinders have come to lend a hand. They get to paint the walls. They love that. They paint with lots of noise and energy.

'Try not to spill,' warns Helen Hedgehog.

Here comes Mister Tie. He's made curtains for the brand-new bakery. Helen is thrilled with them.

Walter Weasel stops by. When Helen tells him she's opening a bakery, he decides to make it a front-page news story in the paper. That way the whole village will know about it.

Meanwhile Daddy Mouse and Bert Beaver have finished their work. It looks wonderful.

The youngsters soon finish their painting too. Now the curtains can be hung and the bakery is set to open.

'It's a lovely shop,' says Mister Tie.

'Yes, and it's going to be a big success, right, Helen?' asks Walter.

'I think so, thanks to you all. And here's something for you from the new bakery owner!' She cuts into a lovely cake she's made as a thank-you present for her friends.

Cream Pie

A long queue stretches out of the bakery that Helen Hedgehog has just opened. Mister Owl waits patiently and when it's his turn, he spots a cream pie and buys it.

'See you soon,' says Helen as he leaves smacking his lips.

But just as he goes through the door, he trips on the threshold and falls. His beak lands right in the middle of the cream pie.

Helen helps him up right away. She wipes the cream from his face with a cloth.

'Did you hurt yourself?' she asks anxiously.

'No, no,' says Mister Owl. 'But my beautiful cream pie is ruined.'

'Please take another,' offers Helen Hedgehog.

Moments later, Mister Owl starts to leave with his new cream pie.

He walks down the path, anxiously peering over and under the box to make sure he doesn't stumble on a branch or step into a hole. He takes his time, thinking happily about the treat he has in store for himself. He just loves cream pies!

He looks carefully as he crosses his threshold. Inside his door, he trips over his door mat. Once again, he lands in his pie, face first.

Oh my! It's just not his day.

Two Chickens

Mummy and Daddy have cleaned the spare room specially, because Granny and Granddad are coming for a visit.

When the bell sounds, the youngsters rush to the door. Alas, it's not Granny and Granddad. Two chickens stand there.

'Good morning,' says one of them, 'have you ordered two hundred eggs?'

The youngsters are astonished. When Mummy and Daddy come to the door, the chicken asks the same question.

'Absolutely not!' answers Mummy. 'What would I do with two hundred eggs?'

'Make a big omelette?' suggests the other chicken.

Nibbles recognises the voice of the second chicken.

'That's Granny's voice!' he cries in surprise.

The two chickens pull off their masks. And sure enough, it's Granny and Granddad.

'We thought we'd play a little joke on you,' says Granddad.

'It was a good one,' laughs Mummy.

'If Nibbles hadn't recognised my voice we could have gone on with it longer,' laughs Granny. 'But he's too smart to fool.'

While Granddad and Granny take off their chicken suits, Daddy and Nibbles carry their suitcases inside. It's already fun having them visit.

October

Storm

29 OCTOBER

'Be good,' say Mummy and Daddy. They are going to a party. Granny and Granddad will stay with Misty and Nibbles tonight.

When it's bedtime, Granny and Granddad take Misty and Nibbles to bed.

'It's going to storm tonight,' says Granny as she closes the curtains. 'I hope it doesn't rain too hard.'

She gives Nibbles and Misty each a good-night kiss. Outside the storm starts.

A bit later Granny and Granddad go to sleep. Just as they are climbing in bed, Misty comes into their room.

'I'm scared,' she says. 'The wind is making scary sounds.'

Granny and Granddad hear how the storm is whistling through the trees and making the roof creak.

'I have an idea,' says Granny. 'Why don't you sleep in our bed tonight? Then you'll be safe from the storm.'

She doesn't have to ask twice. Misty jumps in between them. She falls fast asleep.

'How cute,' smiles Granny. But just as she starts to turn out the light, the bedroom door opens. This time it's Nibbles.

'Are you having trouble sleeping because of the

storm, too?' asks Granddad.

Nibbles nods. Granddad pulls back the bedclothes and pats a spot beside him.

'Here's a safe spot. Your sister is already here.'

Very relieved, Nibbles slips in beside Misty, between Granny and Grandad. It's so nice and warm that he falls fast asleep in a moment. He doesn't hear the storm any more at all.

After the Storm

30 OCTOBER

Granddad is taking Nibbles and Misty for a walk around the village.

'Let's look around to see if there was any damage from that storm last night,' he says. When they go outside, they see that the whole garden is

212

covered with leaves and broken branches. The path is covered too.

A little further on a big fallen tree lies across the path.

'That was blown down by the wind,' says Granddad, pointing to its roots.

'It must have been a big storm,' Nibbles replies. They walk around the tree.

'It's blocking the path, so I'll go and tell the mayor. Then someone can move it away,' says Granddad. He hurries off. Misty and Nibbles want to stay there and look at the tree.

Nibbles goes over to it. He climbs up on the trunk.

'Don't do that, Nibbles,' says Misty.

Nibbles doesn't listen to his sister. He walks along the shaking trunk, his arms stuck out for balance. Suddenly, he slips and loses his balance. He falls behind the trunk.

Luckily Granddad sees this on his way back. He runs to Nibbles and finds him in the middle of a big puddle, soaking wet, crying loudly. Granddad helps him up. Luckily he isn't hurt, but he's certainly scared. He has himself to thank for his scare.

The Catapult

Hopper has found a long piece of elastic. He wants to make a catapult with it and launch himself into the air. Hopper still wants to be the first flying frog.

He gets to work right away. He looks for two trees that will work, then ties one end of the elastic to one of them. He ties the other end around the other. OK, his catapult is made.

Just like a real stunt pilot, Hopper has a helmet on. You never know.

He stands between the two trees with his back against the elastic. Now he just has to stretch it and then it will launch him through the air.

Hopper pushes back into the elastic until it's stretched tight. It's not easy, because the more you stretch it, the harder you have to push to stretch it further. But Hopper is convinced and with one last push back, he stretches it to the limit.

Alas, sometimes elastics just snap when they are at their limits. And that's what happens. Hopper, who was leaning back hard on the elastic, falls backwards as it snaps and breaks. His arms and legs fly around. He lands with a splash in the stream.

'Bah!' splutters Hopper as he climbs out of the stream, dripping wet. 'That didn't work either.'

Poor Hopper. He really wants to fly!

213

November

Granddad's Photo Album

Nibbles sits on Granddad's lap. They are looking at a really old photo album together. There are lots of black and white photos of Granddad when he was a small boy. He looks so different!

In one photo Granddad is in a tree house. It looks just like Nibbles' tree house. Granddad is wearing shorts.

'He looks like someone I'd like to play with,' thinks Nibbles.

Granddad turns the page.

'That's Granny when she was little. Doesn't she look lovely?' laughs Granddad.

'That was a long time ago,' says Granny, who just came by.

Nibbles nods at Granny. 'I think you still look lovely,' he says.

Granny laughs. 'Say, what have we here?'

Nibbles looks at the photo that Granny is pointing to. It looks like it's Nibbles, sitting on a rocking horse. But it can't be, because the photo is old.

'That's your daddy when he was your age,' explains Granny. Nibbles can't believe his eyes. Daddy looks just like him. Or is it the other way around?

'Funny, isn't it?' laughs Granddad. Nibbles asks himself if he will ever be a Granddad himself. Maybe his Grandson will look just like he does now. Who knows?

Saying Goodbye

Two suitcases stand in the hall. Granddad and Granny are going home. Nibbles and Misty think that's a shame, because they love them.

'We'll come back soon,' promises Granny. 'Meanwhile, if you want to come and visit us, you are always welcome.'

As a goodbye present, Nibbles and Misty have made something for Granny and Granddad. They made two little figures of Granny and

Granddad out of toilet paper rolls. Granny and Granddad think they are great.

And Granny and Granddad have goodbye presents for Nibbles and Misty.

Granny takes two bags out of her pocket. When Nibbles sees them, his nose begins to twitch. He smells something, but what is it?

'Nibbles, can you smell what it is?' asks Granny.

He has no idea, but something smells wonderful. To tease him, Granny waves the bag in front of Nibbles' nose, but Nibbles is too excited to really guess well.

Granny hands them the bags and gives them each a kiss. They open the bags.

'Honey biscuits!' Misty exclaims.

'How could I miss that?' laughs Nibbles. 'Thanks, Granny.'

Then it's time for Granny and Granddad to go. Mummy, Daddy, Nibbles and Misty wave until their car disappears in the distance. Let's hope they come back soon.

Ironing

Flopsy's mummy is ironing. A mountain of clothes and things sits on the table next to her. Flopsy wants to help her, but she can't. Ironing is very dangerous. If you don't watch out, you can get burnt badly.

After Mummy has done lots of ironing, she goes to get a cup of tea from the kitchen. Flopsy decides to show Mummy that she can iron too and now's her chance. Flopsy has done a lot of ironing with her toy iron.

Carefully she goes to the ironing board. She takes one of Daddy's shirts and puts it on the ironing board. Then she takes the iron and puts it on the shirt. It hisses softly. Just as Flopsy begins to iron, she hears Mummy's footsteps. Flopsy runs out of the room, but she forgets to take the iron off Daddy's shirt.

Mummy sets her cup of tea on the table. She takes a sip, then turns to the ironing board. When she sees the iron on the shirt, she shrieks and quickly takes it off the shirt.

Too late: the iron has burned a big hole in the shirt and ruined it. Mummy calls angrily for Flopsy. Things don't look good for her!

215

Skeleton

Blinders has fallen on the stairs. He wasn't watching. Now he's crying. Here comes his mummy to help him. She checks to see if he's really hurt himself and takes him in her arms. Luckily it's not too bad, except for one leg. But when Mummy gives him a kiss, the pain goes away.

'You are lucky you didn't break it,' says Mummy.

'Break it?' asks Blinders.

'In your whole body you have a skeleton that's made out of bones,' explains Mummy. 'You have bones in your feet, your legs, your arms, your fingers. They make the frame for your muscles. Your muscles are stretchy and they are attached to your bones and make them move. Feel how when you move your arm, the muscles do the work?'

Blinders moves his arm and feels the muscles getting hard and then soft. That's cool.

'But what did you mean about breaking a bone?'

'Sometimes if you fall, a bone breaks. It hurts a lot. You have to go to the hospital. A doctor puts a plaster on it so the bone can't move for a few weeks. That can be annoying, but it's the way to help the bone grow back together.'

'Skeletons and bones are cool,' thinks Blinders. But not broken bones. He's not interested in them at all.

Knitting

It's getting cooler outside every day. Mister Owl goes to his wardrobe to get a warm jumper. All of his are worn out. He really needs a new one.

But what does he spot at the bottom of the wardrobe? A shoe box with two knitting needles and some balls of coloured wool. Should he knit himself a jumper?

Full of determination, Mister Owl sits down on the sofa and gets to work. It's been a long time since he has knitted. It goes very slowly.

Sometimes the wool falls off his needles. Sometimes the stitches are far too tight. Other times, they are far too loose. Mister Owl is getting upset. He begins to get the feeling that he has forgotten absolutely everything he ever knew about knitting.

Meanwhile, Mister Owl is cold. A chill runs down his back. He's been knitting all morning and has only made a piece as big as a handkerchief. This is going to take a long time.

He's so cold now that he's shivering. He can hardly hold his needles. They finally fall out of his frozen fingers. He's got to think of some other way…

That evening Mister Owl sits on the sofa with a beautiful woollen jumper on. He runs his hand along the soft, warm wool and admires the rich brown colour of the jumper. A big smile spreads across his face and he leans back to enjoy the evening feeling cosy and happy.

He's put his knitting away in the shoebox. He hasn't finished it.

How did he get that woollen jumper? You must be wondering.

He went to Mister Tie's shop and bought one. It's really very simple. That goes a lot faster.

looks out.

Thick, grey clouds hang over the village and drop rain on it all day. The leaves are all gone from the trees now, so the trees look sad.

The village isn't busy like it usually is. The paths are empty, because of the weather.

'What a sad day,' sighs Walter. 'It's high time for a change. It's time for COLOUR!'

Walter goes to his desk and picks up his pen. He begins to write:

'Join *The Village Courier's* colouring contest. Make a colourful picture and bring it quickly to the newspaper shop. Maybe you'll win a prize!'

Walter smiles as he reads his message again.

'I'll hang all the drawings up in my shop. Even though it may be dark and grey outside, I'll be surrounded by lovely, happy, colourful drawings.'

Now all he has to do is print his message in *The Village Courier* to start the contest.

Walter starts smiling again. Isn't it amazing how much happier a good idea can make you feel?

Colour

Walter Weasel sits in his shop window, watching for customers. It's pouring with rain outside, so he probably won't get many today. Walter sighs while he

November

Hard at Work !

Misty and Nibbles are busy at work. They've set a big box of coloured pencils on the table. They're each making a drawing for Walter Weasel's contest. Nibbles has drawn a sun. It's done now. Misty has bigger plans. She wants to cover her paper with colours, so she needs lots of coloured pencils. She hunts through the box. A lot of them have broken nibs.

But Mummy has a good cure for that problem. She gets out an old pencil sharpener. It's so big that you have to screw it onto the table edge. She sets it up. Then she sticks a pencil into it. Now she turns the handle and soon the pencil has a sharp, new nib.

Now Misty can get to work. Her tongue sticks out of her mouth as she works on colouring the paper. It takes a long time. Misty is determined to win the contest with her picture. She colours and sharpens, colours and sharpens, until several hours later, she's done. Just in time, because the deadline for the contest is coming up soon.

When Mummy takes a look, she sees that the coloured pencils are gone.

'Misty, where did you put them?' she asks.

'I sharpened them all up for my drawing until they disappeared,' answers Misty.

Now that's hard work!

The Prize Winner

All the villagers who entered the colouring contest are in Walter Weasel's shop. Today the winner will be chosen.

'… and since it was so grey outside, I thought, why not organise a colouring contest? That way I can hang all the colourful drawings in my shop and it will be bright and sunny inside even if it's grey outside.'

He has succeeded at that. The walls of his shop are full of happy, colourful pictures.

'Now then,' he goes on, 'it's time to announce the winner. Naturally, everybody who drew something will get a little gift, but there is one special winner.'

He is silent for a moment. Everyone holds their breath. He pulls a yellow envelope from his pocket and opens it. Then he reads the name written on the card inside.

'Misty Mouse!'

Misty comes forward as all the villagers clap and cheer. She really didn't expect this. Walter gives her a big package. She tears it open. It's a huge box of coloured pencils. At first Misty is speechless.

'I used all my old pencils up to make my drawing,' she explains. 'Now I have more than enough to do some more. I'll make another drawing for the village and I'll do my best to make it a beautiful one.'

The villagers clap and cheer again. Misty is such a sweetheart.

because it's cold out.

Look! It's Nibbles and his daddy. Their hats are pulled down over their ears and they have warm mittens on their hands. Their cheeks are pink from the cold. Their scarves cover their noses. They keep on pulling the cart.

They stop in front of old Miss Crow's house and unload the cart. They bring the wood inside, then Nibbles shuts the door.

'So,' Daddy says to Miss Crow, 'now you have enough wood to keep you warm for the whole winter.'

'It's so kind of you,' says Miss Crow. 'Can I make you some hot chocolate?'

'That sounds great in this cold weather,' says Nibbles.

Soon he and Daddy are sipping their hot chocolate. They really earned it, didn't they?

Wood for Miss Crow

Whooo, whooo goes the wind through the bare trees. It's a raw wind that comes straight from the North Pole. In the distance, two figures walk along a path. They have thick, warm clothing on. They are pulling a cart that's filled to the top with wood. It's very heavy. But they pull hard and slowly but surely they move along.

Let's look closer. Better get your hat and scarf,

November

Aaat-chooo!

When Nibbles' mummy goes into Helen Hedgehog's bakery, she hears a loud *Aaat-chooo!* It's Helen. With red eyes and a handkerchief, she's standing behind the counter.

'You don't look good,' says Mummy worriedly.

'I'b gut a code,' sighs Helen.

'Poor you,' says Mummy. 'You should be in bed.'

Helen shrugs. 'Who wud open da shop, den?' she asks.

Mummy thinks it over. 'I could do it for you. I can help your customers.'

'Wud you mine?' asks Helen.

'I'd be happy to. Now you make a cup of tea with honey and go to bed.'

She doesn't have to say that twice. Helen needs to get to bed.

Mummy puts on one of Helen's aprons. She looks like a real baker.

Ding-dong, goes the bell as the first customer comes into the shop.

'Good morning,' Mummy says.

'Good morning,' answers Walter Weasel. 'Do you have a loaf of brown bread for me?'

'Of course,' answers Mummy. 'Would you like it sliced?'

Walter nods.

She puts it into the slicing machine. When it's sliced, she puts it neatly into a bread bag. Walter pays for the bread and says goodbye.

'See how well I can do it?' smiles Mummy pleased with herself. 'Helen can rest well and get better faster now.'

No Post Today

Heavy fog hangs over the village today. Mister Sack, the postman, has trouble making his rounds to deliver the post. He can hardly see his hand in front of his face. So he feels his way from tree to tree. He needs to take care not to lose his way. Finally, he sees the vague shape of a big postbox. It's surely the Mole family's postbox, Mister Sack thinks. He had no idea he had gone so far. He thought he'd be at Mister Owl's house by now.

Mister Sack takes out the letters for the Mole family. He looks for the slot in the postbox. He can't see it. What's going on? He reaches out to feel for the slot.

'Help!' yells the postbox in shock. Mister Sack jumps back.

'But…' thinks Mister Sack, 'that's Mister Owl's voice.'

'Mister Sack, is that you?' asks the postbox anxiously.

'Uh, yes, it's me. Is that you, Mister Owl?'

'Yes. I've been waiting for you. With this fog I

was afraid you might miss my postbox. And you did – you thought that I was my postbox.'

'Sorry about that. I can barely see my hand in front of my face,' complains Mister Sack.

'Well, why not come in,' suggests Mister Owl. 'Everyone will understand that you can't work in this fog. You could have an accident or get lost.'

So that's why there was no post today in the village.

So Cosy

It's freezing out. Mister Mouse lights a fire in the fireplace while the youngsters get ready for bed upstairs. Mummy has laid out clean pyjamas for them. They are winter pyjamas and they are nice and warm. When they have them on, they go downstairs.

'Can we sit close to the fire?' asks Nibbles.

Daddy says they may. They go to sit near the fireplace. They watch the dancing flames and enjoy the pleasant warmth.

Daddy lights some candles and turns out the lights. He picks up a thick book. 'Shall I read you a story?' he offers.

The youngsters think that's a great idea. While he reads, Mummy comes in.

'My, it's so cosy here. I have something with me that will make it even cosier.' Mummy has two cups of hot chocolate for Nibbles and Misty.

While they sip, they listen to the story. Mummy comes and sits next to them and they lean on her.

After a while the story ends. Daddy closes the book softly. The youngsters are sleepy. They yawn.

Gently Daddy and Mummy carry them up to bed. They tuck them in and give them good-night kisses. It was such a cosy evening.

November

Cold Hands

When Nibbles comes home, his hands are frozen. He holds them near the fire. That feels wonderful.

'Your hands must be cold,' Mummy says.
'They're nearly frozen.'

'Nibbles, why didn't you wear your mittens?' asks Mummy.

'I had them on, but they are old and full of holes.'

'Why didn't you tell me?' asks Mummy unhappily. 'We will buy you new ones right now. Get your jacket and scarf.'

A little later Mummy and Nibbles are in Mister Tie's shop.

'What can I do for you today?' he asks.

When he sees Nibbles' worn-out mittens, Mister Tie knows the answer. He opens a drawer that's full of mittens and gloves. He takes out several pairs for Nibbles to try on.

Nibbles picks a green pair with little chunks of cheese on them. He thinks they are perfect.

'Do you have a scarf and hat as well?' asks Mummy.

'Oh, yes,' answers Mister Tie. He reaches into another drawer and takes out a matching scarf and hat.

Nibbles puts them on and looks in the mirror. He thinks he looks super cool. 'I want these,' he says excitedly.

On the way home, Nibbles admires his new things. They are soft and warm but they look cool. Now winter can begin.

Ice Bunny

A cold wind blows through the village this early morning. Mister Sack, the postman, is setting out on his rounds.

'Gosh, it's cold,' he groans. 'It's really time that the post office gives me a new winter jacket.'

Shivering with cold, he walks on with his heavy sack. The sack is heavy because he has a big package to deliver today. Mister Sack doesn't know who it's for, but he'll find out soon.

He has only delivered two letters when it begins to rain. The rain runs over his old jacket and soaks in. Mister Sack is even colder now.

He has only one more letter to deliver and then that big package. By the time he has delivered the letter, he is frozen to the bone.

Finally he grabs that big package out of his sack so he can read the address on it.

'Look at that!' he exclaims. 'It's for me!'

He opens the package right away. A letter is enclosed.

'Dear Mister Sack, we are sending you this new winter jacket today. It's really warm and also is waterproof. So stay warm and dry. Sincerely, The Post Office."

'Oh, my. If I had only opened this package this morning, I'd be warm and dry right now, instead of being a frozen bunny.'

Poor Mister Sack. But tomorrow he'll be happy.

Bert Beaver Visits

It's freezing cold in the village. There's frost on everything and everyone is wearing their warmest clothing.

Mister Tie is busy in his tailor shop. The doorbell rings. He looks up from his work. Bert Beaver comes into the shop. They greet each other warmly.

'Cold enough for you?' asks Bert.

'Yes, yes,' laughs Mister Tie. 'It's like the North Pole here. Tell me, friend, what I can do for you today?'

'Here's the deal. I have mittens for my hands, a thick jacket for my body, thick trousers for my legs, woollen socks and boots for my feet, a scarf for my neck and a hat for my head. Only…'

Mister Tie nods expectantly.

'Only my tail has nothing to keep it warm. So I wonder if you can make something for it.'

Mister Tie is glad to give it a try. He measures Bert's tail and gets to work. In an hour he has it done. It's a big sack with a zip on the top side. Bert pulls it on over his tail.

'So, there's your… tail warmer,' laughs Mister Tie.

'It's perfect,' says Bert happily. 'I'll never have a cold tail again. Thanks a lot.'

'Glad to help. What else are friends for?'

That's the truth. Friends help each other keep warm.

223

November

Wood Stove

16 NOVEMBER

The villagers are staying inside as much as they can now because the icy wind is blowing so hard. But now and then, they have to go out. Who's that poor villager with the big shopping basket coming down the path?

It's Nibbles. Mummy asked him to get a few things for her. It's much colder than he thought. Brrr! Finally he gets to Miss Squirrel's shop. Nibbles opens the door and hurries in.

It's so nice and warm inside. Nibbles gives his shopping list to Miss Squirrel.

'Here,' she says, 'let me make you a cup of hot chocolate so you can warm up while I get these things.'

'Oh, that would be great,' laughs Nibbles. When he takes a sip, he can feel the warmth going all the way down to his toes. Lovely!

When the cup is empty, his things are ready. Nibbles heads home. Even though it's still cold, Nibbles doesn't feel it as much.

'That must be because of the hot chocolate,' he thinks. 'It's keeping me warm. I feel like a little wood stove. A stove that runs on hot chocolate.'

A Nice Story

17 NOVEMBER

There's a nice story in *The Village Courier* today.

Sam Stork, the police officer, was making his rounds in the forest. As he went by a deep hole, he heard a voice. To his surprise, the thief, Roger Fox, was trapped in the hole.

Sam carefully helped Roger out of the hole and then brought him to the police station.

'I'll put him in jail,' thought Sam. But the fox was shivering so hard from the cold that Sam decided to let him warm up in front of the wood stove. He gave him a cup of warm soup.

'Thanks, Sam! I was in trouble and you saved me. Without you I might have died from cold and hunger. I promise I'll always do whatever you ask of me.'

'Whatever?' asked Sam.

'Whatever,' says Roger.

'Then promise me you won't ever steal again.'

Roger promised that. He's going to be a good citizen from now on for the rest of his life. And from that day on, Roger was completely changed.

That's what it said in the paper. A nice story, isn't it?

Ice Fun

The whole village is hurrying toward the swimming pool that Bert Beaver made. Bert has told everyone that something special is going to happen. Nibbles and Hopper are on their way too. They wonder what Bert's going to do. It can't be swimming, because the water is frozen.

When they get to the pool, they see Bert standing on the ice. He has ice skates on.

'Dear friends,' he says formally, 'I hereby declare the swimming pool closed, due to the cold weather and the ice rink opened. In that rack over there you'll find skates. Find your size and come skating with me.'

Once everyone has found a pair of skates, they all go out on the ice. But practically nobody knows how to skate. It's one giant falling-down party. Luckily nobody gets hurt and as people fall, they are laughing.

Nibbles and Hopper hold on to each other as they go on the ice. My, is it slippery! They watch what Bert does. He glides over the ice as if it's easy as can be. Nibbles decides to give it a try. He barely starts to move before he's sitting on the ice. Flopsy laughs hard. But her laughing makes her fall down, which makes Nibbles laugh even harder.

If they want to learn to skate, they are going to have to work on it a little more.

Skating Lesson

Bert Beaver is giving skating lessons to all the youngsters in the village. Blinders, Hopper, Flopsy and Nibbles stand on the ice, wearing their skates. They hold on to each other to keep from falling down.

Bert has to laugh. It can only get better!

The youngsters watch fascinated, as Bert shows them what to do.

'See?' he asks. 'Which of you wants to try first?'

Hesitantly, Nibbles raises his hand. Bert takes him by the arm.

'We're going walking on the ice,' says Bert. 'We take long steps and after each step we glide.'

Nibbles does exactly what Bert says. He lets himself

glide over the ice.

'Very good,' encourages Bert. After a while Nibbles can do it by himself. Bert goes back to the others, while Nibbles goes on skating.

'See how easy it is?' he asks. 'Who's next?'

Hopper, Blinders and Flopsy look at each other. They're not so sure.

While they decide, Nibbles comes gliding by his friends. He wants to stop, but Bert hasn't taught him that yet.

'Get out of my way!' he cries in warning. But it's too late. He crashes into them. All of them fall down on the ice.

Silly Bert. If you teach someone to skate, you need to teach them how to stop skating too.

Mister Owl Has an Idea

One evening Mister Owl goes to Bert Beaver's ice rink. He wants to see what it is that has impressed all the villagers so much. He's heard so much talk about how nice the ice rink is and how much fun it is to ice skate. When he sees the frozen swimming pool, a smile appears on his face. It looks wonderful.

Carefully Mister Owl steps onto the ice. It's good, solid ice, he finds.

Then an idea begins to grow in his mind. A really good idea. He goes to Bert Beaver's house and knocks on the door. Bert is surprised to see Mister Owl at his door this late at night.

'Hello Bert,' says Mister Owl, 'I want to ask you something.'

Bert invites Mister Owl to come in.

After a while they both come out.

'So that's arranged,' says Bert. 'See you tomorrow morning, Mister Owl.'

Next Mister Owl goes to Walter Weasel.

'Walter, you need to print something in your paper for me,' he says.

'No problem,' says Walter. He notes what Mister Owl tells him on a piece of paper. When he's done, Mister Owl says, 'Put it in a box so everybody is sure to see it.'

'Good idea. I'll do that,' smiles Walter. 'See you soon.'

Mister Owl heads home satisfied. He can barely wait until tomorrow night. Because something big is going to happen. You'll find that out tomorrow.

November

On a Cold Night in the Woods…

As it gets dark, Nibbles, Misty and their parents go outside. They have their warmest clothes on, since it's still freezing. They aren't the only ones out. The whole village seems to be on the path to Bert Beaver's ice rink. Tonight is the annual Mayor's Ball. The invitation was in this morning's paper. Everyone is welcome. Nibbles and Flopsy run ahead.

'Look how beautiful it is,' cries Flopsy in surprise, when she sees the rink.

The whole ice rink is decorated with coloured strings of lights and ribbons. It looks like a fairy tale.

When everybody has arrived, Mister Owl greets the crowd.

'Dear friends, please get your skates on, because this year I'm giving a different kind of Mayor's Ball. We are going to dance on the ice.'

Mister Owl has barely finished when an orchestra starts playing lively dance music. As soon as they have their skates on, the villagers go out on the ice and start skating.

All around the ice there are little stands offering hot chocolate, honey biscuits and even cream pie. Flopsy and Nibbles watch the fun as they snack. The rink is full of couples skating arm in arm. The Mayor's Ball this year is one that will never be forgotten.

Slippery

Hopper comes out of his house with a bucket filled with water. It's very heavy, but Hopper still manages to carry it to the path in the forest. In the middle of the path he pours the water out.

A big puddle is growing there. Some of the water sinks into the ground, but some stays above. Since it's still freezing weather, a big, slippery spot is left.

Now Hopper hides behind some rocks. 'This will be funny,' he whispers.

Here comes Helen Hedgehog. She's got a huge basket full of bread and she's walking straight towards the icy spot.

'Uh-oh,' groans Hopper. 'This is going all wrong.' He wanted to play a joke on Nibbles, Hopper and Flopsy, not any grown-ups. But it's too late now. Helen steps on the ice and slips. She lands on the ground and the loaves of bread in her basket roll out onto the path.

'Owww!' moans Helen, as she slowly stands up.

'My goodness, it's slippery here,' she says, 'I could easily have broken a bone.' When she notices the bread all over the ground, she cries, 'Oh, no, all my bread for Miss Squirrel's store is dirty. What a shame.' She puts the bread back in the basket and goes home to bake more.

All this time, Hopper is watching from behind the rocks. He realises that he has done something very stupid. Now he sees that playing on slippery ice is not a good idea.

Ice Hockey

23 NOVEMBER

Bert Beaver has built a few rows of seats around the ice rink. They are called the stands. He has set two goals on the ice. The villagers are going to watch a hockey game. Loud applause and cheers come from the stands as the two teams skate onto the ice. The players all have hockey sticks. They'll use them to try to shoot the puck, a flat little black disk, along the ice and into the other team's goal.

One team wears red shirts and the other team wears yellow shirts. Mister Owl is the referee and he wears black and white. He blows his whistle and the game begins.

The red team gets going. Mister Sack, the postman, hits the puck hard toward the other team's goal. But Mister Tie, who's on the yellow team, stops the puck. When he tries to hit it back toward the other goal, the whole red team comes skating toward him. The rest of the yellow team chases them. Mister Tie gets scared and freezes in place. With a smack, the red team crashes into Mister Tie and then the red team crashes into everyone. The whole group slides out of the ice rink and lands in the stands. Groaning and moaning, the players start to get up. They all have bumps and bruises. They've had enough and they leave the rink complaining and grumbling. It was the shortest hockey game in history.

November

Icicles

When Nibbles, Flopsy, Hopper and Blinders arrive at the Friendship Tree, they see something weird. Icicles hang from the tree. They are long sticks of ice.

'Look, it's an ice lolly,' Hopper says, breaking one off. 'Not bad. Try one.'

The friends think they are great.

'Let's sell icicles,' suggests Flopsy. The friends like her idea. While Flopsy and Hopper pick icicles, Nibbles and Blinders build a stand on the path. As soon as it's ready they can start selling.

'Icicles – all shapes, small, medium and large!' calls Nibbles as loud as he can. 'Icicles!' repeat the others.

They stand there calling and calling, but nobody comes. It looks like nobody is interested in icicles. There's nobody but themselves to enjoy them. They each take one and suck on it. My, they are cold! They suck them until they are gone. After a while Flopsy has a stomach ache. It isn't long before the others do too. It must come from the icicles. Suddenly, they aren't interested in icicles either. They want to go to bed. Nibbles throws away the rest of the icicles and they run home. Hopefully their stomachs will feel better soon.

Ice Crystals

Slowly Nibbles opens his eyes. It's already eight o'clock. But that's not bad, because it's a Sunday. The whole village is fast asleep. Nibbles stretches and sits on the edge of his bed, putting on his slippers. He goes to the window. What's the weather like today?

Curious, Nibbles lifts the corner of his curtain. He sees something weird and beautiful on his window. There's a huge, white drawing, with wild leaves and curves and stars. Who drew it?

Nibbles runs out of his room. The window in the hall has another white drawing. Who's been

230

doing this? Maybe it's a joke Daddy is playing on the family?

Nibbles decides there's only one way to solve the mystery: go and ask Daddy. He slips into the bedroom where Daddy and Mummy are still sleeping.

Daddy opens one eye and sees Nibbles standing beside him.

'What is it, son?'

'Someone has painted white pictures with sparkling stars on our windows.'

'What?' Daddy asks in surprise. He jumps out of bed and walks to the window. When he opens the curtains, he bursts out laughing.

'Those are ice crystals, Nibbles. You can feel them. They happen if it's really, really cold outside. Beautiful, aren't they?'

Nibbles nods. He wishes there were ice crystals on his window every day.

One More Time?

26 NOVEMBER

Finally the freezing weather has gone away. The sun is back and it shines like it used to. The ice is melting.

Bert Beaver decides to go skating one more time before the ice rink disappears. He puts on his skates and steps onto the ice. The ice cracks under his weight. Bert wonders if it's safe to skate today. Finally he decides to do it.

Cautiously Bert begins to skate on the melting ice. It is fine until he gets to the middle. The ice snaps suddenly and big lines of cracks burst out all around him. Bert stands still in shock. Then there's a loud crack and Bert quickly sinks through a hole in the ice. The water is freezing cold. Bert loses his breath.

Luckily, he is in a shallow part of the pool. He can stand in the water with his head out of it. He swims to the side and starts climbing out. It's not easy, but finally he makes it.

Dripping wet and shivering with cold, Bert looks back at the huge hole in the ice. He's lucky he could get out. 'It could have been a lot worse,' he thinks with a shudder. Then he takes off his skates, puts his shoes on and runs to his house. It takes him hours to warm up. He learned a lesson today.

To the Moon

We all know that Hopper wants to be the first frog in the world to fly. But now he wants to go to the moon, which this evening is a beautiful crescent in the sky. He knots together all the pieces of rope he can find. At the end he makes a loop. He wants to use the rope as a lasso and catch the tip of the moon. Then he can climb up.

'I have to aim well,' he encourages himself. He swings the rope in a circle above his head. Then he throws it as high in the air as he can. As fast as the rope goes up, it comes down, plopping on the ground. Hopper will have to throw harder and higher. But he doesn't give up. He gathers the rope up and swings it around again, then throws it up. It falls to the ground again.

Poor Hopper, no matter how hard or high he can throw his rope, it will never catch the moon. The moon is far too far away. Alas, this plan isn't going to work either.

Sea Cows

Nibbles is standing by Mummy in the kitchen, asking a million questions. He wants to know all about sea cows.

'A sea cow is also called a manatee. It looks a lot like a big, fat walrus,' explains Mummy while she sets the table. 'They have fins and a tail.'

'Aha,' decides Nibbles, 'it's a swimming animal.' So he moves as if he's in the ocean, swimming and looking for food.

'Mummy, what do sea cows eat?'

'They eat plants that grow on the sea bottom and algae,' explains Mummy while she puts some food on the table. 'Since they live on the shore, they eat now and then as plants go by them.'

So the sea cow called Nibbles acts like he's swimming and eating seaweed.

Suddenly another question pops into his mind: do sea cows moo like land cows?

'They do make a noise, but I don't know if it's like land cows' mooing,' answers Mummy. 'OK now, it's time to stop swimming and come to the table. We're having chips!'

Hmmm. This sea cow loves chips much more than seaweed.

A Dangerous Adventure

Once again an icy north wind is keeping the villagers inside their cosy, warm houses. The paths are empty.

Mister Owl sits in front of his fireplace and reads a book about dinosaurs.

Suddenly, his attention is drawn to a loud groan. Mister Owl puts down his book and goes to the window. Where is that groaning coming from?

He sees something moving through the trees. It… it looks like a giant dinosaur! He has a huge body with spikes and a long neck with a gigantic head. Sharp teeth sparkle in his big mouth. With heavy steps, the dinosaur comes toward the village.

Oh, no, he's coming straight to Mister Owl's house! Mister Owl steps backward and falls over a chair. Suddenly Mister Owl screams. What has happened? He's lying on the floor next to the chair. The terrible dinosaur is gone. Then Mister Owl realises that he fell asleep over his book and had then fallen out of his chair. Luckily it was only a dream.

Clever Questions

Mister Mouse is reading the paper. Suddenly, he stands up and whispers something in Mummy's ear. Then he walks out of the room.

'What is Daddy doing?' asks Nibbles.

'That's a secret,' says Mummy.

Nibbles doesn't like secrets. Maybe the secret is in the newspaper? He looks at the page that lies open. It is the weather forecast for the next day. A bell goes off in Nibbles' head.

'Is the secret that Daddy is going to get something for Misty and me?'

Mummy nods.

'Is it under a whole lot of things and does it have something to do with snow?'

Mummy nods again.

'Is it something Misty and I can sit in while you pull it?'

'Shhh,' she shushes, pointing to Misty. 'It's a surprise, remember?'

Nibbles goes to Mummy and whispers in her ear, 'Is Daddy taking the sledge out of the attic for tomorrow?'

Mummy laughs and says, 'You are such a clever one!'

December

Snow

Misty wakes up early this morning. She hears Nibbles' voice calling, 'Misty, come here quickly!'

'What is it?' she asks, as she comes downstairs a moment later.

'Look! Look!' exclaims Nibbles, pointing to the window. It has snowed!'

Misty runs to the window. A layer of white snow covers the village. Misty thinks it's lovely.

'Get dressed quickly,' says Mummy. 'Then you can go out and play before breakfast. Daddy has the sledge ready.'

Soon the youngsters are all dressed for the snow. Misty picks up some snow in her bare hands. My, it's cold! Mummy brings her mittens so they won't feel cold any more.

Meanwhile Nibbles has found the sledge. 'Let's get on!' he cries.

Misty runs over and sits on the sledge. Nibbles takes the rope and pulls her around. She loves it. Nibbles takes her on a nice, long ride through the snow-covered village.

'Everything looks so beautiful with this snow,' she says.

When they get home they start to build a snowman. Misty has never done that. So she has no idea what to do.

'Here's what you do,' says Nibbles. Together they make the snowman, laughing as they work. Misty loves her first day of snow play.

The Nose

Yesterday, Nibbles and Misty made a wonderful snowman. They rolled three big balls of snow and set them on top of each other. Two snow sausages made the arms, and little stones formed the face. Today they'll finish him. The nose is missing. Nibbles needs a carrot to make that, so he runs to the kitchen.

Luckily, he finds one in the fridge. It's perfect for the snowman's nose.

Proudly he shows the carrot to Misty, then he sticks it in the middle of the snowman's face. It looks wonderful. They play in the snow some more until

234

Mummy calls.

'Did one of you take that carrot that was in the fridge?' she asks.

'I did, Mummy,' answers Nibbles. 'We needed it for our snowman's nose. I didn't know you needed it.'

'Oh, that's too bad,' says Mummy. 'I needed it for dinner tonight.'

'Aw, Mummy,' whinges Misty, 'can't you use something else? It's so nice on the snowman.'

'Oh, OK,' says Mummy. 'If you'll go to Miss Squirrel's shop and get me a new one, we'll all be happy.'

That sounds good to the youngsters. Maybe they'll get a sweet from Miss Squirrel, and the snowman is safe.

A Walk in the Snow

Mister Owl looks out of the window. It has snowed again, but now the storm is over and everything is sparkling outside.

'A perfect day for a walk in the snow,' he decides.

He puts on his winter clothes and goes outside. He enjoys the beauty while he walks down the path.

The sky is clear and blue, and snow lies on all the branches. Birds zoom around, enjoying their wonderful white world.

But just as he walks under a tree, a heap of snow suddenly falls off a branch and lands right on his head.

Mister Owl shakes it off. There's snow down his neck.

'Brrr, that's really cold!' he cries as he brushes it out. Then he continues walking. His boots make squeaky sounds as he kicks through the deep snow on the path.

'Watch out,' he tells himself soon. 'Somewhere here there's a hole in the path. I've got to watch out so I don't fall in it.' As he says that, he suddenly sinks up to his middle in the snow, right in the hole.

Grumbling, Mister Owl scrambles out. Now he has snow in his boots and trousers. It's so cold! After he gets rid of most of it, he continues walking. But he's only gone a few steps when he slips and falls on his tummy in the snow!

'I've had enough fun today,' mutters Mister Owl as he brushes himself off for the third time. 'I'm going home to watch it from indoors.'

Poor Mister Owl. Even if it is pretty, snow can be a problem.

December

The Shop Window

4 DECEMBER

When Nibbles arrives at Miss Squirrel's shop to get things for Mummy, she is standing in her shop's front window.

'Miss Squirrel, what are you doing?' he asks.

'I'm decorating my shop window for the winter,' she explains. 'That makes it more welcoming for my customers.'

Nibbles watches while Miss Squirrel scatters fake snow around. She hangs up silver streamers and tiny coloured lights. Finally she puts a beautifully decorated tree and some presents in the middle. It's done.

'But isn't it too early for a tree?' asks Nibbles.

Miss Squirrel smiles. 'You have a point. But I've learned that if I decorate this early, it reminds my customers to get their cooking and baking started. That brings them to my shop.'

'Hey, that's smart!' laughs Nibbles.

'Could you please go outside and see how it looks? I'll turn the lights on.'

Nibbles hurries out and stands before the large window. The lights flicker on. It looks like a fairy tale. And just then the snow begins to fall again. It makes Nibbles feel like Christmas really is coming soon.

Wonder what he'll get as a present? He wishes it was Christmas today!

Snow Sculptures

5 DECEMBER

'What a great idea. Let's sign up!' says Mister Mouse.

Nibbles wonders what's up. Daddy shows him an article in *The Village Courier*.

'Walter Weasel has organised a new contest. This one's going to be fun.'

Nibbles, Misty and Mummy listen as he continues, 'Every family has to make one snow sculpture. The best sculpture will win a prize. What do you think?'

Nibbles and Misty don't know what to think. They don't know what a sculpture is.

'It's a figure made out of something, like snow, stone, wood or metal. So we will use snow.'

Now they get it.

'But we've already made our snowman,' points out Nibbles.

'I think that Walter wants more than snowmen. Bigger things.'

Bigger things? They have to think that over.

'I've got it!' cries Nibbles. 'How about a snow house? With walls and tables and chairs made from snow. With a mouse family of snow inside it!'

Everybody thinks this is a great idea.

So they start drawing plans. They fill in all the things they want to build. After a lot of drawing and erasing and re-drawing, they are done. It's going to be great.

While Mummy goes to Walter Weasel's shop to sign them up, Daddy, Nibbles and Misty start to work. There's a lot to do, but it's going to be fun.

The Snow House

All the villagers are busy outdoors today. Walter Weasel's newest contest has them all busy making snow sculptures and everyone wants to win the prize.

In front of each house little groups of villagers are working and laughing together as they build their sculptures. They look at the pictures they drew to plan their sculptures, and then get busy collecting snow and shaping it to make the figures they thought up for the contest. The whole village is having a wonderful time.

Walter wanders through the village with his notebook. For each project he makes notes. Mister Sack's family is making – what else? – a postbox. Walter likes that one.

Helen Hedgehog has made a giant snow cake. She has set candles on it. It almost looks real. 'Very nice,' writes Walter in his notebook.

He also likes the statue that Mister Owl has made of himself. It's just too bad that his tummy has fallen off.

When Walter passes by the Mouse family's sculpture, he stands there speechless. They have made a fine snow house, complete with windows and doors. Inside there are snow chairs, tables – everything – even snow food! And in front of the house stand four figures who look just like Daddy, Mummy, Nibbles and Misty.

Walter is certain now. This is absolutely the best entry in the contest. The Mouse family will win.

All the villagers agree. They clap when the Mouse family wins four pairs of warm mittens. Perfect prizes for a snow sculpture contest!

December

Bruno's Souvenir

7 DECEMBER

'Even more snow fell last night,' grumbles Mister Sack, the postman, as he starts on his rounds this morning. The postboxes peep above the snow and Mister Sack is up to his middle in it.

'I'll never get through all this,' he sighs.

Then a light goes on in his head. In the attic he has some souvenirs from his Uncle Bruno. Bruno is a snow hare who lives in Alaska, far away. They have lots and lots of snow there. To get through all that snow they have found a good solution.

Mister Sack runs back to his house and climbs up to the attic. After a search, he finds what he wanted: the snowshoes that Bruno gave him.

When he gets outside again, he puts the snowshoes on. Now he can walk across the top of the snow instead of struggling through it. These snowshoes are just the thing. Thanks to these souvenirs of Bruno's he makes his rounds even faster than usual.

What Flies Through the Air?

8 DECEMBER

What's that, flying through the air over there? It's Sam, the police officer of the village.

'All this snow,' thinks Sam. 'I'm not going to slog through it.'

So now he's flying high, and he looks down at the fairy tale landscape. Below he sees the villagers tromping through the snow. A duck flies below him. Sam has to laugh.

Suddenly he sees Mister Owl, waving to him to come closer. Sam begins a graceful landing. He slows himself with his wings. A few metres before he touches the ground, he sticks his feet out in front of him.

'Ready to land?' he mutters. 'One, two, and…'

Sam touches down. But he has picked a bad spot to land. It's as slippery as glass. As if he is on a slide, Sam races past Mister Owl straight into a huge snow drift. Only his feet stick out.

Luckily Mister Owl is there to help him out.

Poor Sam, that was a bad landing.

December

A Fine Nose

9 DECEMBER

Nibbles is playing with his friends in the snow with the sledge. Nibbles and Flopsy sit in it while Hopper and Blinders pull them around. They are having such fun. Suddenly Nibbles cries, 'Quick, go that way!'

Hopper and Blinders look at Nibbles in surprise. They wanted to go in the other direction.

'No, no, that way, please,' yells Nibbles.

'OK then,' says Hopper. They turn the sledge around and go on.

'Faster, faster,' urges Nibbles. 'I smell something baking! It's coming from that direction!'

Now Blinders and Hopper know why Nibbles wants them to hurry. With his sensitive nose, he is always able to smell treats. They run as fast as their legs can carry them. The sledge flies over the snow.

'Now this way! Hurry!' cries Nibbles.

Helen Hedgehog's bakery comes into view. Of course, where else can those wonderful scents be coming from?

But this is a scent that Nibbles doesn't recognise. When they get to the bakery they all run inside.

'Hello, youngsters,' smiles Helen. 'Has Nibbles' fine nose brought you here?'

They all nod. Helen sets a plate with goodies on the counter.

'Just in time. I've tried a new recipe: cream dreams. You can be my taste testers. Help yourselves.'

They are delicious, of course. Nibbles' nose never lies.

The Flying Frog

10 DECEMBER

A storm howls outside. Hopper sits in his house. The roof creaks and groans under the blows of the heavy wind. Suddenly, with a horrible noise, a piece of the roof blows away. Oh, no! There's a big hole in the roof. Luckily Hopper has a big waterproof cloth handy. If he puts that over the hole, it won't let snow blow in.

Hopper grabs a ladder and climbs up to the roof with his cloth. Just as he unfolds it, the wind hits it and it starts to blow away. But Hopper grabs the four corners. The wind fills the cloth like a parachute and it lifts up, carrying Hopper into the sky.

'Help,' screams Hopper, while the wind blows harder and harder. He goes higher and higher.

240

Suddenly, it occurs to Hopper: he's flying! He can hardly believe it, but he's flying!

'Yippee!' he cries, as he sweeps over the village. Finally, he made it as the first flying frog.

When he gets higher, he looks below. As the wind dies down, Hopper begins slowly to land. He sees the snowy ground coming closer and closer. With a soft plop he lands in the fresh snow.

'Wow, what a wonderful flight,' sighs Hopper satisfied.

Hopper stays there for some time, daydreaming. The storm doesn't matter to him now, since finally, he has flown.

The Winter Garden

When Flopsy, Blinders and Hopper come to the Friendship Tree, they find Nibbles hard at work.

'What are you doing, Nibbles?' asks Flopsy.

'I'm making a garden in the snow,' he says building a wall. 'This is the hedge. If you want, you can help me.'

The friends would love to help.

'I'm going to make a tree,' says Hopper.

'And I'm going to build a bush,' says Blinders enthusiastically.

Flopsy thinks it over. Then she knows what she'll make: a garden bench.

The youngsters work hard and the garden takes shape quickly. Hopper's tree looks great. He made the trunk from snow, then he stuck little twigs into it to make the branches. It's a work of art.

The garden is done now. Flopsy, Nibbles and Blinders sit on the garden bench to admire their work. Hopper keeps on working.

'What are you up to now, Hopper?' Flopsy wants to know.

'You'll see in a second,' Hopper replies, while he makes a whole bunch of snowballs. When he has made ten, he stops and lays them on a plate.

'My tree has produced these snow fruits. Would anybody like a snow apple?'

The others laugh and laugh. They each take a snow apple and bite into it.

'These snow apples taste a little watery,' jokes Blinders.

But even so, they have a wonderful snow garden now.

December

A Big Package for Bert Beaver

Bert Beaver sits in front of his window, looking outside. He sits there for an hour, just watching. He anxiously scans the lovely snowscape out there.

'If he'd just come now,' complains Bert. 'I'm nervous.'

Suddenly someone appears in the distance. With quick steps the figure comes toward Bert's house.

'Finally,' sighs Bert in relief, 'there he is.'

Bert jumps out of his chair and runs to the door. It's Mister Sack, the postman. That's who Bert's been watching for.

Ding-dong! sounds the bell. Bert counts for a couple of seconds before he opens the door. He doesn't want to look too eager.

'Hello, Mister Sack,' says Bert as calmly as he can after he opens the door.

'I have a big package for you,' says Mister Sack, as he shows Bert a long, thin package. 'It doesn't weigh much, but it's really long,' observes Mister Sack.

'A package for me?' asks Bert, pretending to be surprised. He knew the package was coming today. That's why he spent the morning at his window.

Bert takes that package. He would really like to tear it open right here and now, but he doesn't let himself do that.

'Could you please sign here to say you received it?' asks Mister Sack.

Bert scribbles his name and says goodbye to Mister Sack. He closes the door and turns excitedly to his package.

But we'll have to stop the story here. If you want to know what's in the package, you'll have to wait until tomorrow.

Dreams Come True

Bert Beaver stands on a hill above the snowy village. He's warmly dressed, because there is a cold wind blowing.

Bert doesn't mind. Yesterday, Mister Sack, the postman, brought him a big package. There were skis inside. Bert wants to try them out now.

He puts the skis on his feet. Bert is nervous, because he's wanted to learn to ski for so long. Ever since he saw a colourful photo of skiers in a magazine.

'I want to do that too,' he promised himself. He ordered the skis that very day.

Now he's ready. Bert can hardly believe it. He grips his ski poles and pushes off.

Bert slides slowly down the hill. Oh, no, something's wrong. One ski wants to go to the left while the other wants to go to the right. Waving his arms wildly, Bert tries to stay upright. His skis cross now. Bert falls over in the soft snow, popping out of his skis and dropping his ski poles.

'This is harder than it looked,' grumbles Bert. He scrambles to his feet and puts his skis on again. But just as he reaches for his poles, the skis start sliding down the hill.

'Help!' he cries, as he glides away. Soon he loses his balance and falls down again.

It looks like Bert will need a lot of practice.

Fever

Nibbles is lying on the sofa. He feels awful.

'You look pale,' says Mummy worried. She puts her hand on his forehead.

'You feel warm. I'll take your temperature."

Nibbles puts the thermometer in his mouth. After a minute, Mummy takes it out.

'You have a fever,' she says. 'You better get to bed.'

Nibbles crawls upstairs and falls into his bed. He feels hot and cold at the same time. He pulls his blankets up to his chin. Wow, does he feel sick.

Mummy comes into his room.

'I've brought you some medicine,' she says gently. 'If you take this, your fever will go away.'

Nibbles struggles to sit up. His head aches.

Mummy pours some liquid onto a spoon. Nibbles makes a face. He knows that stuff tastes awful.

'I won't,' he says.

'But Nibbles,' says Mummy patiently, 'you know it will make you feel better.'

'No,' wails Nibbles.

'Do you want to spend the whole week in bed while your friends play in the snow?' presses Mummy.

Nibbles gives up. He opens his mouth and swallows the awful medicine down.

'That's what I like to see,' smiles Mummy.

That evening Nibbles feels a little better, thanks to the medicine. Maybe tomorrow he can play with his friends?

December

Christmas Tree

Some of the villagers are going into the woods to get a big Christmas tree today. They want to decorate the village square, because Christmas is coming soon. They have gone quite a way already. They have a lot of work ahead of them. First they have to cut the tree down, and then bring it back to the village.

After they finally get the tree to the village square, they are very tired. But they aren't done yet. They must set the tree upright. Luckily for them, Helen Hedgehog has baked biscuits for them. They gobble them up, then get back to work.

Mister Mole digs a deep hole for the tree trunk. Then with all their strength, they push the trunk into the hole and raise the tree straight up. 'Finally,' they sigh, satisfied, 'the tree is upright.'

Other villagers come to join them. They bring boxes full of decorations and lights with them.

Mister Mouse puts a tall ladder against the tree and climbs up. He hangs the lights from the branches, while below, the others put the decorations on.

When everything is done, the big moment has arrived. Mister Owl turns the lights on. The tree lights up.

Hundreds of lights sparkle and give the square a golden light.

'Ahhh!' sounds around the whole square. It's a marvellous sight to see such a beautifully decorated tree.

Decorating

The whole village is getting ready for Christmas. Yesterday they put up a huge tree in the village square. Today another tree is decorated, but it's a lot smaller. It's in Nibbles' and Misty's house.

The youngsters have been busy all day with bread dough. They have been making figures and shapes like stars, balls, and tiny trees. When they are all made, Mummy puts them in the oven and bakes them.

When they are baked and cool, the youngsters can paint them.

'I want to paint with gold,' says Nibbles. Misty likes silver better.

The youngsters paint their decorations as well as they can. They look like works of art. Meanwhile Mummy puts the lights on the tree.

'We're done,' Nibbles calls to Mummy.

Mummy comes by to admire their work. Their decorations look great. When the paint is dry, they can hang everything on the tree. Misty decorates the lower branches, while Nibbles does the middle ones. Mummy does the higher ones.

'Ta-dah!' crows Nibbles when they finish. 'The tree is done!'

'Not yet,' says Mummy. From a special box she takes a golden star out, then she sets it on the top of the tree. Now the tree is done.

Nibbles and Misty love Christmas time. The tree is lovely.

 ## Snowball Fight

Nibbles and Hopper love snowball fights. They scream and shout while they hurl the balls at each other. And they cheer when they hit each other

Nibbles has hidden behind a hedge. He thinks that Hopper doesn't know where he is. But Hopper saw him slipping away and followed him. He has made a big snowball. He had packed it so it's really hard. That way it is sure to hit his target.

Nibbles tries to peek out over his hedge as invisibly as possible. Hopper spots him, takes aim, and throws the ball at Nibbles' head. Splat!

But Nibbles bursts into tears. The hard snowball landed right on his eye.

Hopper runs over to Nibbles. He can see that Nibbles' eye hurts a lot.

Hopper hugs his friend, but it doesn't help. Now Nibbles' eye is turning blue. Hopper brings Nibbles to his mummy.

She quickly puts some ice on Nibbles' eye. Nibbles stops crying.

'Whatever happened?' she asks. Hopper tells the whole story.

'You must never throw a snowball at someone's head. It's too dangerous. I'm sure you've learned your lesson.'

Hopper promises to never do that again. Meanwhile, the skin around Nibbles' eye has turned totally blue. He looks in the mirror and thinks it makes him look really tough. They go back to their snowball fight, because it's so much fun. But do they throw at each other's heads? No way.

December

Wrapping

Nibbles and Daddy slip into the house.

'Find out where Mummy is,' whispers Daddy. While Nibbles snoops around, looking for Mummy, Daddy takes something out of his jacket. It's a pair of oven gloves. They are a Christmas present for Mummy. But they need to be wrapped. That's why they want to keep Mummy from seeing them.

'Pssst!' hisses Nibbles to Daddy, 'she's in the kitchen.'

'Great,' whispers Daddy, 'then we'll go to your room to wrap them.'

As quietly as they can, father and son sneak upstairs.

In Nibbles' room they start to work.

Daddy takes a roll of wrapping paper and cuts a piece that's big enough to cover the gloves. Then they put the gloves on the paper and fold it up.

But it's hard to make it look beautiful. Daddy folds and folds, but it just doesn't go right. Finally, the paper is full of wrinkles from all his tries. But with a lot of tape, they should be able to get it closed.

Nibbles takes the tape and cuts a piece. He puts it where Daddy points.

'Another piece over here. And there.' Finally the package is ready.

Quietly the two of them slip downstairs. They lay the package under the tree. It looks a little lumpy and sad, but it is what's inside that counts.

A Present for Wilbur

Mister Owl has been thinking all week about what to give his nephew Wilbur, the snowy owl, for Christmas. Wilbur lives in the Far North, because he loves the cold.

That's why it's hard to think of a good present for Wilbur.

For his old Uncle David, the barn owl, he picked a pair of warm slippers. It gets cold in the barn in the winter and he has always got cold feet.

For his Auntie Hanna, a tawny owl, he picked a beautiful pair of gloves, and for his other nephew, Matt, the tiny long-eared owl, a warm hat for when he plays outside.

But what can he give Wilbur? Not clothing, because Wilbur is always too warm.

Suddenly, he has an idea. He runs to Miss Squirrel's shop and buys a big box of ice lollies. Wilbur will love them.

He packs them into a special box that will keep them frozen. Then he wraps the box neatly in paper with penguins and snowmen on it. Won't that please Wilbur?

Mister Owl writes Wilbur's name on the package and puts a lot of stamps on it, then he takes the package to the post office.

Sometimes it's hard to find the perfect present for someone.

Biscuit Boxes

Nibbles helps Helen Hedgehog at her bakery.

Since Christmas is coming, Helen wants to do extra things for her customers. She wants to give each one a little present.

So she's made lots of biscuits. They need to be packed into small boxes. That's what Nibbles is helping her with.

They put several of each kind of biscuit in a box. Then they tie the box with a fancy ribbon, and it's all set.

Each time Nibbles has finished three boxes, he gets to eat a biscuit himself.

That's a great deal for Nibbles. He works hard to pack up three boxes. Then he enjoys his reward. And then he's back to work, packing again.

'It's going well,' says Helen happily. 'We have a whole lot of boxes done now. I'm going to put them in the shop. Can you finish packing up the last biscuits yourself?'

'Sure,' says Nibbles, putting some into a box. When Helen comes back from the shop, she checks to see how Nibbles is doing. He is finishing the last box.

'Well done, Nibbles!' she says. 'All the biscuits are packed up!'

Nibbles laughs with her. It has been fun to help her prepare the presents for her customers. He can imagine how happy they will be when they get their gifts. Won't they be surprised? For him, though, the end comes just in time. His tummy is so full of biscuits that, for once, he can't eat another.

December

Craftwork with Mummy

Flopsy is feeling restless.

'Why don't you make some Christmas cards?' asks Mummy. 'I can help you a bit.'

'Yeah? Why not,' thinks Flopsy.

Mummy collects scissors, coloured paper, pens, brushes and paint, glitter… all the things you need to make a card.

First she folds a piece of paper in half. It looks a bit like a card.

Flopsy cuts a tree from a piece of green paper. Or something that looks somewhat like a tree.

Mummy glues it on the card.

'Would you please bring me a potato from the kitchen?' she asks.

'A potato?' asks Flopsy. 'Are you going to glue that to the card?'

'You'll soon see,' says Mummy mysteriously.

A little later, Flopsy gives Mummy the potato. Mummy cuts it in two. She cuts one piece into a star shape. She cuts the other into a circle. Then she pours a little paint into a saucer and dips the potato pieces in. She stamps them on the green Christmas tree Misty made. Soon the tree is covered with stars and circles.

'Cool!' says Misty delighted. 'Could I try?'

Flopsy covers her card with stars. Then she takes some glitter and scatters it over the wet paint. They'll stick to the paint after it dries.

The card is done and it looks great. Now Misty knows what she will do the rest of the day: make a card for each of her friends.

Christmas Post

'My goodness,' sighs Mister Sack when he sees his post sack, bulging with holiday post.

Every year around Christmas everybody sends each other cards. But who has to deliver them? Right: poor Mister Sack.

He picks the heavy sack up and goes down the path.

He fills postbox after postbox with envelopes. There's a lot of greeting going on in the village. Toward midday the job is done. A few letters remain in his sack, but they are for him. He takes them home, and sinks down on the sofa to open his envelopes.

'Look at that! A card from Auntie Twitch. She wishes us a Happy Christmas. That's sweet of her.'

He picks up the next envelope. It's a card from his nephew Stamper.

Mister Sack opens envelope after envelope. Greetings rain in from all over the world. It gives Mister Sack a wonderful feeling to think that so many friends and relations thought of him.

He hangs the cards on a string and sits back to admire them. It was a big job to deliver those cards today. 'But,' he thinks, 'if everyone gets as much pleasure from them as I have, then it's worth all the work.'

Curious Daddy

23 DECEMBER

Mister Mouse comes into the living room. His eyes land on a present under the tree.

'That's a new present. It wasn't here this morning,' he thinks. He looks to see if anyone's around. Then he goes over and picks it up.

'Yes! It's for me!' he says, when he sees his name on it. The present is pretty heavy. What's in it? Mister Mouse shakes it gently. It rattles a little. What could it be?

'Maybe I can ask Misty about it,' he thinks. 'If I tease her long enough, she might tell me.'

'Misty?' he calls. Misty comes into the room.

'Yes?'

'Do you know what's in that package?

'Which one?'

'You know very well which one. That one under the tree.'

'There are lots under the tree, Daddy.'

'I know that. I mean, the one with my name on it.'

'That one?'

'Yes, that one. What's in it?'

'I know what's in it,' says Misty carefully.

'And will you tell me?'

'I'll whisper to you,' says Misty.

Misty holds her hands around Daddy's ear and whispers, 'Mummy told me that if you asked me what's in that package, I should tell you that you have to wait until Christmas to find out.'

'So that's it?' says Daddy. 'You're in this together, eh?'

Misty grins and goes out of the room.

But she's right: Daddy has to wait until Christmas.

December

Miss Crow's Christmas Eve

24 DECEMBER

Old Miss Crow sits in her rocking chair. She looks outside. She's alone on Christmas Eve.

Suddenly there's a knock on her door. She opens it wide.

'Happy Christmas!' she hears from many voices. Flopsy, Nibbles, Hopper, Blinders, their mummies and daddies, Miss Hedgehog, Mister Tie, Bert Beaver, Mister Owl, Walter Weasel… half the village is in front of her door.

'We've brought you tea and cake,' says Flopsy.

'And honey biscuits and berry juice,' adds Misses Hedgehog.

'And a Christmas present,' the youngsters cry.

Nibbles and Misty give her a large present.

Miss Crow doesn't know what to say. With trembling hands she opens it.

'Oh,' she sighs, 'you shouldn't have done this.'

Inside is a lovely warm jumper.

'Try it on! Try it on!' urge the youngsters.

Miss Crow puts it on. She's beaming with happiness.

It makes a lovely Christmas for Miss Crow. So friendly, warm and cosy!

Christmas Day

25 DECEMBER

It's here at last: Christmas Day. The Mouse family gathers around the Christmas tree to open their presents. Daddy has written everyone's name on slips of paper and put them in a stocking. Misty gets to pick the slips out. She puts her little paw into the stocking and searches around for a slip. Mummy reads the name for her: it's Daddy.

Mummy gives Daddy his package. There is a new hammer in it.

Misty picks out a new slip: it's Nibbles' name. He gets a cool train. He starts playing with it right away.

There are still two names in the stocking. Misty really hopes that she picks her own name next. But it's Mummy's.

Mummy opens her oven gloves.

The last package must be for Misty, so she doesn't need to pick her slip out of the stocking. She tears open the wrapping. It's a beautiful doll. She is thrilled. She gives Mummy and Daddy each a big kiss.

Now it's bed time. It was a lovely Christmas Day.

December

The Last Trousers

Mister Owl is certain about it now: he has to lose weight. He stands in front of his wardrobe, looking for trousers. There is only one pair that fits him now. The others are too tight. He will soon have to buy new clothes from Mister Tie.

No, he doesn't want to do that. He just has to lose weight. If he goes on like this, he'll be as big as a house. That would be terrible.

No, no, he wants to get thinner and he will do it, starting tomorrow.

Naturally he ate far too much at Miss Crow's house. But he couldn't resist; everything was so delicious.

When Mister Owl puts on his trousers, he thinks about what a nice party it was. His mouth waters as he thinks back over the wonderful treats: cake with chocolate sauce, apple tart, and of course, honey biscuits. My, was it wonderful.

He buttons his trousers. Then he picks up a pair of warm socks. When he starts to put one on, it falls out of his hands. Mister owl bends over to pick it up.

'Rrrippp!' There go his last trousers.

Now Mister Owl really has to lose weight.

Mysterious Mister Tie

'I wonder what he's up to,' thinks Helen Hedgehog one evening, as she and Mister Tie finish dinner. 'He slips out to his workroom every night. What is he making?'

She decides to find out. She fakes a big yawn. 'I think I'll go to bed early,' she says.

'Please do. You need your rest,' says Mister Tie with a smile.

Helen gives Mister Tie a kiss and pretends to get ready for bed. Mister Tie hurries off to his workroom. Quietly, she follows him.

She can see him busily working away. But she can't see what he's working on. She needs to get closer. She tiptoes in. As she gets nearer, she bumps into a dressmaker's dummy and it falls over. Mister Tie jumps in fear.

'What are you doing here?' he asks in surprise.

'Just trying to find out what you've been working on,' answers Helen a bit embarrassed.

Mister Tie looks like he's trapped. Then a big smile breaks across his face.

'You've been wondering what I've been doing on these evenings, right?'

Helen nods. He points to the dressmaker's dummy. A beautiful evening dress is draped over it. It shimmers in the light.

'That's what I've been working on. It's for you. It's a present.'

How sweet of Mister Tie! Helen has never received such a lovely surprise as this in all her life.

Polar Bear

At the North Pole there lives a polar bear. He's the biggest, scariest bear of them all. His name is Nibbles. And he's hungry.

(You've already guessed it: Nibbles is pretending to be an animal again.)

On all fours he crawls through the living room. He's searching for prey to satisfy his roaring hunger. He rears up on his hind legs.

'I want a delicious penguin,' he growls.

'A penguin? Such a sweet animal? One of those funny-walking birds?' interrupts Mummy.

'A polar bear has to eat,' whinges the polar bear. 'He likes to eat penguins.'

'I think that's a problem,' says Mummy.

The polar bear looks angrily at Mummy. In a deep voice he asks, 'What do you mean?'

'Look. Polar bears live at the North Pole. Penguins live at the South Pole. That's the other end of the earth. If a polar bear wants to eat a penguin, he has to travel halfway around the world. I think he'd die from hunger first.'

'How about seals, then?' asks the polar bear.

'That's what polar bears really like.'

'Then I don't want to be a polar bear any more. I don't want to eat a seal.'

Well, nobody said it's easy to be a bear.

December

Day-by-Day Calendar

Nibbles is looking at the calendar. Every day, Mummy tears a page off and the new day shows up. Today he tears a page off, and he notices there are only two pages left for this year.

'Mummy, the calendar is almost over.'

'That's true, and so is the year.'

'What do you mean?'

'Each year has 365 days. The new year begins on the first day of January and ends on the thirty-first day of December. Then the new year begins.'

Now Nibbles gets it. So now they need a new calendar or else they won't know what day of the year it is. Imagine if they think that it's Tuesday when it's really Sunday. That would be annoying.

'Let's go,' says Mummy. 'We will buy a new calendar at Miss Squirrel's shop.'

A little later they are in the shop. There are lots of day-by-day calendars in a rack.

Nibbles picks one and Mummy pays for it. They take it home.

Nibbles is happy with the calendar. Now every day, he can tear off a new page. And Mummy can tell him what day it is.

Getting Ready

Nibbles is helping Daddy and Bert Beaver. They are carrying a long table to the village square. They set it up right in the middle of the square.

Then they bring chairs and all the other things they will need to help the village celebrate New Year's Eve.

As they go by Helen Hedgehog's bakery, Nibbles smells that Helen is baking something for the big feast.

'We are going to have wonderful things to eat,' he exclaims.

As they pass by Walter Weasel's newspaper shop, they see him inside, busy unpacking all kinds of fireworks.

'Walter and Bert Beaver are in charge of the fireworks tomorrow night,' explains Daddy.

'So we will have delicious treats *and* fireworks? Cool,' says Nibbles.

When they get back to the village square, they see that Mister Tie has set up a stand where berry juice will be served tomorrow night.

'Oh, wow! Food, fireworks, *and* berry juice!' cries Nibbles, who really can't wait now.

Sam Stork, Roger Fox and Mister Owl are standing on the tiny stage in the square. They have their musical instruments with them. After they tune them, they start to warm up, playing some songs they want to practise for tomorrow

night. It sounds great.

Food, fireworks, berry juice, *and* music for dancing. What more could anyone want?

New Year's Eve

On the village square tonight, the feast is starting. Sparkling lights shine on the trees.

The whole village has gathered. They are ready to say goodbye to the old year and welcome the new year in.

Old Miss Crow is enjoying some cake and berry juice. She's chatting with Walter Weasel. Walter is wearing his finest suit for this feast, because soon he'll be dancing with Miss Squirrel's sister Bitsy.

Miss Squirrel and Bitsy are chatting with Helen Hedgehog. They share cake recipes with each other.

Nibbles' mummy and daddy are talking with Flopsy's mummy and daddy about how fast this year has gone by and what happened in it.

Sam Stork, Roger Fox and Mister Owl play lively music, and Mister Tie walks around with a big platter of snacks that he offers the villagers. His best customer is Nibbles, who samples something every time Mister Tie passes by.

'Where do you put all that food, Nibbles?' he asks. But Nibbles doesn't know, or care. He is dancing and jumping around with Flopsy, Hopper and Blinders. They are having the time of their lives.

In fact, they are having so much fun that they have no idea of the time. It's just so much fun to celebrate the coming new year with your friends and family!

Suddenly there's a loud *PSSST* sound. A flash lights up the sky.

All the talking stops while everyone looks up in surprise. There is a boom and fireworks start to explode overhead.

Bert Beaver, who's lit the fireworks, cries, 'HAPPY NEW YEAR, EVERYONE!'

All rights reserved
© Yoyo Books, Olen, Belgium
www.yoyo-books.com
Printed in China